PACIFIC THUNDER

DECKER'S MARINE RAIDERS SERIES
BOOK FIVE

SCOTT W. COOK

SPINDRIFT PRESS

Pacific Thunder
Decker's Marine Raiders, Book 5

Copyright © 2025 by Scott W. Cook

All rights reserved.

Formatting and book cover provided by Trisha Fuentes

No part of this book may be reproduced in any form or by any electronic or mechanical means, including information storage and retrieval systems, without written permission from the author, except for the use of brief quotations in a book review.

CONTENTS

Prologue	1
1. Henderson Field	13
2. September 30, 1942	23
Chapter 3	31
4. Guadalcanal interior	41
Chapter 5	50
6. Mount Austin – 2320	60
7. Team One	71
Chapter 8	84
Chapter 9	94
Chapter 10	105
Chapter 11	115
12. Guadalcanal	125
Chapter 13	136
14. Kokumbona	147
15. Fort Travis	158
16. Kokumbona	169
17. Fort Travis	182
Chapter 18	193
19. Matanikau River Valley	210
Epilogue	221
Before you go…	227
Other Books by this Author…	229

PROLOGUE
GUADALCANAL – SEPTEMBER 28, 1942

Corporal Marlin "Whitey" Groft hated long range patrols.

The painful welts on the skin where an endless variety of insects gobbled his flesh right through his utilities… the slimy, sticky sweat that flared into fiery chafe at every joint… the oven-like heat so thick with humidity it was a wonder a man even *needed* a canteen… oh, and on top of that, the incessant itching between his shoulder blades as, at any moment, a Jap round might burrow into his body like a rabid mole.

Most of his time on the Canal had been spent either in assaulting enemy positions or defending the perimeter. On the few long-range patrols he'd made, things had been miserable at best and nail-biting at worst.

And worst was pretty much the order of the day on this God forsaken rock.

But the life of a Marine, and a Marine Raider at that, was one of diversity as well as terror. With the failure of both Colonel Puller's and Colonel Edson's push across the Matanikau recently, the Old Man himself was struggling to play catch up and to figure out ways to keep the Jap from flooding across the muddy river in a great yellow horde.

Units had been shuffled, men reassigned… and many men who had yet to venture out into the malodorous jungle were now being sent in patrol squads to try and root out any crafty Nips who might be sneaking into U.S. held territory.

Fair was fair and everybody had to take their turn. Nothing wrong in that… but it didn't make sleeping out in the wild any easier. Those long nights where strange beasts called out to the darkness… where insects chittered and buzzed… and where bloodthirsty enemies might be tiptoeing up to slit a man's throat before he could say Jack Robinson.

Guadalcanal by day wasn't much better than Guadalcanal by night, either. There were less mosquitoes, but more centipedes. Less crushing darkness but greater heat and the very land itself seemed to exhale a foul, diseased breath as the sun rose and began to cook the night's condensation from the rainforest.

It was morning now, although barely. While the sun ought to be poking up over Sealark Channel at any moment, little of the dawn light penetrated the dense jungle south of Henderson between the Matanikau and Lunga River basins. The canopy was damp and thick and redolent of the heavy, cloying reek of chlorophyll, ceaselessly damp loam, and the sharp tang of animal skat and decaying vegetation. In the trees above, parakeets and macaws began their morning song, chirping and cawing and flooding the environment with their racket.

And drowning out the Marine's footsteps… and any Jap's that might be skulking nearby, too.

Sergeant John Basilone was leading the squad on a circuitous route that moved up the Lunga and would come back north closer to the Matanikau. All the way up to where the northern flatlands… or what passed for them on Guadalcanal… began to terrace into the highlands at the base of the jagged central mountains. The thought was, or so Basilone explained, was that the Jap would probably attack Henderson again and do so from the south. If so, they'd be cutting their way east from the upper Matanikau, maybe even as far south as Mount Austin. A longer run but easier to cross the river with heavy equipment.

Groft didn't know Basilone well. The sergeant, attached to the Seventh Marines, had only come in recently and, like everyone else, had been shuffled like a deck of Hoyle's ever since. Somebody probably figured the new sergeant needed a little seasoning, in spite of his former Army experience. Show him exactly what they were all facing here.

As the squad tromped through the dripping foliage, Groft found himself next to last in the single column. As noncom in charge of fire team three, he was positioned to cover the squad's rear, keep an eye on his two riflemen ahead and his newly assigned private in the rear. He himself carried a Thompson, one of the few in the entire platoon, and was ready and willing to use it. After what he'd seen on the rock, especially that horrifying night at Alligator Creek a million years ago back at the middle of August, Groft never relaxed either his eyes or ears when away from the relative safety of the lines.

The team was moving south along a low, flat ridge of coral paralleling the two rivers. Such ridges were everywhere on the island, cutting jagged swaths through the softer ground like the bones of some gargantuan beast that had been buried long ago. Perhaps the very skeleton of the island itself, bits and pieces protruding from the earth or their counterparts… rough-edged ravines and canyons that bisected the landscape as if clawed out of the rock by unimaginable, monstrous beasts.

This particular ridge didn't have much elevation. Not like the prominent Lunga Ridge just south of the airfield. Now being called Edson's Ridge and for good reason.

This one was just a flattish track of limestone and was quickly descending back into the ground, leaving only soft loam and plenty of vegetation ahead.

Something nagged at Groft. Something he and Leckie and their friends with Major Decker's squad had talked about more than once. *That* team had certainly earned its stripes. They'd traversed more of Guadalcanal than anyone else. They'd seen more of what the Jap had been up to than anyone else, too.

"Gotta watch the soft ground, Whitey," Joe Treadway had said.

"Yeah, that's where the little buggers like to dig their hidey-holes," Ted Entwater had added.

Soft ground… where the squad was headed now. Of course, every hardwood tree, every bird of paradise, every viny bush or leafy shrub could hide an enemy, so it wasn't as if the danger was any more or less in any one place… but still…

Whitey would swear to his dying day that he knew it was coming even before it happened. No matter how keen was the vision of hindsight, he swore that his mind sounded the alarm a second before the shot rang out… but not soon enough to do anything about it.

A sharp crack split the morning air, followed by an epithet shouted in a foreign tongue… and then the agonized, heart-rending scream of a man in mortal pain. In one sinuous motion, Groft spun, dropped to his belly, aimed his Thompson and fired.

He'd also swear that he didn't remember zeroing in on the smoke from the shot. Yet he must have, because his three-round burst ripped through the camouflage and burst the Japanese soldier's head like a ripe watermelon. The entire incident took no more than two seconds.

Shouts raced up and down the line. Alarm, fright, and fury-fueled curses snapped like rifle shots. Marines dropped to their knees, bringing weapons to bear on the greenery all around them, frantic to set their teeth into targets. Ahead, near the front of the column, Basilone's deep voice rumbled for quiet, calm, and for a goddamned report.

Groft crawled forward and found Jimmy Bixby, lying face down on the leafy ground, a dark, blackish patch rapidly spreading between his shoulder blades. Gritting his teeth, Groft gently rolled the eighteen-year-old Marine over, revealing a ghost-pale face twisted into a rictus of torment.

"Jimmy," Groft said gently. "Hey, Jimmy… talk to me, pal…"

"Whitey, what—" the man who'd been in front of Groft began.

"Jap," Groft snapped and pointed and then returned his attention to his man. "You're gonna be okay, Jimmy… I know it hurts, but—"

"It don't hurt that bad now, Whitey," the kid wheezed and coughed, splattering his cheeks and chin with bright red speckles. "I don't feel much of nothin'… just… hard to… breathe, is all…"

"Just lie easy, kid…" Groft's eyes simmered, and he had to blink rapidly to keep them from brimming over. Bixby was not much more than a year younger than himself, yet Groft's time on The Canal had aged him far beyond his years. At that moment, he felt as if he were comforting a son.

A shadow fell over the two Marines and a broad-shouldered figure hunched down beside Groft. John Basilone was only twenty-five himself, but like Groft, had seen too many hard moments in his days and his soul, if not his body, was twenty years senior.

"How is he, Corporal?" Basilone asked.

Groft looked over at his sergeant and shook his head back and forth ever so slightly. Basilone nodded just as slightly and then smiled down at Bixby, brushing a lock of the young Marine's hair from his forehead. It was a tender gesture born from true feeling and Groft nearly lost control again.

"Hey… Sarge…" Bixby said. "I think…"

"Shh…" Basilone said quietly. "You just relax now, chum. We're gonna get the medic over here and get you patched up and in a nice, comfy bed real soon, hear?"

Another man dressed in sweaty green BDUs slid down next to Bixby. Petty Officer Bill Lang, the platoon's Navy corpsman, quickly examined the wounded man's face, the dark exit wound in his chest and his face went taut. His head shake confirmed what the two Marines had already known.

Lang opened his pack and removed a tiny syrette of morphine. He glanced at Basilone, and the sergeant nodded. The dying man would not be denied a last moment or two of comfort.

"How you feelin', Bixby?" Lang asked, mustering a smile for the man.

"Hey… Doc… okay, I guess," Bixby's breathing seemed slightly easier, but with every word, more bright blood appeared on his lips. "Hurt like heck at first… but now… feels okay. Tired, though… real tired…"

"You get some rest, kid," Basilone said.

"Okay, Sarge… sorry for gold-brickin'…" Bixby tried to smile, coughed, coughed again and then his breath rattled out with a sound that was like none other. The sound of the gossamer-thin veil between life and death temporarily parting and then closing once more.

"No sign of any more of the bastards, Sarge," another Marine said as he walked up. "Just the one in his hole. Whitey's rounds blasted his head clean off."

"Good," said the sergeant. He drew in a steadying breath and rose to his feet. "Radioman! Call this in, give our position and request a collection detail. We've still got work to do. Christ… maybe from now on, the rear guard walks backward… ons of bitches…"

HENDERSON FIELD

"Come on in, gentlemen... take a seat wherever," General Alexander Vandegrift said, sipping from a steaming mug for once filled with real coffee.

General Thomas and Colonel Twining were already there, along with General Roy Geiger. Filing in were some of the unit's most notorious and courageous fighting commanders.

There was Edson who now commanded the Fifth Regiment along with Puller commanding the second. Sam Griffith was there, Edson's former XO now commanding the first Raiders. Still recovering from his wounds and waiting for an evac to the hospital in new Caledonia, Griffith insisted he was well enough to pull at least some of his weight.

As the final man, a broad gauged bulldog known as William "Wild Bill" Whaling entered, Vandegrift frowned. He liked Whaling, the man was a hell of a field commander... yet he and his former CO, Colonel Hunt, had not done a notable job running their regiment. One of the reasons it'd been given to Edson.

However, Whaling was far too valuable and had far too much experience to be dismissed the way Hunt had been. Vandegrift needed him... wanted him... he just wasn't sure what to do with a colonel without a unit.

"As you all know," Vandegrift began, doing away with preamble as usual, "the Jap is massing west of the Matanikau. Intelligence reports have it that while Kawaguchi and Oka's forces have been decimated and are verging on starvation... Mr. Moto has been sending reinforcements down The Slot every goddamned night. HQ thinks this is the prelude to a massive push and I agree."

"Trouble is," Thomas put in, "our patrols are being beaten to shit every time they get anywhere near that God forsaken river. We need better boots-on-the-ground intel, and the beshitted Jap ain't giving us a break."

"Go figure," Lou Puller snorted.

"What about my special unit, sir?" Edson said. "They've gathered plenty of intel in the past."

Vandegrift nodded, "True enough, Merritt. However, Al Decker and his team are off on a jaunt to Santa Isabella and all we know now is that they've achieved their objective at the airfield and are waiting for a ride. I've been informed that USS *Bull Shark* is on the way down from Truk to pick them up and they'll hopefully be here tomorrow or the next... but that still leaves us with a gap."

"Those fellas will need to rest," Griffith added. He smiled and added, "Then again... don't we all..."

"Precisely," said Vandegrift. "Jerry, Merryl, and I have been talking it over... which is why we've asked you here, Bill."

"Sir?" Whaling asked. At forty-six, Whaling was still in full command of his youthful energy. A native of Minnesota, his Norwegian heritage was evident in his square features and jaw.

"Now look here, Bill," Thomas said. "We know that fifth reg has had its troubles. Admin troubles. A unit command needs more than just blood and guts... it needs a man who can organize. With Red Mike here, we've got both."

"Understood, sir," Whaling said stiffly.

"But you're still a damned fine Marine, Bill," Vandegrift said. "And based on no small amount of recommendation from Merritt and Jerry here, we've decided to create a special unit that we want you to command."

"Sir?" Whaling asked, cautiously optimistic.

"Between all you colonels," Twining said, grinning slightly, "there's more than a hundred years of fighting experience. The kind of up close and personal stuff that seems the order of the day on this rock. But as mentioned, we lack good scouting. Even squad-sized units are being hit hard. We need a special detail created. A scouting and sniper unit to spread out past the perimeter, penetrate enemy territory, and bring back usable intelligence. That sound like something you can put together, Colonel?"

"Absolutely, sir," Whaling replied instantly. "You can count on me, General."

"Outstanding," Vandegrift declared and then frowned, lifting a sheet of paper from the pile in front of him. "Because I just got this little piece of… correspondence… from Admiral Turner."

Everyone did their best to hide wry smiles. They could tell that whatever Turner had written it had pissed Vandegrift off… royally.

"Our illustrious commander," Vandegrift said tightly, "urges us to continue to push against the Matanikau perimeter. He says that more Japs are being sent and are massing for an attack. We simply cannot dismiss such *insight*… he's right, though… but doesn't really have a full idea of what we're up against. I *do* want to hit the Matanikau again. I want to establish a position on the west side, near One Log Bridge if possible. And I don't think we need to stretch our imaginations too far to guess that Kawaguchi, backed by *his* boss Hyakutake and Yamamoto too, want to do the same on the east side in preparation for a massive attack on us."

"Which is what I'm to find out," Whaling said.

"Precisely," said Vandegrift. "Now, on a lighter note… we do have a distinguished guest coming in tomorrow. The Old Man himself. Chester W. Nimitz."

"Holy Christ…" Puller muttered.

"Seems *our* leader isn't too happy with Gormely over there in New Caledonia," Vandegrift said. "Frankly, Rich Turner isn't either. So Nimitz wants to see things for himself. Besides, a little birdie tells me he might have a few citations to give out. All right, gents, that's all for now. Lou, Merritt, stand by to assemble your men for another push. But this time, we're going to do it *right*. More men, better placed, and a full artillery and aerial bombardment."

"Damned straight," Geiger said.

Vandegrift nodded, "We will not have another travesty like the other day... not that I'm blaming anyone. Circumstances were poor, but we can't allow that again. You two scratch something together and we'll review it in the next day or two. Dismissed."

Just before stepping out, Whaling turned back, "Sir... Jerry... how many men am I being assigned?"

"About a hundred and a quarter, Bill," Thomas said. "You arrange them how you like. We're picking through every unit we've got to find woodsmen, hunters, trackers, you name it."

Whaling smiled and went out.

TRUK LAGOON

"Come in gentlemen, come in," Admiral Isoroku Yamamoto said, waving an arm at the conference table already laid out with his China tea service. "Take a seat and enjoy a cup of tea. Thank you for coming on such short notice."

Yamamoto sat beside his chief of staff, Matome Ugaki. Across from him, General Harukichi Hyakutake and his aides took seats. One of them, a fresh-faced lieutenant, poured tea for his superiors.

"We are grateful to have this opportunity to speak to you, Admiral san," Hyakutake said. "To iron out a plan for the recapture of Guadalcanal and the extermination of the Yankee *pests* there."

Yamamoto smiled thinly, "Yes, General. And we in the Navy are pleased by the Army's cooperation. As you know, our efforts so far have been... less than satisfactory."

The other army officers contrived to appear shame-faced. All but Hyakutake, however. He calmly shook a Golden Bat from a pack, dropped that onto the table, and used the decorative lighter to ignite it. He leaned back and eyed the two admirals coolly.

"The situation on Guadalcanal," said the general, "is far more complex than we were led to believe. A logistical nightmare, to be frank."

"True enough," said Ugaki.

"And we do not blame Kawaguchi," Yamamoto said. "We understand that things in the field are less than ideal. Indeed, I am currently gathering assets to support what we're here to discuss today, General. A full battleship squadron to bombard what the Americans are calling Henderson Field. To obliterate their air assets, which have been hampering our ability to send in troops and supplies by day."

Hyakutake nodded appreciatively, "That is good news, sir. Intelligence reports at least ten thousand Marines at that field. This is one reason Kawaguchi has encountered so much difficulty."

"Yet he *has* accomplished something vital," Ugaki said. "He has kept Vandegrift from crossing the Matanikau and establishing forward positions there."

"Do you have a recommendation for a decisive victory, General?" asked the grand admiral.

"I do, Admiral san," said Hyakutake. "I estimate that a force doubling that of the Americans... perhaps 22,000 in total, should be sufficient to break their perimeter and overrun the base. If naval gunnery can eliminate the Cactus Air Force... such names... we should be able to get the additional 17,000 troops, equipment and additional tanks and heavy artillery to the island by the second week of October. I call this Plan X. I will send generals Nasu and Maruyama in to begin the organization."

Ugaki smiled.

Yamamoto nodded curtly, "Very good. I have also ordered the completion of a forward air station at Bougainville, on the island of Buan. From Rabaul to Guadalcanal is just under a thousand kilometers. No problem for our bombers... but the escorting Zero has but a few scant minutes over the target. Buan is nearly halfway there. Should we be able to assemble a fighter contingent there, this will provide sufficient cover for the bombers as well as give our superior fighters far more time over the enemy."

Hyakutake nodded, "Very good, sir."

"Additionally," said Yamamoto. "I will be gathering the combined fleet to mount an assault from the sea."

"And *I* shall lead the ground offensive myself," said the general. "The men already on the island are sick, hungry, and weary. Even Kawaguchi himself."

"Whatever happens," said Ugaki sternly. "We *must* re-take Guadalcanal in the next few weeks. It is pivotal to our success in this conflict."

The army officers bowed, and Yamamoto rose, "Now, gentlemen… we shall adjourn for the time being. Men must not plan such important destinies on an empty stomach. We dine and then we shall return and hash out the details. To victory!"

They all aped Yamamoto's enthusiasm.

"To the Empire of the Rising Sun!" Hyakutake proposed and everyone cheered.

Even Matome Ugaki did not suspect how much hope rather than confidence his superior clung to. Just as the Americans had taken Guadalcanal on what they considered to be a shoestring, so now did Yamamoto believe that this combined operation was to do the same.

After all, the American shoestring had overwhelmed his forces in early August and no attempts thus far had been successful at dislodging them. And just a few days earlier, the fifth ship in his proposed battleship contingent had been torpedoed no more than ten kilometers from his very own battleship fortress of *Yamato*.

Victory was by no means certain, and the grand admiral was uncomfortable having to rely on so much luck. Yet one made best use of the tools at one's disposal.

1
HENDERSON FIELD
SEPTEMBER 29, 1942

"Hell's bells…" Captain Andy O'Dell cranked as he leaned forward over his yoke. "Like pea soup down there…"

"Least we know we're over land, Skipper," his co-pilot, a reedy young lieutenant from Ohio said. "This'n's ninety miles wide… heck of a lot better'n the last few days."

The B-17 flying Fortress angled in over the southeastern corner of the big island, almost entirely covered by thick, charcoal gray thunderheads. Both pilots knew they'd have to swing in low, below the cloud deck, if they were to have any chance of finding the airfield.

The trouble was that the cloud deck was very low, and the clouds were violently active with whipping wind, heavy rain, and frequent lightning. And both pilots as well as the rest of the crew were more than a little anxious, seeing just who it was they were flying in for a visit to the Marine base.

Both pilots were secretly wishing that the Navy had used their own jocks for this tour. It wouldn't look good, the Army Air Corps losing the Commander of the Pacific Fleet due to piloting error or inclement weather. The B-17 was built like a brick shithouse, and could handle just about anything thrown at her… but mother nature could always find a way to assert her dominance over Man's hubris.

"How we doin', fellas?" Admiral Chester W. Nimitz asked from the jump seat behind O'Dell and beside the flight engineer.

"Oh… just fine, sir," O'Dell said pleasantly. "Just make sure you're nice and secure, though, huh?"

Nimitz grinned. No coward and no stranger to aberrant flying conditions, the admiral shrugged elaborately and struck a match off his thumb. He used this to light his pipe, "All set, son. Got my seat upright and my tray table secure."

The flight engineer was a stern-faced, ruggedly built Navy chief aviation machinist's mate named Parkins Denny. The twenty-year veteran chuckled. He had to hand it to the Old Man. Nothing perturbed him… at least outwardly.

"Chief, get me on the horn to Henderson control," O'Dell decided as he throttled back and angled his nose down.

"What about the radio silence, Andy?" asked Lieutenant Jim Barnes from beside the pilot. "On account of our V.I.P.?"

"Considering the conditions and that we're less than a hundred miles out," O'Dell said. "Low risk with this nasty weather about. Go ahead, Park."

Denny already had the radio set up for Henderson's tower and switched the set on. He spoke briefly into the handset and then put the call on the pilot's mic, "Go ahead, Skipper."

"Henderson Field, Henderson Field," O'Dell said. "Navy Flight one-niner-five… are nearing feet dry and requesting radar vector, over."

The radio crackled, *"One-niner-five, Henderson tower… be advised we have severe weather over the field. Can you orbit, over?"*

Denny snorted and even Nimitz chuckled to himself. O'Dell shook his head and squeezed the mic, "Ah… that's a negative,

Henderson. We are a baker-one-seven heavy flying special delivery. Request altimeter, wind speed, and approach vector, over."

"*Oh shit...*" someone said in the background, bringing a smile to all four men's faces. "*Uhm... stand by one-niner-five...*"

"Sure take your time, pally..." Barnes cranked, nervously rubbing his palms on his trousers. "We've got nothing better to do..."

"Can you get in without info?" Nimitz asked.

"Oh, yes, sir," said O'Dell confidently. "I've flown into Henderson before... in good weather. Know the general layout, but I'd rather have a course to fly than follow the coast. Shortest distance between two points and all that."

"*One-niner-five, Henderson.*" This was a different voice. An older and far more authoritative one. "*Understand your sitch. Altimeter is one-one-hundred, wind is three-six knots out of the west, northwest. We're foregoing the standard approach, as there's nobody else up... have you on radar now. Continue on course for another... six minutes and then come left to three-double-oh. That'll take you right in. Just watch the downdrafts. Pouring cats and dogs over here, over.*"

O'Dell snorted, "Roger that, Henderson. Will advise upon our turn. One-niner-five standing by."

"Hope no Japs heard that," Denny chuckled.

"Who'd be a Jap pilot on an afternoon like this?" Nimitz smiled.

The big four-engine bomber descended into the heavy clouds and was instantly blanketed in dense gray nothingness. The big plane's airframe shivered and shuddered as roiling convections of air seized her in their teeth and shook her like a ragdoll.

Just as the ship was about to break through the storm, the cockpit was bathed in a brilliant flash of lightning as a gargantuan thunderclap rattled the plane so violently that everyone's teeth clattered. Barnes went a little pale and Denny glanced over at the admiral who sat, placidly smoking his pipe and seeming not to have noticed.

"Least we're gettin' a bath out of it," O'Dell said as he jockeyed the plane beneath the gray clouds and into the heavy rainfall.

Thousands of fat droplets exploded against the bomber's olive drab aluminum skin. They struck the windshield with such force that the drops shattered and streaked overhead, making the wipers unnecessary. Through the watery haze, the men could see the dark form of the island and the slightly lighter gray form of the sea stretching out before and below them. O'Dell advised the field that they were on their new course and within minutes, Henderson's lights could be seen glowing through a hazy nimbus.

"They must really not be worried," Denny said. "Runnin' them lights hot like that."

Barnes scoffed, "Them slant fighters wouldn't stand up to this slop, Chief."

"Okay, here we go, gentlemen," said O'Dell. "Jimmy, give me flaps and gear down."

"Gear down," said the co-pilot after the faint hydraulic whirring and thunk of the landing gear extending ceased. "Flaps set."

O'Dell throttled back even more, taking advantage of the headwind to shed some speed. Ahead of them, what few runway lights the field could boast outlined the main strip. To the right, several bulky transports were anchored near Lunga Point and tied to the wharf.

"Christ… is that the runway or somebody's patio?" Denny snorted.

"Little short," Barnes commented.

"It'll be muddy, though… might help," O'Dell added.

"You boys working up a comedy act?" asked the admiral.

"We'll let you know, sir…" O'Dell said, adjusting his angle of attack. "Okay… lined up… airspeed's good… stand by on the brakes, Jimmy…"

The big plane plowed onto the muddy runway hard enough to rattle every piece of gear aboard, bounced once and then bumped again, throwing up great sheets of dingy water as she slewed down the Marston mats, her brakes squealing and the engines roaring as O'Dell applied reverse thrust.

The bomber jinked left, then back to the right and then centered again as O'Dell fought with the sloppy controls. Just before they ran out of official runway, the B-17 slowed to a gentle stop, juddering slightly over an uneven portion of the runway that had recently been repaired.

Everyone in the cockpit heaved a sigh of relief and exchanged sheepish smiles as the pilot whirled the bomber around to face down the strip and shut down his engines. Even as he did so, several Jeeps sped across the muddy field and pulled beneath a large, hastily erected tent a few yards from the edge of the runway. Half a dozen Marines jogged out from under the canopy, formed themselves into a twin line bracing the plane's main hatch and came to rigid attention, seemingly unconcerned that they were already drenched to their skivvies.

"Gotta love me some Marines," O'Dell chuckled.

SEALARK CHANNEL, OFF LUNGA POINT

"Hello the submarine!"

"Hello back, sailor!" said Lieutenant Porter Hazard from the bridge of USS *Bull Shark*. "Pickin' up or droppin' off?"

"Little birdie tells me you got a passel of devil dogs needs a lift, sir," said the beefy petty officer at the helm of the Higgins boat pulling alongside the submarine.

Two more officers appeared on the bridge, both wrapped up in rain gear. Both men were tall, broad in the shoulder and fit. The taller one spoke first.

"That you, Mac?"

"Captain Turner!" said the petty officer. "Nice to see you again, sir. And Major Decker?"

"That's me, Mac," said Decker. "What've you been up to?"

"Oh... the usual, sir," said Mac as he helped his engineer to take lines thrown to them from a couple of sailors on deck. "When I'm not out here drivin' the V.I.P. hack... we're stormin' the beaches."

"Little excitement recently, Mac?" said Turner as he followed Decker down to the main deck.

Mac snorted, "A heller, sirs. Colonels Edson and Puller pulled an assault the other day. Another unit tried goin' ashore at Point Cruz... got pretty nasty. Me and the Coasties had to go in and bring the Marines off. Touch and go."

The word was passed, and Decker's Raiders came on deck, packs loaded and wearing what foul weather gear they could lay claim to. As they filed into the LCP, Gunnery Sergeant Phil Oaks grinned and shook Mac's hand.

"Hiya, sailor, come here often?"

Mac chuckled and helped the Marines to get situated. Finally, Decker and Turner clambered aboard as well.

"You goin' to see the boss, Captain?" Mac asked Turner.

"Seems the polite thing, Mac..." Turner noticed that in spite of his oilskin jacket and floppy rain hat, the boat's skipper was soaked through. "Humid today, huh?"

"That's funny, sir."

Decker guffawed, "Hey, Mac... was that a bomber we saw come in a few minutes ago?"

"Toss 'em, Charlie!" Mac ordered his mate and engineer. He waved to the men on the submarine and throttled up, guiding the square boat toward the wharf half a mile away. "Scuttlebutt is that God Himself is come for an inspection, sir."

"Nimitz?" Turner asked.

Mac nodded, "Lot of political stuff goin' on with the upper

echelons, sir. Seems like the CNO ain't so happy with Gormely, and neither is Admiral Nimitz… or Turner for that matter."

"You sure know a lot for a lowly cabbie, Mac," Decker jibed.

"Pays to keep an ear to the ground, Major," said Mac and flashed a grin. "All right, folks… we're nearing our destination. Please keep all arms and legs inside the vehicle until we come to a complete stop. Gather all personal belongings and watch your step as you disembark."

"Crackin' wise must be a survival mechanism in the armed forces," Oaks commented.

Sergeant Dave Taggart snorted, "Why we're all still alive, Gunny."

"Thought it was cuz we was good," Sergeant Charles Lider said.

"Yeah, good at bein' smart asses," Oaks glared.

Presently, Mac found docking space and he and his mate helped to unload the dozen men and their gear. Standing by on the wharf not far from where the Higgins boat pulled up was a six-by-six truck with its engine running. The driver opened his door and waved.

"Major Decker! Got you a ride, sir!"

The Marines piled into the back of the truck, allowing Decker and Turner to clamber into the front with the driver, who turned out to be none other than PFC Robert Leckie.

"Thanks for the lift, Leckie," Decker said.

"Yeah, Bobby… how is it you always seem to turn up?" asked Turner.

Leckie did a double take, "Captain Turner! Well I'll be… talk about always turnin' up, sir!"

"Like a bad penny," said Turner.

"Where to, sirs?" asked the Marine as he put the Deuce and a half in gear.

"The Pagoda," Decker said. "You can drop me and Art off and then take the fellas to our quarters… if we still got 'em. I imagine the captain here will need a ride back to the wharf shortly, too."

"Aye-aye, Major," Leckie stepped on the gas. "Say… you don't mind me askin', sir… what happened to that beautiful sailboat you guys had last week?"

Turner cocked an eyebrow, "Sailboat?"

Decker sighed, "Blown up. Weren't on Santa Isabella more than an hour or two."

"Shame," said Leckie. "Was hopin' to go sailin' sometime… Oh… did anybody tell you sirs that we got a guest?"

"Admiral Nimitz is actually here?" Turner asked.

"Yessir… just got in not long before you did," said Leckie. "General's gonna give him a tour of the perimeter when the rain lets up. Word is he's got a bucket full of medals to give out."

"God knows you all deserve one," Turner mused.

"And how…" Decker added softly.

In short order, the truck pulled up to the admin building. Known as the Pagoda, the structure was originally built by the Japanese and had been spared destruction during the initial invasion of Guadalcanal and ever since. Many of the Marines considered it to be sort of a lucky charm for that reason. The structure featured the classic Japanese architecture with upswept eaves and decorative trim.

The two O4's were shown into the conference room and immediately overwhelmed by the display of brass. Most of the field's commanding officers were there, from admin to individual battalion commanders. ComCincPac stood out in his khakis, white hair, and piercing blue eyes.

"Al!" General Vandegrift boomed. "You made it back! And brought us a guest, I see."

Both Turner and Decker snapped to, trying not to fidget with their sopping covers in front of so many senior officers.

"The other way around, sir," said Decker with a smile. "Captain Turner was kind enough to give us a lift home."

Vandegrift stepped over and shook the two men's hands vigorously, "Damned fine work, Al! Damned fine! And I hear you bagged yourself a battleship, Art! Hot damn! Anvil Art strikes again, huh?"

Turner blushed slightly, "Thank you, General… although word is that we're being credited with sinking a battle *cruiser*, not a wagon."

"Oh, horse shit!" Vandegrift thundered, appearing genuinely displeased.

"I agree, General," said Nimitz as he ambled over and stuck out his hand. "Bunch of bureaucratic nonsense, you ask me. Far as I'm concerned, Art… you got one of Mr. Moto's wagons. Damned good piece of work. You too, Major. Your general here's been talkin' my ear off about you and your team."

"Uhm… thank you, sir… sirs… that's very kind," Decker said, visibly daunted.

"How long you here, Captain?" Nimitz asked.

"Oh… just long enough to make a delivery, sir," Turner said ruefully. "We've got to steam for Brisbane and get reloaded."

"And back here, I hope," Vandegrift said. "Goddamned slants are getting ballsy with their Tokyo Express runs. Every damned night, the yellow bastards."

"Big buildup underway," Nimitz said. "Word from Hypo is that Yamamoto and the Army want to push for a final, all-out assault to retake Henderson."

"That can't be allowed to happen," Turner mused.

"No, it cannot," said another man, a barrel-chested Marine Colonel Turner knew. Chesty Puller shook hands as well. "Welcome back, Major."

"Thank you, sir," said Decker. "Things have been hot around here, I take it."

"Putting it lightly," said Edson, moving over and joining the clutch. "Glad to have you back, Al."

"Uh-oh…" Turner muttered.

Vandegrift chuckled, "Whenever the higher-ups start patting you on the back… you know that you're in for it."

"My team's ready for what needs doing, sir," said Decker. "As always."

"Well, we're not asking just yet, Al," said Edson. "You and your boys will get a little down time. Sam Griffith will clue you in soon. He's in command of First Raiders now. Light duty, though… he got hit a few days ago and I'm worried they're gonna evac him and we'll lose him for good."

"Yeah," said Puller, patting Edson on the back. "Red Mike did such a good job on Bloody Ridge… they gave him a regiment. Then put poor Sam in charge of the Raiders. On his feet though. One tough monkey."

"No rest for the wicked," Turner said.

"Why does that seem to be a theme of late, Art?" asked Decker.

Nimitz chuckled and shook his head, "And it doesn't seem like that's going to change anytime soon, gentlemen."

2

SEPTEMBER 30, 1942

"Last but certainly not least," Admiral Nimitz said from the makeshift platform that had been erected for his awards presentation. "I've got one more award to deliver. But before I do, I want to say a few words."

The hellacious storm of the previous day had passed and now a bright, clear tropical morning constituted an almost perfect backdrop for the ceremony. A bright robin's egg blue dome without even a hint of cloud curved above the rich greenery and turquoise waters of the Solomons. A light but steady breeze kept the several hundred assembled Marines if not exactly cool, at least less miserable at zero-eight hundred.

Less than five percent of the total compliment of more than 23,000 Marines were in attendance, however. The fact was that every man was needed on the perimeter that could be spared and while a third or so were on duty, another third slept near their posts and the remaining went about other duties before or after what sleep they were able to snatch. That included Decker's Raiders, who were still on the no-duty list but had been asked to attend the festivities.

This was due to the fact that Nimitz had presented Decker's top-heavy little unit with a citation along with a distinguished service cross for their CO and a silver star for their gunnery sergeant. Additionally, every other man received his own Navy and Marine Corps medal. Both Travis and Lider also were awarded their purple hearts. Further, Joe Treadway and Ted Entwater were promoted to grade 5, corporal.

There had been a few other changes since Decker and his men had sailed for Santa Isabella. The aircraft of *Enterprise* flight 300 had departed just a few days earlier. Those men and their aircraft, stranded on Guadalcanal after the Battle of the Eastern Solomons, had bravely and vigorously defended Henderson and were honorary members of the Cactus Air Force. Although they would be missed, the Navy had contrived to ferry in more aircraft from Neumea and Espiritu Santo with more to come.

War was, if nothing else, never stagnant.

"There simply aren't enough medals or ribbons to adequately shower you and all of your comrades," Nimitz said. "The struggles, sacrifices, and dedication of this division has been nothing short of historical. Your officers, your president, and your nation are and will be forever grateful to you men. And although the struggle is far from over… I promise to do all that I personally can to ease it for you. You've established and held a vital toehold in Japan's territory here. The door to ultimate victory may only be open a crack as yet… but thanks to you, that breech is there, and we *will* exploit it until the nation of Japan and their emperor are on their knees."

A chorus of cheers, cat calls, and whoops rose up among the assembled Marines. No sergeant or officer tried to hold it back. It was well-deserved and hard-earned. Only when Nimitz himself raised a hand for quiet did the assembled leathernecks rumble into silence once more.

"Finally," said CincPac. "I have one last award to give out. General Alexander Vandegrift, front and center."

Vandegrift, who'd been standing off to the side with the other senior staff, stepped forward, a neutral expression revealing nothing of his inner feelings. He stood before Nimitz at attention.

"General," said Nimitz, holding out a small case. "By order of the President of the United States, the Chief of Naval Operations, and the Commandant of the Marine Corps, I hereby award you the Navy Cross in recognition of your tremendous efforts here on Guadalcanal."

"Thank you, sir," Vandegrift was heard to say before the uproar rose into the morning sky once again.

Nimitz smiled and leaned in, still holding Vandegrift's hand, "I know that this little bauble doesn't amount to a hill of beans against what's been done and still needs doing, Alex. What do medals mean to men like us… but this is from the heart, you can believe that."

Vandegrift smiled, "Coming from you, Admiral, that means a *helluva* lot. To me and to my men."

The ceremony ended and the makeshift band played *Stars and Stripes Forever*. Within minutes, the Marines were dismissed and scattered. In their wake, the Navy's construction battalion, the Seabees, were setting up for another Tojo time. It would be coming, as it always did, and their readiness and efficiency was one of the key factors that kept the Cactus Airforce in the sky.

"Major, got a minute?"

Al Decker turned to see Sam Griffith striding over out of a gaggle of Marines. The ieutenant colonel appeared a bit pale and he moved a bit slowly, but other than that, hardly revealed how much pain he was truly in. Decker stopped with Oaks beside him and the rest of his squad came to attention behind.

"Sir!" Decker saluted. "I hope you're feeling better, Colonel."

"At ease, fellas," Griffith held up a hand and smiled. "I'll live, Al. Christ, if you can come back after being shot in the chest I can stand a little soreness for a few days. Anyway, I just wanted to say good work on that airfield assault. Really knocked the Jap for a loop."

"From the sound of things, though, Colonel," Decker said a little glumly, "they're pulling the same schtick at Bougainville."

Griffith sighed, "Yeah… but that's war for you. Move and counter move. Or maybe more accurately, you rush around trying to put out fires before they burn out of control."

Oaks harrumphed, "Like the damned Matanikau, sir?"

Griffith scoffed, "And how, Guns. Can I borrow you two men for a few mikes?"

Decker suppressed a groan and nodded, "Of course, sir… guys, why don't you head off. The gunny and I will catch up with you later."

"Aye-aye, sir!" the eight men said, saluted and then fast walked toward the far end of the field.

"Walk with me a minute, gentlemen," Griffith said and strode carefully but confidently toward the base's mess. "I won't take much time, Al. I know you and your boys are on a few days Furlough. No doubt you've got someone you'd like to visit."

Decker's relationship with Lana, a pretty native woman from the nearby village of Norambao was no secret. It was also no secret that Lana, like the now famous Jacob Vouza, was notorious for being a top-notch scout and damned near warrior goddess. Decker hadn't seen her since they had delivered the New Zealand missionary back to his family near Morah Point on the island's weather coast.

"My men and I are always ready for duty, sir," Decker said, yet wishing he didn't have to.

"I know, Al," said Griffith. "And unfortunately, you'll be needed all too soon… there's a lot happening and about to happen. You've heard about our little scuffles along the Matanikau the past week or so?"

Decker and Oaks both nodded. Oaks said, "Bits and pieces, sir."

"Well, the Old Man wants us to go at it again," Griffith said. "We have to. That damned river is the key to the whole shootin' match. Japs are running down hard at night on their damned Tokyo Express. Rumors and intel say there's gonna be a big push in the next few weeks… and getting men across that frigging river is the key."

"Sort of surprised they ain't tried going the long way around," Oaks said. "Bypass the dammed thing altogether."

Griffith chuckled, "They would, Gunny, except that moving ten or twenty thousand men that way would take a lot of effort and time. The advantage we have over the Japs is that their supply lines and logistics for this island are worse even than ours. Scouts report that hundreds of Kawaguchi's troops literally dropped dead on their way back from Bloody Ridge. And in spite of our failure last week to cross that damned river… his troops, Oka's, and the others are still trapped over there."

"We need better intel," Decker said.

Griffith nodded, "Colonel Whaling's in charge of a new scouting company… but I want my own intel. So does Edson and Puller. We want the kind of dope and the kind of capability only you and your boys have been able to achieve so far."

"On account we've been between here and Cape Esperance," Oaks said. "Least part ways."

"Right," said Griffith, leading them into the dining tent and to a table where Martin Clemens sat by himself. "You know how to get into Indian country and have enough manpower to not just gather information… you can hit the Nip where they live."

"Wizard!" Clemens said, getting to his feet and grinning from ear to ear. "Al! Philip! Glad I am to see you lot again."

"Hiya, Marty," said Oaks.

"Up to no good, I hope, Marty?" Decker asked.

"Depends on you, Cobber," said Clemens. Although English by birth, he'd been raised in Australia and spoke in that accent.

"Have you and the Colonel been plotting?" Decker asked.

"Al, I know that a man with your rank and experience ought to be commanding a battalion," Griffith said. "Not a small guerrilla squad, but…"

"Colonel," said Decker, holding up a hand. "When the Japs attacked Pearl, I was just a first looey. I got these oak leaves as a gift, nothing more. I didn't go up the ranks the usual way and I'm perfectly satisfied doing the job we've been doing. Feel useful, at least."

"Humility from a Marine?" Clemens teased. "Gods my life. Good on ya', mate!"

Griffith smiled, "Your time will come, Al. In the meantime, Marty and I have come up with a hairbrained scheme we'd like you fellas to put into play."

"Seems to be our specialty, sir," Decker said.

"Part and parcel for this bloody campaign, eh?" Clemens smiled.

"I want you to take your team in and get behind the Japs," Griffith said. "Make your way along the mountains to the south and then drop down and penetrate their territory somewhere west of Point Cruz. I want to know what kind of numbers we're facing and how well the Jap is equipped, Al."

"Just a simple recon, sir?" Oaks asked.

"Primarily," Griffith said. "But if you find an opportunity to do damage… an opportunity that doesn't get you fellas so far in Dutch that there's no way out… bloody their noses."

"I'd also be obliged did you locate a proper spot for a watch station in that sector," Clemens added. "Would be convenient if I could place a few of mine in a position to permanently clap eyes on the yellow buggers, Al."

"I'm sure there's somewhere," Decker said. "Trouble is,

communicating that back here and supplying them once established."

"Leave that bit to me," Clemens said.

"As for communicating... you're right," said Griffith. "I want you traveling light, Al. Focus on rations and ammo. I'll give you a pair of handheld field radios, but not the backpack job. Too heavy."

"With all due respect, Colonel," Oaks said, "the range on them things is only about three or four klicks in good conditions."

"I know, Guns," Griffith said. "I've arranged with General Geiger for a pair of overflights every day through the western sectors of the island. You'll be able to make contact with the pilots and report anything you need to. Your codename for this mission is Bashful. Ten days, Al. That'll be enough for you to get plenty deep."

Both Oaks and Decker frowned. Clemens smiled knowingly and Griffith nodded, as if all four men were in perfect telepathic sync.

"I know you'll be stretching your chow load," said Griffith. "But by now you know how to do this better than anybody, Al. We can also drop in a resup if need be."

"Aye-aye, sir."

"Well, now that's settled..." Griffith trailed off when the air raid siren began to blare. "Christ... damned slants are nothing if not consistent."

"Let's hope Admiral Nimitz takes off before the first wave hits," Decker said as the men bolted outside to get to the nearest foxhole.

The big B-17 had just powered up. In spite of the impending attack, Marines stood by, waving and cheering as CincPac's aircraft roared to full power and rumbled down the strip toward the palms at the far end.

Like baby ducks following their mama, several dozen Wildcats and SBDs taxied into the line and were quickly sent aloft to greet the incoming enemy aircraft. Thanks to Henderson's radar installation, the Marine pilots had just enough time to get into the air and up to angels twenty in preparation for the onslaught of Japanese fighters and bombers.

On that day, however, things would be different. Frustrated by their inability to permanently affect the field and with a need to shift the odds into their favor, the Japanese were employing a new aerial assault strategy.

In spite of the fact that the Zero was a superior fighter in terms of speed and maneuverability, it had a scant few minutes near Guadalcanal after the long haul from Rabaul. The Americans, on the other hand, need only hover over their home base, with hours of fuel to burn and the ability to choose their position thanks to the early-warning capability of the radar.

In previous attacks, the Zeroes were employed mostly to defend the Betties as they made their bombing runs on the airfield. On that day, however, the bombers were held in the rear and the fighters came in first, their goal not to ward off the Wildcats… but to shoot down as many as they could.

Like a broom, sweeping the sky clean of pests.

3

"Dog pound, Dog pound, Watchdog flight has reached Angels two-zero. No joy on bogies. Repeat, no visual contact, over."

"*Dog pound, Guard dog flight… same report.*"

Captain Marion Karl banked his Wildcat into a slow, lazy loop above New Georgia Sound. From his position above the waters between Savo Island and Tulagi, he had a horizon of over 150 miles. Theoretically, he should be able to see the incoming Japanese aircraft. However, there was only so much the human eye could do, even the sharp eye of a fighter jock.

His friend and fellow squadron leader Captain Dick Amerine had just confirmed the same odd lack of enemy contact from his position thirty miles to the east. In between were several other squadrons, too. Yet it would be Amerine and Karl out in front.

"*Watchdog, Guard dog… Dog pound.*" That was the Henderson fighter director. "*Confirm we have both you and the bogies on our scopes. Incoming units approximately five-zero out… and fainter contacts one-double-oh miles out.*"

"What the hell...?" Karl asked himself. He moved to press his mic, but Amerine beat him to it.

"*Dog pound... can you give counts and speeds on bogies?*"

There was a pause and then: "*That's a Rodge... first wave possible twenty-nine units, second are eight moving at one-five-zero... first wave two-five-zero.*"

"I have visual!" Karl broke in. "Watchdog flight to all... have visual on bandits. Eleven o'clock high... they're above us! Watchdog flight climbing to intercept!"

"*It's a fighter sweep!*" Amerine blurted. "*They're sending the Zekes in first to tackle us and to keep us busy while the Betties slip under!*"

"*Dirty yellow sons of—*"

"*Maintain radio discipline, dammit!*" That was none other than General Geiger himself. "*Watchdog, Guard dog, climb to intercept. Fox sections seven, eight, and nine, begin long orbit back toward field, descend to Angels one-five. Go get 'em, gentlemen!*"

"Watchdog-2, on me," Karl said. "Watchdog-4 on three and break right. Remember the Thatch weave... ready... break, break, break!"

Karl shoved his throttle to the stops and inhaled deeply from his O2 supply. High-altitude maneuvers always made him giddy and seemed to flood his entire body with a sizzle of excitement. Logically, he knew that was a combination of adrenaline and O2... but he knew part of it was psychological for him, at least. After all... high altitude meant plenty of room, and with plenty of room, meant Karl had plenty of opportunity to wipe Tojo's eye!

He banked his plane left, arcing away from his two wingmen in a long circle that slowly added altitude. The Zeroes were going to try their own trick on the Americans, come in high and dive down on the enemy, using speed and surprise in their favor.

In previous runs, the Japanese fighters stayed with their bombers, and so generally came in at much lower altitudes. This allowed the slower Wildcat to gain height and swoop down on them. That advantage often made all the difference and would be denied the Americans on this first run.

However Karl and his fellow pilots had another advantage over their incoming foes. Since the war began, Japan had suffered considerable losses in aircraft and pilots. And unlike the Americans, they were not able to make up these losses with men of equal or grater experience. Further, the experienced pilots, rather than being rotated home to train new men, had been killed, permanently removing that experience from the pool.

The long the war went on, the better the Allied pilots became and the worse the Japanese skills became. It was an experience gap that would continue to grow and prove deadly.

"And here are our first contestants, Watchdog-2." Karl said.

"*You want we should split and tag 'em, Skip?*" Watchdog-2 asked.

"Negative," Karl replied. "See them other two behind? The first two are gonna come for us. Ignore 'em and come straight up under them others' belly. Then we'll circle back and tag the eager beavers."

There was a laugh, "*Roger that!*"

As predicted, two of the four approaching Zekes broke off and dove down toward the American fighters. Neither Karl nor his wingman did a single thing. They simply let the smaller, more nimble fighters wing over, accelerate and flash by, their 7mm guns sparkling in the morning sunshine but hitting nothing.

Their two wingmen, apparently waiting to see what would happen, did not expect such steadfastness. It took considerable nerve to let an aircraft come roaring out of the sky directly at you and not flinch away. When the surprised Japanese pilots realized what had happened, their reaction was to throw their birds into a steep wing over in an attempt to roll away and swoop down into an advantageous position over the Wildcats. Unfortunately for them, all this succeeded in doing was to present a broader profile to the American's .50 caliber machine guns.

Eight streamers of tracer fire tore through the blue, ripping into the delicate aluminum of the Japanese aircraft, tearing away hunks of metal, peeling back the skin and burrowing into the fuel tanks where they sparked off devastating explosions.

Both Zeroes bloomed into ugly orange balls of oily fire as bits of burning metal and flesh plunged out of the sky.

"*Ya-Hoo!*" Watchdog-2 cheered.

"Don't get cocky, kid!" Karl called out. "Follow me in, we got them other two to worry about!"

Both aircraft rolled up onto their starboard wings, pivoted and angled in, diving out of the sky at the first two Zeroes that had flashed by. By this time, the two Japanese pilots had realized their mistake and were muscling their birds into tight climbs in order to try and come up under the bellies of the Americans. What they saw froze their blood… but not for long.

As the two Zeroes banked over and nosed up, they flew straight into the maw of two F4F wildcats diving out of the sky directly on top of them. Triggers were pulled and rounds exchanged. One Zero exploded and the other spun away, half its vertical stabilizer obliterated and its engine cowling peppered with cigar-sized rounds. The pilot lost control and the plane began to auger in toward the concrete-hard water seventeen thousand feet below.

Thirty miles to the east, Dick Amerine had spotted another flight of Zeroes vectoring in over the Florida Islands. At first he was caught off guard by the absence of bombers but the realization of what was happening drove him into immediate action.

"Guard dog-2, stick to my six," Amerine said. "The Japs are finally startin' to learn."

"*What's going on, Dicky?*" came the reply from his wingman, even as the other Wildcat snapped over and settled in behind him.

The wingman was a new arrival to Henderson. A young Marine retread named Bruno Santino. Santino had done a hitch that had ended a little before the war started. Upon hearing about Pearl

Harbor, he'd rushed to the nearest Navy recruiting office and signed up again.

He'd been sent through flight training and had shown remarkable natural skill. A New York city native, Santino's accent often got him teased for being in the mob. Taking it good naturedly, the young pilot would often wink and intimate that maybe it *was* true… and that any man busting his babbalones might do well to watch his ass.

"Fighter sweep, Bruno," Amerine said. "They want to clear us out before sending in the bombers. Three, four, get high as fast as you can. Me and two are gonna run up and intercept. We'll draw them back to you. Tallyho!"

Amerine went to full power and banked his aircraft into a swooping right turn. He angled up a little, just enough to get another thousand feet of altitude before the four onrushing Zekes pounced. "Four bandits," Amerine said. "Two at twelve o'clock high and two at eleven o'clock low, Bruno."

"*Want we should split and take them lower two mamelukes out?*"

"Negative," Amerine said. "Never leave your wingman, pally. Them two up high are gonna dive down on us and try to force us to run. Then when we do, their pals are gonna hit us in the belly."

"*Yeah, hah… I mean… Roger that… so what's the plan?*"

"We go after the two high, let 'em pass and then we invert, roll, and dive on the lower two," Amerine said. "Table the turns. Ready? We might take some rounds."

"*I ain't a'scared.*"

Amerine laughed, "Good man. Hold on… here they come…"

Just as predicted, the two leading Zeroes, perhaps a thousand feet higher than the two F4Fs, wheeled over and dove, their 7.7mm machine guns flashing and sending out blue tracers. The Japanese pilots expected the American planes to panic, throwing themselves into a hard roll or tight turn to get out of the line of fire. However, the two larger aircraft simply stayed on course, only jinking left and right to avoid most of the fire. In spite of this, however, several rounds struck each plane but did no lasting damage.

That was yet another thing that new Japanese pilots didn't have the experience of. They were used to their own light, nimble, and admittedly fragile aircraft. Although the Wildcats were sneered at for being clunky by comparison, they were also robust and could take a great deal of punishment as well as dish it out.

So when the two Zeroes zipped past, the pilots did not suspect that the Wildcats would suddenly wing over, roll onto their backs and then drop out of the sky like avenging angels. The two lower fighters, still waiting for their prey to appear in their gun sights, were caught unaware as Amerine and Santino dropped out of the morning sun, eight streamers of red tracers reaching out with taloned claws to rip them to shreds.

"*Oh, Marrone! Scratch two type-1 lightiz!*" Santino whooped.

"Nice work, kid, but don't get too big for your britches… here come their pals," Amerine warned.

In the distance, the first two Zekes had recovered and formed back up. They were banking around to confront the Americans once more. Amerine grinned, flexed his hands on his controls and angled in toward them, nearly head on. As he did so, two more Wildcats raced in from above, seemingly out of nowhere. They vectored in behind the Zeroes and lit them up, turning both into flaming balls of debris.

"Ha!" Amerine shouted. "So much for the fighter sweep!"

"*All aircraft! All aircraft!*" That was the fighter director. "*Vector in for the field! Incoming bombers!*"

"*Never rains but it pours, huh, Dicky?*" Santino asked.

"You got that right, pal."

∼

On the ground, what precautions that could be taken had been taken. All valuable equipment had been moved as far from the runways as possible. Construction equipment was staged to spring into action immediately. Along the beach and at strategic points throughout the field, Marines manned their anti-aircraft guns.

At the wharf and anchored out in the Sound, transports and their escorting warships manned their guns as well and began throwing up a curtain of flack to discourage the incoming Japanese bombers.

The mechanical roar of angry hornets as several dozen aircraft wheeled about one another in the sky was drowned by the cacophony of hundreds of rounds of ack-ack fire banging into the morning sky. Machine guns clattered, 20 and 40mm cannons thwacked and the sound of expended brass tinging and pinging rose as one giant chorus. The song of war being sung to the exclusion of all others.

In the skies, the fighters swooped and danced and sent burning debris raining down on Iron bottom Sound and the rest of Sealark Channel. Twin engine Betty bombers slipped in, coming in low and trying to get in under the curtain of lead. Some were smashed by .50 caliber rounds from vengeful Wildcats, a few were torn to bits as merciless explosive AA rounds dragged rivulets of destruction through the skin, frames and flesh of the attackers. Yet in spite of all of this, some got through.

Added to the song of weapons' fire was the thunder of exploding ordnance. Great billows of dust and blasted coral flew into the air in great cones of ejecta as Japanese ordnance struck the field. A pair of bombs struck the end of the runway not far from where Admiral Nimitz's plane had been just an hour before. An eighty-foot section was blasted into a pair of craters that through burning bits of Marston mat into the sky.

A Marine ack-ack position near the wharf spotted an incoming Betty angling down from over the Sound. The team swept their

Oerlikon around, lined up and emptied an entire magazine into the approaching aircraft. Their aim was perfect, the big explosive rounds virtually obliterating the nosecone and cockpit of the plane as it vectored in.

Although the pilot was killed, his plane continued on the course he'd set. Pilotless, out of control and beginning to auger, Betty arced down, flipped over once and then slammed directly into the center of runway two, its full load of ordnance exploding into a hellish ball of white-hot fire. A shockwave of superheated air raced away from the crash site, choking the air with dust so thick that men a hundred yards away had to cover their mouths and shut their eyes against the furnace blast.

That's when the shells began to fall. From off to the west, from behind the Matanikau, Japanese 80mm artillery lobbed explosive rounds over the perimeter and into the field. This happened almost with every air attack and could be even more deadly as the Americans began to take stock and begin the repair process.

Of course, once the planes in the air were able to home in on the source of the shelling, their strafing runs would generally put a stop to it, but the danger was still present, especially for the Seabees.

Commander Joseph Blundon watched through a pair of binoculars from his foxhole as the last of the Betty bombers wheeled away and fled for Rabaul. Gritting his teeth and offering up a prayer, he rose and bellowed the order.

"Seabees! Fall to!"

Blundon and his assistant and the half platoon worth of men in the foxhole with them leapt from cover and sprinted. By this time, Blundon and his Navy construction battalion had honed their activities into a plan of both preparation and swift action.

First were waves of men with shovels to fill in bomb craters even as the few bulldozers and power shovels and trucks loaded with gravel got underway. Other men were tasked with hauling in new

Marston mats from the stacks set up along the runway like extra rails beside a railroad.

"Incoming!" somebody shouted even as the whistle of a shell screamed through the morning air and plowed into the ground on the far side of the runway with a thunderous boom and cloud of dust and pebbles. It was close enough to a squad of Seabees that they were thrown off their feet… some coughing, some gagging, and some crying out for a medic. Blundon raced forward, waving his arms and shouting directions. He saw that no one had been killed and waved them on.

Even as he did, another arcing screech froze his blood. Almost with pinpoint accuracy, the second shell burrowed into the crater left by its fellow… but did not explode. It simply sat there, surrounded by staring, running, and cursing men.

"Wait for it!" Blundon shouted.

One trick the Japanese had learned was to lob in a shell, wait just long enough for unsuspecting Seabees to begin working on filling in the crater and then send in another right on top of the first. Of course, the Japanese couldn't see what was happening from their positions miles away, but they knew… the yellow bastards just knew…

"Arnold! Travers! Osteen!" Blundon roared as he moved toward where the remnants of the crashed Betty still burned. "Get that damned dozer over here! Get the water truck, too! Hose that down and plow it under, for Christ! C'mon, c'mon! Our boys are running low up there!"

On and on it went, day after day and week after week. Dedication, bravery, and sacrifice.

"It's a madhouse," Al Decker said as he and Oaks helped a group of Seabees haul a stack of mats to the runway.

"The whole world's gone bananas," Oaks said. "Why should we be left out, sir?"

"Some day off," Decker cranked as he picked up a shovel

dropped by a wounded Seabee who was being hauled to the infirmary, even as he shouted his protests to be able to finish his job.

"Just think, pretty soon we'll be back in the jungle fighting bugs and Japs coming at us outta the dark," Oaks said.

"Ah… back to normal," Decker couldn't help but laugh.

4
GUADALCANAL INTERIOR
OCTOBER 2, 1942

"First day's always the easiest, huh, Ed?" PFC William Gartrell teased before gulping down three large swallows from his canteen.

PFC Edgar Jones cocked an eyebrow at his teammate, "Easy, huh? Gotta be well over ninety in here, ninety-five percent humidity and I already got something bit me on the back of the hand. Lookie that som'bitch."

Jones held out one of his large dark hands and Gartrell whistled softly at the puffy red lump on the back. He smiled and shrugged, "Yeah but ain't no Japs around… not this close to Edson's Ridge anyhow."

"Don't be sure about that, boyos," Sergeant Dave Taggart said around a half-smoked Camel. "Was only a couple weeks back. For all we know that Kawaguchi could've left some scouts back here to keep an eye on things."

"Everybody knows when they come back in force it's gonna be the same route," Sergeant Charlie Lider added as he walked up. "Only way to hit the field is from the south. Leastways without a major logistical undertaking."

"Listen to this guy over here," Phil Oaks said as he strolled up, reaching under his boonie hat and wiping at his forehead. The mosquito netting hanging around his head gave him the general appearance of a beekeeper. "Guy gets a few chevrons and suddenly thinks he's Dugout Doug MacArthur."

"You mean like a gunnery sergeant, Phil?" Taggart jibed.

"Exactly," said Oaks.

"What's the word from the skipper, Gunny?" Jones asked.

"To sit tight and take five," Oaks said, finding a deadfall and easing himself onto it. "Know we've only gone three klicks or so… but we're startin' to see signs of the aftermath at the ridge. Skipper's a hundred yards up. Established a temporary OP with Evans and Joey. Travis and Teddy are scouting toward the river."

"Which one? Lunga or Teneru?" Lider asked.

"Both," said Oaks. "Skipper wants to push west past the Lunga to the Matanikau, too. Had to be the way the Jap went after we gave 'em that pasting couple weeks ago. Already seen a couple of bodies out here… or what's left of 'em."

That silenced the men for a moment and sent involuntary shivers up their spines in spite of the warmth. It was known by now that when Kawaguchi attacked the long ridge just south of Henderson, once known as Lunga Ridge and renamed Edson's Ridge in honor of the former Raider commander's gallantry, he'd come across the log bridge over the Matanikau and then had his forces split to come at the ridge from the south and along the Lunga River. After the defeat, the remnants of the force, which had already been near starvation when the battle started, had to retreat through the harsh Guadalcanal climate. Many wounded did not make it. Many walking wounded became so ill they could no longer walk, and many healthy Japanese soldiers came down with dysentery, malaria, dengue fever, and other sicknesses that permeated the dense and malodorous tropical rainforest.

After three weeks, the only signs of those who'd fallen along the path back were fragments of moldy clothing and stark white bones, their flesh having been scoured clean by thousands upon thousands of white ants, fire ants, and other insects.

Enemy soldiers or not, it was a gruesome sight. No soldier wanted to be reminded of the all too real possibility of dying… not to mention the horrors of what happened afterward.

"So we got a marching plan yet?" Gartrell asked.

"Well," Oaks said, "considering how much time we got… there's only one real choice, ain't there? See, what your Jap fails to appreciate is that the further inland you go on this rock, the easier it is to move laterally. Sure, along the northern coast, the land is flatter… but the rivers are wide, and you still got ridges and ravines and shit. You go in, toward the high country, and them same rivers are nothin' more'n narrow streams. Not to mention water's cleaner. You go south, cut over, and come north again. Maybe it's no faster… but a lot less effort."

"Plus we seen a lot of this land since the beginning of August," Taggart said. "Before anybody."

"Not this part," Oaks said. "Where we're goin' is mostly new territory for us."

"What about that time we went after Captain Amerine?" Gartrell asked. "Remember? We was not far from Kokumbona and all that."

Oaks drew a long pull from his canteen and pointed more or less west, "That way. We'll be further inland, crossing south of where we went before. Skipper wants to see how far west we can get. Word is Mr. Clemens wants to set up a watcher station out that way. And maybe even man it with a platoon. Rear observation post and jump off point for some raids. Lotta Japs comin' down the Express lately… and they're all bunching up near Matanikau village and Kokumbona."

"We in for another hullabaloo?" Jones asked.

"Looks that way," said Oaks.

"It's a damned war, Jonesy," Lider grinned. "Sooner or later, you gotta put a few twenty, thirty thousand guys up again' one another."

"Hey, y'all," a voice called from the gloomy jungle just to the south. "Skipper says c'mon up!"

James Travis stepped out of the foliage, one moment he wasn't there and the next he was. He hadn't even been trying to conceal himself and yet the vegetation had done a good job for him. Not a man lounging about missed that and once more, they shivered.

Travis led the men back through the path he'd pushed through the jungle. Presently, they emerged into a partially sun-dappled clearing where the denser trees, vines, and broad leafy arms of the jungle gave way to a few hardwoods and short kunai grass. What might be something of a game trail pushed through the clearing roughly west to east. To the south, the jungle began to encroach again, but not as thickly as the direction from which they'd come.

"Sir?" Oaks asked.

Decker stood in the center of the clearing with Ted Entwater beside him. Both men were collapsing the antennae of their radios and storing them. Off to the right, Joe Treadway stood with two Marines not assigned to Decker's unit.

That was rather jarring, finding two comrades out in what felt like the middle of nowhere. Oaks recognized one man, but not the sergeant with him.

"Hiya, Whitey," Charlie Lider said, moving toward the trio and extending a hand. "Whatcha doin' out here in fruit city?"

"Hey there, Charlie," Whitey Groft smiled. "Me and the sarge here is out on patrol. Temporarily assigned to Colonel Whaling's scouts, we are. This here is Sergeant John Basilone."

Basilone stuck out a hand, "Pleasure, Sarge. Heard lots of good things about you boys."

"Sergeant Basilone has some intel on the territory hereabouts, Guns," Decker said, striding over and gathering all of the men around.

"Understand you all are headed deep into Indian Country," Basilone said. "Sure wish we could join ya'."

"Not all it's cracked up to be, Sarge," Oaks said. "How long you fellas been out here?"

"Since yesterday," Groft said. "Doin' a circle between the two rivers… Lunga and Matanikau, that is. Tryin' to keep up with the Jap buildup at the log bridge."

"They on our side?" Oaks asked.

Basilone sighed, "Some. Maybe a platoon's worth. We hit 'em pretty hard a while back. Colonel Puller and the artillery section… but like damned cockroaches, they come back again. Massing on the left bank, too."

"Way I heard it, there was some trouble at the bridge not long ago," Taggart said.

Basilone nodded, "Yeah… our guys got pushed back hard. Lost Major Bailey on that one."

"Yeah…" Decker sighed. "We were off island on a search and destroy… from this position, Sarge, what's our best choice? We've got to get over the Matanikau."

Groft frowned but let the higher-ranking Marine speak.

Basilone sighed, "You take this trail here… one we came out of, and you'll come to a small ford across the Lunga. Easy going, never gets more'n knee deep. On the other side, there's a clearer trail that leads right to one log bridge. Cutting across that is a couple near the river and further in that'll take you to Mount Austin. Easy to get across the river there. Matanikau River, that is… but the Japs probably have that manned again."

Decker jerked a thumb over his shoulder, "And this way? To the south?"

"Probably decent going about a half mile down," Groft said. "But you gotta scale a pretty big coral ridge first. Goes right up to the Lunga above the ford… some rapids there… and goes east, too. Not sure how far."

"Can't be too far," Entwater observed. "We've tracked up and down that part of the island before."

"Still…" Decker said. "Might take a good day just to get around the ridge. Going's slow as molasses in here."

"If you want, Major, I'll guide you over the Lunga," Basilone said. "Or me and Whitey'll climb that ridge and stick with you the rest of the day. Be good intel to bring back."

Decker frowned, "We've got too much ground to cover to spend the next couple of hours scaling a wall we don't have to… let's gain as much ground as quickly as we can. Sergeant, I'd be obliged if you showed us the ford across the Lunga."

"Aye-aye, Major."

It wasn't long before the jungle thinned out once more as the muddy Lunga River wound its way toward the beach several miles to the north. As Basilone had indicated, a short, steep coral ridge butted against the river to the south, creating a ravine through which the waters surged and frothed. Almost immediately after, however, the waters subsided and became the placid, reflective surface they were all used to.

"Just at the mouth of the ravine there, sir," Basilone pointed. "Where the ford's the easiest. About a foot deep. Just watch the current, though. It's calm there but there are still some good eddies coming out of the rapids."

The men were gathered in the shadows at the edge of the jungle and looking across the calm river at the shadowy line of foliage on the other side. Basilone's ford was no more than 200 yards to the left. Before them, the river was perhaps fifty yards across and about two-thirds that wide at the ford. Thus far, there appeared to be no movement on the other side save the usual fauna of Guadalcanal.

"Have the Japs come across, do you know, John?" Oaks asked.

Basilone shook his head and glanced at Groft, who nodded, "Not so far as we can tell, Gunny. They're a lot more interested in holding One Log Bridge, I think."

Decker glanced up and saw that the sun was well beyond its zenith, "All right, we need to move. I'd like to get past Mount Austin before dark and find a place to camp… Joe, Ted, set yourselves up here with good cover and a clear firing arc for the ford and the bank beyond. Ted, you keep the radio. Cover our crossing and once we're over, we'll call you up."

"We'll hang with them, sir," Basilone offered. "See you boys across before heading back to the barn."

"Thank you, Sarge," Decker clapped the man on the shoulder. "And you two, Corporal. Appreciate the intel as well. Fall out."

Decker turned and led the remaining eight men of his unit along the tree line toward the ford. As he went, Treadway and Entwater found good sniper positions in the shadows where they could rest the barrels of their 1903 Springfields in the crotches of teak trees and cover the ford.

"Ought we should tell them about the Japs, Sarge?" Groft asked as he and Basilone readied themselves beside the two Raiders.

"What about the Japs?" Treadway asked.

Basilone harrumphed, "Yeah, that's right… few days back, me and Whitey was out on a dozen-man patrol. We were between the log bridge and Mount Austin, as it happened, when we passed a Jap sentry."

"Uh-oh…" Entwater mused, never taking his eyes off the far side of the river.

"Yep…" Groft sighed. "I was in the rear with the sarge here nearby. We go past this Nip, see… guy was hiding under cover. So we go past, like I say… and he pops up and drills the guy directly behind me. Last man in line. Me and the sarge we wheels around, see… drop and snaps off a few shots, but…"

"But the bastard got our buddy," Basilone said. "Poor kid… just arrived on the rock few weeks ago. Point is, these slants is tricky. Devious. You gotta watch yourself every second."

"Believe me, Sarge," Entwater said, pushing his glasses up on his nose. "We know that."

"Yeah…" Basilone mused. "You fellas have got a reputation. Still, never hurts to learn about a new trick."

"No, it doesn't," said Treadway. "If the Jap is anything, he's… hey, Teddy… you see that?"

That was all that was needed. Both Groft and Basilone shouldered their rifles and took to scanning the jungle across the river. All four men held their breath for a moment before Entwater finally responded.

"About a hundred yards to the right of the far side of the ford… azimuth… twenty left. That a khaki sleeve?"

"Hang on, I got binocs…" Groft let his rifle hang in its sling and brought up a pair of field glasses. He quickly scanned the foliage and nodded. "Yeah… a pair of Nips, dug well in but with a clear line of fire. Well I'll be dipped… you got good eyes, Treadway."

"Think they see your guys?" Basilone asked.

"Ain't gonna bother to ask," said Entwater, zeroing in. "I got the left one, Joey…"

"Roger that… got the second one… up in a tree," Treadway said. "On three… one… two… three…"

The two reports were so simultaneous that they might've been one weapon. The crack echoed gently across the water and faded quickly, not even disturbing the cacophonous song of parakeets and the occasional squawk of parrots on both sides of the river.

There was a brief, shrill cry and then something crashed down in the foliage. The second man made no outburst, he simply pitched over, tumbling as he fell and splashed into the water creating a brief silvery fountain. He did not move, except to begin a lazy float to the right, along with the flowing current of the river.

Basilone was just about to compliment the two young men on their shot when another splash erupted across the water. Something large, greenish black and sinewy broke the surface, rolled and disappeared so quickly that a single eyeblink would've missed it.

But not one of the four men had blinked. They'd seen the creature take the Japanese soldier in its jaws and vanish below the muddy surface. All that remained was a spreading ring of foam and a curtain of ripples moving north.

"Holy… Jesus…" Groft breathed, visibly shaken. "What…?"

"Croc," Entwater groaned. "God help us all… saltwater croc."

"Of all the damned places to fight a war…" Basilone shook his head.

"*Blue, Red… Blue, Red… sitrep?*"

Entwater reached down and pulled the handheld off his belt, "Red, Blue… we read. Located and eliminated two enemy targets, over."

Decker and his men were already nearly across the ford by then and the four could see Oaks with his radio held before his face, "*Understood. Good eye. No other signs. Will take up cover position. Actual says to rejoin. Over.*"

"Acknowledged," said Entwater and collapsed the antenna. "Well, that's it for us, fellas. Good to see ya. Thanks for the support, too."

Hands were shaken and Basilone said, "Good luck. Hope we see you guys again soon. Wish we were comin' with ya'."

"That's okay, Sarge," Treadway grinned. 'We'll go out and do the hard work. You fellas go back and hang around at the cushy airbase for a while."

That drew a laugh and Groft said, "Yeah, just gotta keep an eye out for Washing Machine Charlie."

5

"There's gotta be *somethin'* we can do, sir..." Phil Oaks hissed in frustration.

Beside him, Al Decker scowled and pressed his binoculars to his eyes, "I'd say we're looking at a platoon-sized unit here, Guns. Bivouac, machine gun emplacements... at least half a dozen guards... about all we'd accomplish is getting ourselves killed."

On Decker's other side, Henry Evans tried not to fidget. The three men lay on their bellies on a small rise overlooking One Log Bridge and the Matanikau beyond. They could also easily observe the activity of the Japanese soldiers on both sides of the river. There were a lot of them, with perhaps the rest of an entire company located on the western side of the water course.

Evans had seen his fair share of action in his short time with the unit. Yet looking at such a large force, so well organized... it gave him pause. More than that, Evans felt the distinct and icy fist of fear digging into his gut. The idea of attacking such a large force scared him... and left him with the sour taste of shame in his mouth, too.

"What about after dark?" Oaks asked. "We range the unit here and open up on 'em. We could take out ten, fifteen in the first volley... maybe even seize a couple of them Nambus. You know this is a set up for another push at the base, sir."

"Yeah..." Decker said. "But look across the water, Gunny. They've got a couple of halftracks and mobile guns over there... and look, coming out of the jungle to the right..."

They heard it before they saw it: the low, rumbling growl of a large diesel engine. As the three men watched, a trio of tanks rolled out from the jungle path and arranged themselves at strategic positions in the cleared area that represented a large camp on the left bank of the Matanikau.

"Christ..." Oaks said. "They're better equipped than before..."

"They can cover the whole approach on this side just with them three monsters," Evans said. "All we got are a few pineapples and a couple of satchel charges."

"Exactly," said Decker unhappily. "If General Vandegrift wants to push across the Matanikau it's gonna take a couple of battalions. Sorry, Phil... much as I'd like to tan these bastards' hides for them... we don't have the firepower."

"Phooey..." Oaks said and chuckled.

For Evans's part, he was relieved. He knew that it was possible to attack a larger force, especially with the element of surprise. They'd done so on Santa Isabella just a few days before. Yet that had been different. The force was split, and the Raiders had been able to whittle away at the Japs there as they'd crossed the island. The scenario at the log bridge was an entirely different kettle of fish.

And there were worse things than dying in battle...

"What's that?" Oaks asked, nodding toward the river.

On the other side, a pair of flatbed trucks rolled out of the jungle next. Their beds were piled high with a heavy load of logs. The two vehicles stopped not far from the existing bridge and a score or more of soldiers ran up and began casting off lashings.

"I think they're expanding the bridge," Decker said. "Gonna make it wider, sturdier… uh-oh…"

"So they can get vehicles over here?" Evans asked.

"Looks that way," Oaks grumbled.

Decker sighed, "Nuts… we've seen enough. Let's backtrack and find out how our guys are doing up at Mount Austin."

A string of harsh Japanese stopped the three Marines. A man, obviously an officer, stood behind one of the Nambu nests shouting at a small group of soldiers. Beside him, a larger sergeant stepped forward and added his own words. The six soldiers snapped to, saluted and turned and began marching past the bivouac area of the camp and into the jungle to the south.

"Patrol, sir," Evans mused.

"Yeah… and do we recognize those two fellas, Guns?" Decker asked, pointing.

"That wouldn't be Lieutenant Hondo and Sergeant Makai, would it, sir?" Oaks asked with a crooked smile.

"I think maybe so," Decker smiled. "Would love to say hello… but I suppose it's not in the cards now. I'm sure we'll meet again, however. Let's move."

The trio slid backward until the camp was out of sight. They then picked themselves up, brushed off any freeloading insects they'd collected and double-timed it through the jungle and to a narrow path leading more or less north and south. Waiting there were Lider, Travis, Entwater, and Treadway. Entwater had the radio activated and was listening intently, although there was currently no chatter to hear.

"They're dug in," Decker announced at the men's expectant looks. "A good company's worth, with a platoon on our side. Got tanks, halftracks, and guns. And they're adding to the bridge."

Lider groaned, "Sounds like we need to get on the blower, sir."

"Think you can, Teddy?" Decker asked.

Entwater frowned and shook his head, "Been scanning the

freqs, sir. Found a couple of convos… probably guys on the southern perimeter doing a little chin-wagging… but mostly static. I'll need some elevation."

Decker frowned. That was the trouble with the Signal Corps Radio - 536. A good, solid walkie-talkie but its range was limited, even in the AM band. With open ground or open water, it could transmit and receive over several miles. But in the dense jungle of Guadalcanal with its many hills, ravines, and ridges, the range could be as low as a few hundred yards.

"All right, then let's move south," Decker decided. "We can catch up with Blue team and—"

Entwater's radio squawked and then crackled to life, "*Red, Blue… Red, Blue, come in, Red…*"

Entwater looked at Decker who nodded. The young Marine held up the unit, "Go ahead, Blue. We read you five by five."

A crackle and Jones said, "*Have eyes on objective… enemy occupied.*"

"No surprise there…" Lider muttered.

Decker took the radio from Entwater and thumbed the transmit button, "Blue, Red actual… numbers? Equip status?"

"*Assess platoon strength, actual… include rifle sections, heavy weapon section and mortar section,*" Jones replied. "*Some limited fortification and what look like a radio aerial. Over.*"

"Uh-huh…" Decker mused and then pressed the button again. "Potential target?"

A pause and then Taggart's voice, "*Red, Blue… Roger that. Over.*"

Lider chuckled and Oaks grinned. Decker smiled and said, "Understood. Rendezvous point Able. Two Hows. Out."

"We gonna hit 'em, sir?" Evans asked.

"Looks that way, PFC," Decker said. "But not until after dark. C'mon, let's Charlie Mike. We've got to make camp before dark."

Point Able was an arbitrary spot approximately half a mile southeast of Mount Austin. Mount Austin was not, in fact, an actual mountain. It was merely a jagged outcropping of limestone near the south end of a hill approximately seventy feet above sea level. Point Able was nothing more than a spot picked out on the map. There was no good intel on it, and Decker had to hope that there was space to sling a few hammocks and possibly rig some cover from the weather.

The geographical advantage was that Point Able was located just south and east of the Mount Austin crag, which would hopefully provide radio range as well as be high enough that the team would be out of the thickest of the jungle.

As it turned out, Point Able was located along a spine of coral that ran parallel to the coast and intersected with the Mount Austin crag. The ridge was perhaps twenty feet above the jungle to the north and more sparsely populated with hardwoods and less dense tropical foliage.

In order to reach the ridge, the team had to hack their way through dense jungle east of the Japanese position at Mount Austin. Then they had to climb a near vertical cliff face. Decker opted for this, as trying to find a better way up would eat too much time and the sun was already only a few handsbreadths above the rainforest. To add spice to the proceedings, a line of rain squalls was gathering over Iron Bottom Sound and moving south.

Fortunately, the cliff of coral was relatively low. Jones and Gartrell, having had recent experience with such endeavors, were sent up first without any gear. Once on the ground above, they hauled up the team's packs while the rest climbed the knotted rope. Although hot and sweaty work, the entire evolution took less than half an hour.

"We should only be a few hundred yards away now, sir,"

Charles Lider said, conferring with Gartrell and their hand-drawn maps. Both men were from Georgia and had extensive backwoods experience.

Decker nodded, "Let's get set up and then you fellas can give us the lay of the land. With that rain coming in, it might be our best chance to clear out Mount Austin. I think these Japs could do with a bloody nose."

The spot they chose for their camp was decent enough for The Canal at that elevation. There was a clearing in the denser foliage dominated by teak, rosewood, and a few mahogany trees. In enough number and close enough together that hammocks could be slung off the ground and kept bunched together. The Marines then used their individual rain flies to rig cover over the sleeping area. There was even a small open section in the center where the ten men could crowd together.

By then, the sun was nearly gone, and the rain had reached the northern coast. Distant rolls of thunder and a slight increase in the breeze heralded what was to come. Decker gathered the men around and let Taggart brief them on the target.

The sergeant used a stick to draw a rough outline of the Japanese camp in the dirt, "Looks pretty much the same as what Colonel Puller reported the other week. A semi-open area with a good number of large, hardwood trees. The Japs laid out four sections of deadfalls on the north, south, east, and west sides, with the whole camp backing up close to the outcrop. Sort of like horizontal palisades, you might say."

He began to dot the rough image and put an X on the north side and behind it, a larger X. He also drew several small circles at various points.

"That's the Nambu nest and directly behind, and a little above, a field piece," Taggart explained. "Nothing huge, maybe a 37mm job. The whole camp rises on a slope from north to south. These circles here are knee mortar men. All in all, I'd say we're looking at thirty slants manning this post. There's a bivouac area near the rear and that's where the radio antenna is located."

"Okay…" Decker said, tapping his chin.

"They're expecting trouble from the north," Oaks noted.

"Yeah, another push from Henderson," Decker said. "How about the approaches?"

Taggart looked to Jones and Gartrell, "I sent these two fellas to do a little scouting, sir."

"The north side is jungle with a few trails leading north toward the river and paralleling that, sir," Jones said. "Dense right up to about ten… fifteen yards from the north log wall. I could see signs of the previous battle everywhere… dense, like I say, but ain't much cover. Cover in terms of protection from that machine gun, sir."

"Coming in from either side would be better," Gartrell added. "Plenty of jungle still and some more hardwoods. Plus, if we go after dark, them squalls comin' in will blind the Jap but good."

"And us, too," Oaks said. "Be blacker'n a coal miner's nose tonight."

A valid point. When heavy rains came to the Solomons, the islands could grow dark in the extreme. Without artificial light and covered by clouds, Guadalcanal could not just be difficult to manage… it could be deadly.

Decker looked into the twilight sky, out to the dark gray blanket rapidly gathering to the north and frowned. He had two choices. Either he and the team went immediately in hopes of gaining position before it grew too dark… or they wait out the storm. Were it earlier in the day, the decision would be easy. However, the days on The Canal were long, hot, and miserable… leaving him with only one choice.

"No… we wait," said Decker with a sigh. "Weather will give us good cover. Let's gather fuel for a fire. Least we can have a hot meal… probably gonna be our last for a while. Then we'll bed down for a bit and catch a few Zs. My guess is… we're gonna need 'em."

The men gathered enough fuel for a small fire just before the wall of heavy tropical rain raced across the land and smashed into them in a chaotic blast of wind and warm water. With so much darkness and the rain to mask the smell of burning wood, the team was able to heat a can of rations and enjoy hot coffee. There was little danger of being discovered, as one could hardly see behind the edge of the makeshift tarp roof.

Henry Evans climbed into his hammock between Jones and Gartrell and settled in. Although Guadalcanal in October was still summer warm, the rain and breeze made it cool enough to warrant wrapping himself up in his thin Army blanket.

"All tucked in?" Jones asked.

"Gonna tell us a story, Jonesy?" Gartrell jibed.

The two men had started out badly. Back in the beginning, when Gartrell, Jones, Travis, and the former Evans joined the team, Gartrell's southern upbringing and bigotry quickly created a rift between himself and the two Black Marines. After Jones practically saved Gartrell's life at Taivu point a few days later, Gartrell's thinking had begun to change.

Yet when he'd thanked Jones and offered what he thought was an olive branch, the other Marine had told him off. It was Travis, the other of the two Black men in the unit, who'd had to explain to Gartrell that they didn't want his offer to think of them as equals. They already *were* equals.

Although it took Gartrell some time to come to understand the nuances, he had come to them at last. He, Jones, and Travis had developed a respect and even a friendship after so many trials and adventures together.

"You want one?" Jones asked. "How about you, Hank?"

Evans was silent for a moment and both of the men pressed close to either side of him noticed. It was Jones who asked.

"Hey, Hank... you okay?"

"Sure," said the midwestern Marine Raider. "I was just... thinkin'."

"Broads?" Gartrell asked and chuckled.

"No... forget it, it's nothin'," said Evans and sighed to himself.

"Aw, now c'mon, Hank," Jones pressed gently. "You got somethin' on your mind, let it out. We ain't gonna laugh, huh, Bill?"

"That's right, pal. We's a team."

"Well... it's just..." Evans prevaricated and finally leapt in. "Sometimes I wonder... wonder about dying out here."

"Sure," said Jones. "We all do."

"But it ain't just that," Evans went on. "I don't want to die... but after so much shit we done... it don't bother me as much as some other stuff."

The three were silent for a moment until Gartrell asked, "You mean like being taken prisoner or somethin'?"

Another heavy silence fell. Beyond the tense lack of conversation, fat raindrops pattered the canvas overhead and splattered on the moist ground. The sound was like the world's largest steak fry, the hiss of water flowing through leaves and the splash of drops exploding reminding the men of dozens of juicy steaks sizzling on the world's largest grill.

"Yeah..." Evans said almost inaudibly. "You hear things... what they do to prisoners. Slave labor camps... food and sleep deprivation... beatings, keeping you in a cage in the hot sun with no water..."

"Take it easy, Hank," Jones said softly. "That ain't gonna happen."

"Nah... we're too crafty to catch," Gartrell said wryly.

Evans shivered and hunkered down into his blanket, "I hope not. I dunno, fellas... I guess that scares me more than fighting... even dying."

"That natural," Jones said. "Natural to be scared, Hank. But always remember… you ain't alone out here."

"That's right," Gartrell added, patting the other man on the shoulder. "You got your buddies, and we got the best CO and Gunny around. We gonna be A-okay."

Evans smiled, "Thanks, Bill… thanks, Jonesy."

"Good," said Jones. "Now enough chin-waggin'. Let's catch some shut-eye whiles we can."

6

MOUNT AUSTIN – 2320

The rain lasted well into the night and only began petering off just before eleven. Decker, Oaks, Lider, and Taggart took turns on watch in pairs, allowing the rest of the men to get four hours of uninterrupted sleep. Although the four highest ranked only got two each, it was enough and kept two pairs of eyes on watch at all times.

In spite of the fact that there was a Japanese contingent no more than half a mile away, the dark and the weather ensured that it might as well be a hundred miles. However, one could never be too careful.

At 2300, the skies were partially clear. There were plenty of stars and the crooked smile of the moon somewhere between a quarter and a half shone down from almost directly overhead. Not brilliant, but enough light for the Raiders to make their way toward the Japanese encampment and find their positions.

Decker's plan was hasty but simple, and it also took into account fields of fire and eliminating dangerous crossfire. The unit's three best sharp shooters, Treadway, Entwater, and Gartrell, would make their way to the northeast corner of the camp, find adequate cover and set up as snipers. Their job would be to pick off targets of opportunity while doing their best not to be targeted.

The main assault would come from Decker, who would take Lider and his BAR, Travis and his BAR and Jones and his Thompson, which would match up with Decker's own Thompson. Joining them would be Evans, who was also a crack shot with his Springfield. All of this automatic weapons' fire would distract the Japs from the three snipers and also give team three a chance to work in close from the south.

Oaks with his Tommy gun and Taggart with his Springfield 1903 would work in from the rock and make a stealth… at least at first… assault on the bivouac area near the upland and rear of the camp. Taggart, as one of the team's ordnance men, would also carry incendiaries to set the tents on fire.

The squad traveled light. No packs and only limited reloads for their long guns and pistols. Each slung a bandolier and a canteen, and each man also wore their KA-bar and stiletto on their thighs. Decker's idea was to strike hard, fast, and with deadly intent. Take out the heavy weapons and then pick off the Japs while chaos reigned.

The team worked their way along the ridge, which eventually shortened and vanished near the Mount Austin camp. They moved silently, having learned from practical experience and having been trained by the many islanders who accompanied them on their early missions.

With the rains gone, the jungle was once more a sauna. Thick air, heavy with steam and humidity clung to the plants, the ground and the men. All around, insects chittered and screeched and everywhere, heavy drops of moisture dripped and plopped and splattered everything and everyone. Occasionally, a bird would caw, or a large, ancient lizard would croak a call into the damp tropical night.

And then the voices came.

It was faint at first, the cottony air swallowing sound and dulling any possibility of echo. Yet as they drew close to the enemy, ghostly Japanese voices rode the heavy air right to the Marines straining ears. Sometimes quietly, sometimes in a high, angry quip or guttural string of words that, while unintelligible to everyone but Oaks, clearly indicated displeasure.

Decker halted the team, and they huddled close together, "All right… we can hear them, which means we're close. Phil, you break off now. You're team three. You won't have a radio, so you'll have to make your own decisions. Don't act until you hear me open up, though."

"Aye-aye," said Oaks. "We'll be careful, sir."

Decker nodded, "Good man. On your way. Now, Ted, you're in charge of team two. Same order. Don't fire until we do. I'll give you fifteen minutes to find good cover. And I mean good, because you won't be able to fire and move. I want you three to shoot only when there's fire being exchanged. Hopefully in the dark, the Japs won't notice they're being sniped."

"What if they do, sir?" Treadway asked.

"Then make sure you three have an escape route planned," Decker said. "Idea is to rendezvous back at the camp. Hopefully we'll be able to clean up this Jap camp completely… but you never know. Got it?"

"Aye-aye," said the three men and they vanished into the brush.

"As for us," Decker told the four remaining men. "We're gonna space ourselves out along the eastern perimeter. Hank, you'll be working behind us, moving up and down the line and offering pinpoint shots. Your job is to pick off any uppity Nips that try to zero in on our muzzle flashes. Once we open up, they're gonna try and get us with that Nambu and field gun. Those are our first targets. Travis and Chuck, you stick to either side of me. We move as a unit. Jonesy, since you got the other BAR, I want you on the far left of the line. Us three will concentrate on the heavy weapons, and you focus on hosing down as many loose Japs as you can. Keep them from getting any big ideas about rushing us. We clear?"

A quiet chorus of yessirs and Decker nodded. He offered each man a smile and a thump on the shoulder, and they moved into the darkness.

TEAM TWO

The Raiders knew from conversations with their fellow Marine buddies who'd been serving at Henderson about the general layout of the area. When Colonel Puller and his three companies attacked Mount Austin several weeks earlier, they'd brought back decent intel on the lay of the land.

Entwater and his team knew that there was a rough path leading to the eastern side of the Japanese camp. Major Decker would use that. There was also a path that led right up to the camp's northern face along the Matanikau. Neither of these would serve, as they'd put team two in the wrong spot.

However, extrapolating from this information and making their best guess at night, Entwater led his men ahead of Decker along the path that opened onto the eastern flank. Partway down, they cut out and picked their way into the brush, using the glow in the dark numbers on a handheld compass to track a roughly northwesterly path through the dense and dark rainforest.

The going wasn't easy. The Solomon Islands jungles were a living tangle that almost seemed intentional in their ability to slow men down. Movement often required hacking through with multiple machetes just to make a few dozen yards per hour. However, with only three men, and all of them young and fit, they were able to climb through, over and go around vines, leafy birds of paradise and other jungle foliage steadily enough that progress was admirable. The trouble was that Entwater had to balance speed with stealth. Creeping around a jungle at night wasn't exactly a quiet endeavor and trying to make headway with only a few minutes to do so meant that some sacrifices in silence must be made.

Presently, however, the three men found themselves at the edge of the jungle and almost exactly at the northeastern corner where they were to set up. The three exchanged silent grins and began easing into potential firing positions. Now that they could see, not to mention *here*, the enemy, quiet was vital and the going was slow.

Near the corner, team two found a large mahogany tree nearly completely covered in a thick curtain of vines. It had a low crotch, perhaps no more than four feet high and Gartrell set himself up here to use the crotch as a ledge upon which he could steady his barrel. In spite of the vines, he had a fairly good view of the camp and the shadowy wraiths that moved within.

"Okay..." Entwater said quietly. "There's an old log just to the right... I'm gonna set up there. Joey, what do you think about climbing up into this tree? If you can use the vines and the branches, you could get some elevation."

Treadway looked up into the dark canopy. Very little light filtered down, and the three were drenched in almost pitch dark. He'd have to feel his way and the thought made his belly shrivel.

"Sure," he said in spite of himself. "I think I can find a spot up there."

"Better you than me," Gartrell snickered.

"Superior obstacles... superior ability," Treadway thumped Gartrell on the shoulder and climbed cautiously and as stealthily as he could manage.

"Damn..." Gartrell grumped as Treadway's movements showered him with fat, earthy droplets.

Entwater grinned and pulled the antenna on his radio. He kept the volume low and said, "Actual, team two... in position. Over."

There was no response. There wouldn't be anything verbal. However, a quick double burst of static indicated that Decker had thumbed his mic twice in acknowledgment. Entwater slid the antenna back down, clipped the radio to his belt, and moved to kneel behind his log. Although he and his friends were in darkness, the camp ahead was lit enough for the snipers to identify individual targets, spectral as they were in the dark. Especially the men who stood near the machine gun and field gun emplacements.

"Here we go..." said Entwater and sighted in.

TEAM ONE

The path that led to the camp was easy enough to follow. It was obvious that a large number of men had pushed their way through the jungle not long before. However, as Decker and his team drew close, he was disappointed to find that there was little in the way of cover.

The density of the jungle thinned somewhat near the camp, either naturally or by having been cleared. There was perhaps fifteen or twenty yards between the edge of any substantial foliage and the line of logs that had been laid down as the eastern wall. There was enough plant life to hide behind, but nothing in the way of a defensible position.

Decker and his four men crouched low and huddled together near the head of the path. The major observed for several minutes and scowled.

"Not much cover," Lider pointed out.

"They's them logs, though," Jones said.

"Say what?" Travis blurted, albeit quietly.

Decker grinned, "You're saying we get right up to that wall and use *it* as our cover, Jonesy?"

"You smokin' somethin' funny?" Travis jeered.

Decker nodded, "He's got a point... We open up and make our way to the wall. Look there... two men at the Nambu, two more at the field gun. There's another half dozen or so spaced out inside the perimeter. Rest are probably sawing logs in the tents to the left.

Nuts... new plan... Lider, Travis, you're with me. We're gonna snake our way up to the palisade. Hank, you stick with Jonesy back here. When we get close, you two open up and take down as many Japs as you can and fast. Team two is in place now. Then we'll pop up and lay down some heavy fire and you two join us. If we're good, and lucky... we might be able to take out the men at the two guns and then turn them on the Japs."

"What about Davie and the gunny, sir?" Hank asked.

"They'll have to figure it out and stay low... but we'll avoid hitting the eastern side of the bivouac," Decker said. "Okay... stand ready. Chuck, Jimmy... let's go!"

Cursing, Jones moved to his left, putting distance between himself and the path of his comrades. So far, their luck had been good, but he knew it wouldn't last. It simply *couldn't*.

Jones stopped, took a knee between a pair of leafy trees and sighted in. He swore and got to his feet. The log wall was at least four feet high and he needed the elevation.

Evans was right there, so close that Jones could feel his body heat, "When do we open up, Jimmy?"

"Sight in on the Nambu nest, Hank," Jones said. "They be the ones that—"

A shout rose, and then another. They were quickly followed by more shouts and angry Japanese snapped between several men who immediately took to running and diving behind cover. Half a dozen Arisaka rifles cracked, and half a dozen rounds flew into the jungle in seemingly random patterns.

"Uhm... I guess... *now!*" Jones barked out and pressed his trigger.

The Browning automatic rifle fired heavy .30 caliber rounds. Each magazine held twenty, so Jones was careful not to simply hold down the trigger and burn through his bullets in a matter of seconds. Instead, he located a target, fired off a two or three round burst and then switched to another.

Even as he did so, Evans's Springfield, which also fired the same caliber rounds but was limited by the bolt action, crackled. There were shouts and screams… the Marines couldn't understand the words, but a death scream was the same in any language.

Decker and his two men were more than halfway across by then. Jones wasn't sure who'd spotted whom, but somehow the alarm had been raised. He bit his lip and kept firing, itching to move but knowing he couldn't. Not just yet.

The Japs were figuring it out, though. The men hiding behind trees were sighting in on Jones's and Evans's muzzle flashes and more than one Arisaka swung around to their general location. Five or six rounds zipped past, hissing through the jungle and missing the two men by mere yards.

"We gotta move!" Evans whisper-shouted. "They're homing in!"

From off to the right, three shots cracked the night open. Jones and Evans had already cleared the Nambu nest and the men at the field gun. They didn't see who'd been hit, but three men all cried out in pain and tumbled from behind cover.

"Cmon!" Decker shouted as he and his two comrades stood.

As they did so, an entire squad of Japs burst from the tents and fanned out, seeking pre-established points of cover and bringing weapons to bear. Decker, Lider, and Travis brought their own automatic weapons to bear and open fire, the sounds of a BAR and two Thompson's belching heavy .45 caliber rounds tore the night open.

"Go, go, go!" Jones shouted and took off toward the wall, low-running and somehow keeping his weapon level. Behind him, Evans swore a blue streak and dashed after his partner. Nowhere but right into the hornet's nest.

TEAM THREE

Oaks and Taggart found their way to the rear of the camp fairly easily. The jungle was thinner there, and the craggy outcropping that made up Mount Austin stood in a somewhat clear area south of the main camp. Bordered on either side by hardwoods and low brush, the way to the edge of the camp was easy to navigate. Just below them down a low but steep incline was the Japanese living space.

There were a series of tents laid out in parallel, half a dozen to either side of a central path leading north to south. To the left of these was another larger tent off by itself not far from an even larger wooden and thatched structure that was probably a communal area. The mess or a storage shed.

The two sergeants eased their way closer, darting between trees and melding with the shadows as best they could. Soon enough, they were hunched behind a heavy mahogany tree, panting and staring down at the tents fifteen feet below the steep coral slide only a few yards ahead.

"What's the plan?" Taggart asked. "You just gonna start hosing them tents down with rounds?"

Oaks grinned, "Eventually… but I want to clear them tents, too. No way of knowing how many Nips is hiding in there. So I say that when the balloon goes up, we slide down and make our way to the first one, that one closest to us. By then, any Japs inside will be scrambling. I'll come around the corner and pump 'em full of lead as they come out. You cut your way into the tents, one at a time, and make sure no clever slants is hidin' inside."

"Sneaky," said Taggart.

"War is hell… you ready?"

Taggart grinned and slung his Springfield and pulled his .45 and drew his KA-bar with his left hand, "Me and ole Bertha here'll give 'em what for."

Oaks chuckled, "Which one is ole Bertha?"

"Both. I got two Berthas… three if you count my stiletto… oh, and my rifle."

Oaks shook his head, "Everybody from new Jersey as screwy as you?"

"Nah… I'm special."

"And how… all right… let's roll!"

"Banzai!

The two Marines hadn't taken more than two steps out from behind the tree when a pair of slim, dark shadows exploded out of the night. They'd been hiding in the shadow of a boulder nearby and rushed out of the darkness with bayonets raised.

Taggart reacted, instinct taking over. He threw himself sideways, rolling on the hard, leaf-strewn ground and coming up on one knee, pistol raised. Oaks, for his part, whirled around, instinctively trying to bring the barrel of his SMG to bear… but far too late.

Several shots cracked the night open, bright flashes from multiple muzzles casting the four combatants in harsh relief. Taggart's shot plowed into one of the Japanese soldiers, bursting his heart and blowing out of his back, carrying with it shards of bone and a geyser of thick blood that gleamed as it sprayed through a shaft of moonlight.

Oaks's man fired too, but not before the barrel of Oaks's weapon smashed into the barrel of the Arisaka. The gunnery sergeant cringed as the bullet breezed past his ear and the razor-sharp blade of the bayonet slid over his shoulder, missing his flesh by mere inches.

The two men crashed together, hot bodies hard with tension colliding and bouncing apart. Oaks used his momentum to drive the barrel of his gun sideways and into the Jap soldier's throat, pushing the man back toward the tree. As he did so, another large shape materialized out of the night and the world throbbed as a heavy caliber handgun discharged, blowing the Japanese soldier's brains sideways into the night.

"You okay, Phil?" Taggart gasped.

"Yeah, you?"

"Just swell... but the shit's hit the fan now!"

Oaks heard the battle raging a hundred yards or more to the north. He wondered if it'd been the brief fight with the two soldiers that had lit the fuse. Not having time to ponder it nor caring at that point, he pointed, and the two Raiders half ran, half slid down the hill and right into the Japanese camp.

7
TEAM ONE

Things were beginning to get heavy. More and more Japanese soldiers were appearing seemingly out of nowhere. Although Decker and his four companions had superior firepower, the enemy had superior numbers and better mobility.

In addition to the hardwood trees inside the fifty- or sixty-yard-wide perimeter, the Japanese had established sandbag nests at various points as well. As the soldiers moved out of their tents, they ran or crawled toward these positions. Slowly but surely, they were finding cover and snapping off shots at the five Americans in ever increasing intensity.

"They's too many of 'em!" Travis griped as he peeked over the logs and tried to bring his weapon to bare on a target.

For his pains, he received a rather sharp and rapid response. No less than eight 7.7mm Arisaka rounds slapped into the log wall just above his head, throwing up small clouds of jagged splinters.

"Jonesy, go—" Decker never finished his order. The Raider was already shuffling away, staying low and putting some distance between himself and the other four.

Travis saw and broke off in the other direction. He hefted his BAR and made his way toward the northern corner.

Decker cursed. He didn't like breaking up his concentrated fire that way but knew there was little choice. He and Lider still had their automatic weapons, and Evans could still pick off individual targets… if they let him.

"Like prairie dogs!" Decker snapped. "Every time Jonesy or Travis pops up and fires, we do the same. Charlie, our job is just to lay down suppressive fire. Maybe we get lucky, but we give Hank a chance to pick a target. Ready, Hank?"

"Aye-aye, Major."

Jones stopped thirty yards away as did Travis. The latter was now nearly in the direct line of fire of team two. Decker crossed his fingers and hoped that Entwater and his sharp shooters didn't hit Travis in their zeal.

Jones popped up and roared out a string of curses as he swept the barrel of his Thompson over the top of the logs. The muzzle belched fire as he sent heavy .45 caliber rounds into the Japanese camp. Travis, inspired by his friend's grit, stood and began doing the same with his BAR, paying close attention to the two heavy weapons that had been temporarily cleared.

"Now!" Decker said, standing and pulling his trigger.

No one was firing on full auto, but even using controlled bursts, a man could burn through a twenty or thirty round magazine in seconds. Evans, understanding that he only had three or four seconds, leapt to his feet and swung his barrel back and forth, seeking any target he could find in the dark.

He found one. A shadowy figure thirty yards away popped out from behind the trunk of a tree. The Japanese soldier found Evans at the same time as the American found him, and the two rifle shots came so closely together they might've been one.

The soldier cried out, a gurgling, agonized screech as Evans's round punched through his throat just above the notch of his sternum. The Japanese round did not hit the American but slammed into the wood just in front of him, blasting out several razor-sharp splinters that plowed into Evans. One raked his cheek and sliced across his left earlobe. Warm blood flowed down his jaw and poured from his ear, down his neck, and soaked into the collar of his BDU. Another piece, perhaps eight or nine inches in length, drove through the flesh of his left forearm and lodged there, setting up a huge, throbbing pain.

Evans yelped, cursed, gritted his teeth and dropped down to his knees, breathing heavily. He surprised himself that even through the pain, he could marvel at how just a couple of little hunks of wood could make it feel as if they'd been on fire when they'd hit.

"Move!" Decker shouted. "Left five yards! Hank… you all right?"

Evans grunted something that might've been an affirmative and duck walked after Decker and Lider. He couldn't be sure what good they'd done, but the Japanese inside the perimeter had taken to shouting and throwing wild shots into the night. The bees were pissed now, that's for sure…

TEAM TWO

"Christ on a soda cracker, Ted!" Treadway said from his perch. "It's a madhouse down there!"

Entwater and Gartrell maintained a steady rate of fire, when they could. Following Decker's orders, they only fired when fire was being exchanged. Thus far, the two of them had taken down at least five Japs and hadn't yet been sighted.

Treadway, for his part, was being more conservative. Ten feet up in the tree as he was, his muzzle flashes would be far easier to spot. He chose his targets more carefully and had eliminated at least two.

Yet he also acted as lookout and passed down vital information to the other two.

"Skipper's at the eastern log wall," Treadway said. "More Japs are fanning out into the camp, too! They got trees and some sandbag or rock pile firing nests, too. Oh… and now two from team one are splitting off! Hey, one's coming toward us! Watch him, fellas!"

"I see him," Gartrell said. "Think it's either Jones or Travis… can't see nothin' but a silhouette."

"That's a big word for you, Billy!" Entwater said and squeezed his trigger. An enthusiastic Japanese soldier who'd broken from cover and was making a mad dash for the machine gun went sprawling when Entwater's round burst his heart.

"I been readin'!" Gartrell said. "Even an ignant country boy can sound shit out!"

"Uh-oh…" Treadway groaned from above.

"What?" Entwater urged.

"I think they're setting up a knee mortar line near the rear of the camp!" Treadway said. "About sixty yards in… behind that pair of big trees on the left."

"Shit…" Gartrell drawled. "I don't see 'em!"

"Me either!" Entwater cranked. "Can you get a shot, Joey?"

Treadway watched as three shadowy figures, partially concealed by trees and other obstacles, knelt down in a line. There wasn't enough light for him to make out details, but when the three figures suddenly glowed brightly as three short muzzle flashes lit them, he knew what they were and what they'd done.

Not hesitating, Treadway homed in on one flash, adjusted his aim slightly up and right and fired. He couldn't be sure but thought that one of the shadows disappeared.

A second later, three small explosions flashed and banged and sent up three plumes of dirt and rock near the edge of the jungle.

Although Decker's men were no longer there, the three 50mm shells landed nearly in line with their positions at the wall.

"Sweet Jesus!" Gartrell blurted.

"You see *that?*" Treadway asked. "I think I mighta got one…"

"Let's shift!" Entwater decided. "Joe, stay up there, Bill, you and me go right until we can get a clear shot at those mortars!"

"Roger that, I'm ready!"

"Go!" Entwater said and broke to his right, noisily crashing through the jungle. Treadway cringed at the racket, but he understood the logic. They probably wouldn't be heard anyway, and speed was of the essence. All it would take would be one or two lucky shots from those mortars and team one could be wiped out in a second.

A sizzling shiver danced across his spine as Treadway also came to the conclusion that a lucky shot or two could ruin his team's day also…

Treadway bit his lip and searched for another target. He chuckled at how easy Taggart and the gunny must have it.

TEAM THREE

The two Raiders slid to a stop no more than ten feet from the closest tent. They paused for a moment in the shadows, listening as multiple Japanese voices shouted and called out to one another. They heard men pushing aside tent flaps and boots thumping as they ran.

Oaks tapped Taggart on the shoulder and pointed and then he tapped his own chest and pointed left. Taggart nodded and moved toward the tent, KA-bar at the ready.

Oaks darted to his left, racing across the open space between the two lines of tents and melting into the shadows again. Taggart pressed the blade of his knife into the moldy canvas before him, starting at head-height and working down. The razor-sharp combat blade sliced through the fabric with ease and within seconds, Taggart had created a large enough slit to push through.

Taggart pushed his bulky frame through the slit and found himself wrapped in inky blackness. He took a single step and painfully barked his shin on something unyielding. Cursing under his breath, the Marine went tumbling, landing on what must be a cot and then rolling to his left onto the canvas floor. He'd contrived to lose his pistol in the tumble but held onto the knife. He grinned in the darkness, ignoring the throbbing in his left shin and almost laughed at the foolishness of the situation.

The hard fist that crashed into the side of his head drove out any mirth, however. Taggart's heart leapt to full speed as he cursed and tucked himself into a ball and rolled once more, trying to avoid his invisible attacker.

A hard, compact form dove on top of him, low, guttural Japanese curses peppering the air with malice and a faint scent of bad breath. Somehow, the bastard got his hand around Taggart's left wrist while he used his other fist to beat at the American in the dark.

"Shit… fuck…" Taggart swore as he grappled with the tenacious enemy soldier. "Can you see in the dark, ya' little yellow prick!?"

In response, the soldier let fly with a string of rapid Japanese that, while unintelligible to the American, left little to the imagination. Taggart had probably just been given a crash course in Japanese vituperative.

Growling with frustration, the Marine heaved with his left hand and brought a knee up hard into the mass of the other man. The knee drove into softness, eliciting a rank but satisfying whoosh of air. Taggart got one knee under himself, pushed up and back and brought the heel of his right hand around as hard as he could right into where the other man's face should be.

There was a crunch, a nauseating give and a muffled howl of pain.

Pressing his advantage, Taggart grabbed a handful of the man's tunic in his right hand. He jerked his wrist free and swung the blade of his knife, dragging its finely-honed edge across the man's throat and through his carotid artery and jugular vein. A brief gurgling cry, gagging and choking, and the body went limp.

For a second, Taggart just knelt there, panting and collecting his wits. When his opponent did not move, the Marine fumbled in his pockets until he located his Zippo, pulled it out and flicked it to life.

He was in a tent with two cots and a couple of foot lockers. A Japanese soldier dressed only in skivvies and a T-shirt lay half atop one bunk, his clothing appearing black from his neck to his crotch, stained as they were with his life's blood. Taggart cringed and slipped the KA-bar back into its sheath and switched the lighter to his left hand.

He scanned the ten-by-ten shelter until he located his Colt 1911 lying on the righthand bunk. This he scooped up and looked around, still catching his breath.

"Hell…" he said. "I ain't doin' this every time…"

Taggart shoved the left bunk up against the tent wall until it bulged outward. It had appeared from outside that the tents were pressed up against one another, or nearly. Piling blankets and pillows onto the bunk, he applied the flame of his lighter until the fabric caught.

It didn't take long. Even in the damp, humid environment of Guadalcanal and even after a heavy rain, the bedding was quickly consumed by the flames which then hungrily spread to the tent itself. By the time Taggart pushed out through the slit he'd made, the inner wall and pointed ceiling were already ablaze. He hoped Oaks was faring better.

Thus far, the gunnery sergeant hadn't met any trouble. Wishing to take a more efficient approach, Oaks pulled one of his grenades from the bandolier, yanked the pin, and tossed it up and over the tents. He didn't know where it landed, but he hoped it'd be on or between them somewhere in the column at whose head he now stood.

The grenade flashed and thundered and set up a howling from ahead.

Grinning, Oaks knelt, shouldered his Thompson and pulled the trigger, spraying heavy caliber rounds into the tent before him and, as the fabric was in no way adequate to stopping them, the bullets passed through all of the tents, ripping open fabric and, based on the screams and cries of agony he heard, more than one man, too.

The weapon dry fired, and Oaks quickly swapped in a new magazine. A flickering orange light caught his eye and he looked right in time to see the tent Taggart had entered whoosh into a writhing, flaming torch. He chuckled to himself, imagining Taggart growing frustrated and applying his usual subtlety.

"Phil!" A voice shouted from the right and a figure materialized from behind the burning tent and raced across to Oaks.

"What happened?' Oaks asked.

"Went inside and met up with an optimist who tried out his karate on me," Taggart griped. "Little bastard jumped me, but I cut his throat. Then I figured… why do things the hard way?"

Oaks grinned, "Might as well burn these too. Shit's hittin' the fan ahead. I say we light these tents and then go left toward those bigger structures. Maybe we can come in from behind and give the major a hand."

Taggart returned the smile and bent down, applying his lighter's flame to the tent's fabric, "Sounds good to me."

"Keep your pistol," Oaks said. "We beat feet to that communal tent and see what's what. Ready?"

"Born ready."

"Then move out!" barked Oaks and took off running, a

flickering yellow flame devouring the canvas behind the two racing shadows.

They reached the large tent in seconds. Moving quickly and biting his lip the entire time, Taggart tore the flap open and poked the barrel of his pistol inside.

The tent was lavish, by the standards he'd seen from the others. A larger cot, writing desk, and two heavy chests sat to either side of a wooden armchair. No doubt this was the camp commander's quarters.

"Light it up," said Oaks, gazing around. "Then we gotta move."

Taggart applied his lighter once more. He smiled to himself, thinking that by the time they got someplace where he could have a smoke, there'd be no damned fuel left in it.

The final structure was a hastily built mess or communal area made from bamboo poles, palm fronds, and a thatched roof. Just beyond this were several Japanese soldiers, some crouching behind trees and rock piles and several kneeling in a row. Oaks put a finger to his lips and pointed to the corner of the structure.

"I'm going inside," he said. "You start picking off targets while I make my way through. Start with those damned mortar men."

"This is crazy," Taggart said, slipping his .45 back into its holster and unslinging his Springfield.

"Yep… screwy," was all the gunny said before plucking a grenade from his bandolier, pulling the pin and easing to the opening in the little building.

It was open at either end, although some sort of screen had been set up on either door. Oaks had no idea what was inside, but he wasn't about to poke his head in and find out. Gritting his teeth, he tossed his grenade and back pedaled several steps.

"Grenade!" he called out even as Taggart pulled his trigger.

"Christ!" hollered the sergeant and stumbled back, throwing himself to the dirt as the pineapple whoomped from inside the structure.

Parts of the walls blew outward, and a section of roof blasted upward, belching flames and coughing thick smoke. From within, several men screamed and cursed and ran... straight through the walls and into the night!

"Holy shit, Gunny!" Taggart rolled onto his knees and started firing.

Oaks got to his feet and shouldered his weapon. As he gawked, the entire structure leaned and then slowly, almost majestically, collapsed to one side, beginning to burn as its dry components were touched off by the fire started by the grenade. Oaks laughed maniacally even as he began sending rounds downrange and into the scrambling, terrified Japanese.

TEAM ONE

"What in the world..." Decker mused as he popped up to shoot and saw the fires to the south.

"The gunny!" Jones whooped from ten yards away. "Gotta be, sir! Got them Japs all in a heap!"

"Open fire!" Decker said, searching for targets and squeezing his own trigger.

Although not quite panicked yet, the remaining Japanese were close to it. Several knee mortar shells flew, but they went wide and deep into the jungle. Even as they whistled through the air, a trio of rifle shots crackled from Decker's right. Team three must have zeroed in on the mortar throwers. From the left, more fire crackled and rattled. Evidently, Team three had joined the fray.

Decker knew that in order to win this, a bold move was called for. Given the time, the Japanese would regroup and overwhelm his men with numbers. There was only one thing for it.

"CHARGE!" Decker roared even as he scrambled up onto the wood wall and leapt down into the Japanese camp.

He ran, firing at anything that moved even as he pushed toward the center of the camp and the greatest concentration of enemy units. Without seeing but feeling it, he knew that Lider and Evans were right beside him, their weapons cracking and chattering as they, too, laid down deadly fire.

Soon Jones and Travis were over the wall, angling toward their CO and their own muzzles jabbing white-hot jets of flame into the night.

The scene grew crazy, chaotic, and maddening. Light and dark flashed as muzzles lit up the ground and trees and men in a strobe light effect that was the stuff of nightmare. Men shouted, cursed, and screamed. As Decker ran, seeking a place to set up with cover, he prayed that those screams of agony weren't being torn from his men.

From nowhere, almost as if by sorcery, three Japanese soldiers materialized out of the night. They rushed Decker, Banzai battle cries in their throats and bayonets fixed.

Out of the corner of his eye, Decker saw another pair of Japs running across his path… right toward the Nambu nest. He had no time to ponder this, however, as he, Evans, and Lider were suddenly set upon by enraged Japanese.

Decker planted his feet and used the barrel of his smg to bat the rushing Jap's Arisaka aside. As the man came in, teeth bared and eyes burning, Decker spun to his right, shoved the man away with his weapon and planted his boot in the man's ass. With a mighty shove, he heaved the smaller soldier forward, the man flailing and trying to regain his footing.

Unfortunately for him, the soldier stumbled right into Evan's path. With his Springfield's stripper clip empty, Evans let the weapon hang in its sling and had drawn his 1911. The stumbling Japanese man's head blew apart as a .45 round penetrated his ear and blasted the rear of his skull into a fountain of chunky gore.

Lider hadn't used any such finesse. When the Japs rushed him, he'd simply squeezed his trigger and dumped the rest of his magazine into the two rushing men, blasting them open from their bellies to their throats. A horrifying tableau of glistening blood and gory fragments spun through the strobing light of the muzzle flashes.

"Good God…" Evans wheezed. "What the—"

Three wordless battle cries rose from the right. Decker turned to see three dark figures emerge from the trees and fire their rifles almost in unison. The two Japs Decker had seen earlier had nearly made it to the Nambu but failed to reach their goal. A trio of .30 caliber rounds ended their attempt with ultimate finality.

"The gun!" Decker roared to Entwater and his team unnecessarily.

The three young men leapt onto the log wall and over in one fluid motion. By the time they reached the Nambu, Travis had gained that position, too. The four quickly got the heavy weapon into the fight, spinning it around and pouring its rounds back into the camp and at the now fleeing Japanese.

What followed did not last long. Perhaps two or three soldiers managed to reach the safety of the jungle and vanish. But all of the rest of them… an entire platoon… were cut down wherever they were. To a man they were killed and their encampment burned, casting their dead and dying bodies in stark, unforgiving relief.

"Congrats, sir," Oaks heaved as he jogged up. "Camp's clear."

Decker shuddered as he took in the full extent of the death and destruction all around him, "My God… good work, Top. The radio gear?"

"Survived," Taggart said, still trying to catch his breath. "Antenna's set up on a truck with a radio set."

"Very well," said Decker. "Take me to it. I want to report this to HQ. The rest of you do a quick scavenge and meet us near the crag. We'll contact HQ and get the hell out of here. Let's hope Tojo doesn't find his balls and come back in force tonight. What's everybody's status?"

All the men were uninjured except for Evans, who still had a nasty cut on his face and a splinter in his arm. Entwater examined it and said that he could patch Evans up if he could get to where there was enough light.

"Make it quick," Decker said. "We're buggin' out back to our camp. Fifteen minutes, fellas. Damned fine work."

8

After reporting into Henderson, Decker made sure that all structures were burning and that the Nambu and field gun were spiked and useless. They also blew up the truck that held the radio gear just for good measure. If the Japanese decided to come back and dig in at Mount Austin again, they'd have to start from scratch.

Once done, the Raiders proceeded back to their camp and a watch was set. Some reluctance was expressed at being so close to the attack, but after conferring, Decker and Oaks decided the risk was minimal. That, and they had a wounded man to attend to.

"Can I rig a light, sir?" Entwater asked. "I think Hank's gonna need stitches."

Decker frowned, "Can he wait until morning, Ted?"

Entwater frowned this time, "Sir... he's got a pretty good slash on the face and ear... and that splinter in his arm looks nasty. I'd rather get those wounds attended to asap."

Decker nodded, "Agreed. Find as closed off a part of this area as you can. Throw up a couple of tarps to block as much light as possible. You need some help?"

"Joey can give me a hand," Entwater said.

"All right, let's get to it and then bed down for a few hours," Decker said. "I want to put some miles between us and this area tomorrow."

"Aye-aye, sir."

Entwater and Treadway rigged a temporary exam room. Charlie Lider helped and volunteered to stand by. Evans was in his fire team, after all. In truth, every man in the team wanted to stick by and see how things went, but Oaks put the kibosh on that.

"Okay, Hank my boy..." Entwater began as he sat Evans down on a log and used a flashlight to inspect his face. "Looks worse than it is... although that ear's gonna need a couple of stitches."

"Can you do that?" Evans asked.

"Sure... swallow these pills for me, though..." Entwater handed Evans his own wound pack. "Take all of them. Help with infection and pain. I've got a bit of procaine in my kit. It'll dull the pain. Your face is mostly superficial... so we'll clean it up and put a bandage on near the ear after I sew that up."

"Do I gotta get a shot?" Evans asked, grinning crookedly.

"Oh... yeah, like half a dozen," Entwater chuckled. "But you be a good boy and after you'll get a nice sucker."

"Aww, gee whizz... was hopin' for a B-girl."

The three men laughed and Entwater was glad for that. Field surgery, even minor surgery, could be a painful and stressful experience. Good spirits always helped.

"How about that splinter in his arm?" Lider asked. "Gonna pull it out?"

Entwater shined his light on Evans's arm. The splinter that hit was nearly six inches long. It punched through the sleeve of his utilities and part of it stuck out a couple of inches. Gently, Entwater explored the arm with his fingers and felt the nub of the splinter sticking out of the arm just beneath the fabric. Evans flinched.

"Sorry, Hank."

"It's okay, Teddy… do whatcha gotta do."

Entwater sighed, "Okay, so it's like this… we gotta get that sleeve up. I don't wanna cut it, and based on what I can see and feel so far… I'll want to cut the long end of the splinter off anyway, as close to the skin as I can. Anybody got a set of sharp dykes in their pack? I can do it with a KA-bar… but I'd rather have a snipper."

The end of the splinter that Entwater referred to was a good half inch wide. Upon his declaration, the other three men drew in a hissing breath.

"Hang on…" Lider said and vanished. A minute later he returned, smiling. "Jimmy and Ed got some tools. Jonesy had a set of dykes. These do?"

Lider held up the heavy, blunt-nosed snips. Entwater nodded.

"Can you cut that splinter nice and close, Sarge?" Entwater asked.

Lider blinked, "You ain't gonna pull it out?"

"Oh, I will," said Entwater and drew in a breath. "But look close at it. The grain… I pull it out from that end and it's gonna barb. Hurt like the devil and might do more damage, maybe even leave pieces behind. Nope… I'm gonna have to pull it out from the other side, Hank. Continue the motion."

Evans groaned, "Geez… like I said, Teddy… do whatcha gotta do."

"Okay, Sarge, start cuttin'," Entwater said. "Real easy now. Don't try to get it in one go. Lemme grab the plyers here…"

Treadway held the light for Lider while Entwater used his flash to locate more tools from his medical kit, including alcohol, needle and thread, and a small pair of plyers. Even as he did so, he could hear Evans's heavy breathing as Lider gently cut the splinter off just above the skin. The pressure and movement were painful, and Entwater cringed inwardly at the agony he was going to inflict next.

"Got it," Lider said, holding the piece of wood up before the light and grimaced.

"Good, now let's get his sleeve rolled up," Entwater said.

They did so, getting the sleeve past the wound. Treadway drew in a sharp breath and Lider groaned. Entwater glared at them.

The shaft of wood had punched through Evan's forearm, but beneath the ulna and radius, through the muscle. In truth, the wood was only in perhaps an inch below the skin and maybe two inches of it was buried. Not quite superficial but probably not having done too much damage to the muscle.

Entwater rubbed procaine, commonly referred to as Novocain, on either side of the wound. He also applied some to Evans's face and split earlobe. After several minutes, he glanced at Evans.

"Feel any better?"

"A bit… kinda numb like," said the wounded Raider.

"Good," said Evans, taking hold of the slimmer end of the splinter with the plyers. "Now, Hank… I'm gonna draw this out. It's gonna hurt like a bastard. Sarge, Joey, hold his arm still so I can get some leverage. You ready, Hank?"

Evans drew in a steadying breath, "As I'll ever be. Maybe you do it fast?"

Entwater smiled, "Don't want to jerk it and do more damage… let's see how it goes. On three. One… Two…"

Entwater applied pressure and Evans hissed in agony and clamped his teeth together. A fresh sheen of sweat broke out on his face and his breathing became deep and heavy.

Entwater gritted his own teeth and pulled harder. At first there was no movement, and he began to think that he might have to cut the splinter out. Then it moved. Just a millimeter at first, but then it came, sudden and quick, sliding out of the arm accompanied by a low, long moan from Evans, tears trickling from beneath his clamped eyelids.

"Got it!" Entwater exalted and held up the three-inch long, bloody sliver of wood before Evans's eyes. "Phew, Hank! You did great, pal. Double tough. Wanna keep it?"

Evans was still breathing hard, the throbbing agony in his arm like waves of fire. Yet he opened his eyes, dashed his other sleeve across them, and managed a weak grin, "Sure… impress the ladies…"

"You can take that to the *bank*, Mug," Lider chuckled. "Say honey, lookie what were stuck in me! But that ain't nothin' compared—"

"I got it, Sarge," Evans shook his head and chuckled. "Brother."

"Jesus…" Treadway said, eyes bulging. "Looks like a damned railroad spike."

"You done real good, Hank," Lider patted the other man on the shoulder. "Real good. Teddy, you got something for the pain?"

Entwater smiled, "I'll put a little more procaine on it and wrap it up."

"I meant for me," Lider chuckled. "Just watching that made my nads shrivel up."

"Sorry you had to go through this, Charlie…" Evans jibed.

"Screwballs… let me get that ear attended to…" Entwater said. "Joey, get me one of those morphine syrettes, huh?"

Ten minutes later, bandaged and pain medication applied, Evans was led to his hammock where he promptly fell asleep. Treadway and Lider went to theirs and Entwater was met at his own by Decker and Oaks.

"How'd he do?" Oaks asked.

"Everything okay?" Decker added.

"All fine, sir… Gunny…" Entwater said. "Got him stitched, bandaged, and pumped full of pain killer and medication. The wounds were mostly superficial. He might need another injection tomorrow, but he should be able to stay on duty. For all his mild manners, that kid's one tough monkey."

That drew soft chuckles. Partly because they agreed and partly because the difference in age between Evans and Entwater was less than two years.

"Good work, Teddy," Decker said. "All right, let's get some shut eye. Gonna be a long day tomorrow."

Dawn was still nearly a half hour away when Kiyotake Kawaguchi rose from his cot in his private hut. Although certainly better than a tent, the Kokumbona home was still primitive and almost always too hot. Only in the hours after midnight could Kawaguchi usually find restful sleep. Yet his nature and long years of warfare forced him to rise before dawn with unswerving regularity.

Being as regular as he was, it was no surprise when a gentle knock came at his door five minutes after rising. He bade the visitor to enter, admitting Yoshi Shimodo, his chief aide de camp.

"Good morning, sir," said Shimodo and bowed deeply at the shoulders. "I've brought you a fresh cup of tea."

"Most kind, Captain," Kawaguchi said, accepting the steaming mug. Already the temperature outside was above twenty-six degrees Celsius, yet the flavor of Japanese tea was such a comfort that Kawaguchi never complained. "Have we news of the attack last night?"

"Hai," said Shimodo. "Colonel Oka has requested to see you, sir."

Kawaguchi grunted, "No doubt. I will speak with him out of doors, Captain. At least there is a possibility of a breeze."

Shimodo nodded, bowed and held the door open. He frowned and glanced at his commander, "General… sir… are you… are you well?"

Kawaguchi's first impulse was to lash out at the man's impertinence. To inform him that a general did not require a nursemaid and that his aid should mind the business to which he was assigned. However, he knew that Shimodo's concern originated from a genuine place.

"I'm fine, Yoshi," said Kawaguchi and offered a lean smile. "The ordeal has passed. I am well… physically. Not that this will mean much for long, of course."

"Sir?"

Kawaguchi headed out, "Come, we have work to do."

Shimodo was no fool. Knowing he'd already overstepped and was fortunate not to have been raked over the coals, he simply remained silent and followed his general dutifully.

Oka's own hut, along with several other battalion commanders was close to Kawaguchi's own. The general occupied what had been the village headman's house, of course. Yet the dwellings were so much alike the difference was hardly worth noting.

Oka had several men erect a sort of covered patio outside his house and had even slung mosquito netting around the three open sides. Within were a set of bamboo chairs and a fire pit, currently flickering in readiness for the colonel's morning meal preparation.

Once more, a wave of irritation rose up inside Kawaguchi. Here was Oka, enjoying what few luxuries Guadalcanal could offer while most of his men and others slept on the ground and barely had enough food to eat. Yet rank had always come with privilege. It was the way of things, after all. And the time would come, as it had already, where even Oka would have to get his hands bloody.

"Good morning, General," Oka said, standing and smiling. "Please do sit and breakfast with me."

Kawaguchi bowed slightly and slipped through the netting. Oka offered the general his own padded chair and took another beside his own aid, Captain Same Nakira. "Please sit as well, Captain Shimodo."

"I'm told there is a report on the Mount Austin contingent?" Kawaguchi asked without preamble.

"Yes, sir," Nakira replied. "Their last report was that they were under attack shortly after midnight. Soon after, radio contact was lost. Major Roantai sent out a pair of scouts at zero-three-hundred in spite of the darkness. They were able to follow the river and confirm that the camp had been attacked, and the structures were burning. No doubt the Americans struck and overwhelmed the platoon there."

"Any sign of the Marines?" Oka asked.

"Negative," said Nakira. "Even when we still maintained radio contact, there was no way to tell. The last report indicated that there may have been as many as three individual sections attacking from the jungle."

Oka sighed, "A difficult position to occupy with only a single platoon. An entire company would be more effective."

"And therein lies the rub, Colonel," said Kawaguchi bitterly. "The one problem we seem to face over and over again on this miserable rock. We lack manpower and logistical support. We are to hold and attack an entrenched enemy of unknown strength. They have men, aircraft, and even vehicles. In spite of our efforts by day and night, supplies are brought in by air and sea."

"As does the rat delivery do for us," Oka said wryly.

Kawaguchi grunted, "Yes... one destroyer at a time. A hundred and fifty men and a few barrels of supplies per ship. Given time, given enough time... we might accumulate enough men and equipment and *food*... to mount a true assault."

"That is the plan, is it not, sir?" Shimodo dared to ask.

Kawaguchi's laugh was cold and bitter and humorless, "That is the plan, Captain. And should it succeed... should we gather enough to mount an assault on Vandegrift with a genuine hope of success... it will not be *I* who leads it. All that has gone before has been my responsibility and my fault."

"That is most unfair, sir," Oka offered.

Kawaguchi shook his head, "It is the way of things, Colonel. I'm given barely enough to work with and if I don't bring back an overwhelming victory... I am the one to bear the shame. Whatever we've accomplished here... whatever inroads we've made… it will be another man who uses them to claim victory for himself."

"Surely not, sir," said Nakira.

"Surely so, Captain," Kawaguchi said. "General Hyakutake himself will arrive shortly. He will relieve me and take over and I will be sent back to Rabaul in shame. Perhaps I will be allowed to keep my life… such as it is… but eventual victory here will not be credited to me."

Oka and the other men opened their mouths to commiserate but Kawaguchi held up a hand to stay their protests. He was not interested in commiserating nor in their pity.

"Let us get down to business," said the general. "We know that after our relative victory along the Matanikau recently, that Vandegrift has been sending out more scouts. Yoshi's idea to have a man hide and attack their rear has worked and has the Americans scrambling."

Shimodo contrived to look humble. Kawaguchi resisted the urge to smile.

"However, we also know that Vandegrift has under his command a special force," Kawaguchi went on. "A small but effective fighting unit which has plagued us here on Guadalcanal since the beginning. I also suspect it was this unit that attacked the construction of the airbase on Santa Isabella."

"A man called Decker," said Oka. "Intelligence says that he is part of the Marine Raider regiment."

"Just so," said Kawaguchi. "Several of our men have had direct dealings with this Decker. Lieutenant Ata Hondo. Where is the lieutenant now, Yoshi?"

"Stationed at the log bridge command post, sir," said the aide.

"Where he cannot get into so much trouble," Nakira added.

Kawaguchi did not miss the disdain, "Indeed, Captain. I wish a message sent. Inform Hondo that he is to put together a squad, including his sergeant. That man, at least, seems to know his business. Have the sergeant…"

"Makai, sir," said Shimodo.

"Yes… Makai… have him assemble the men," Kawaguchi said. "Tell Hondo I want him to report to me directly. I have a special mission for him."

"Sir?" Oka asked.

"I have a suspicion, Colonel… call it a hunch, call it divine inspiration… call it what you will," said Kawaguchi. "But I suspect that our old adversary Decker and his Raiders may have attacked last night. It fits their profile, does it not? And perhaps… just perhaps… Hondo would like a chance to gain his revenge on Decker… and regain some of his *honor* as well."

9

"Lieutenant Hondo reporting as ordered, General."

Kawaguchi and Oka were still finishing their morning meal when a truck arrived, and a pair of men climbed out and hurried to Oka's dwelling. One man, Hondo, was typical in build for a Japanese man. Average height and slender in carriage. The other, older man… the sergeant, radiated experience. He was somewhat taller and more stockily built. His face, though still youthful in its early thirties, was set into hard lines that hinted at the travails he'd experienced in his long career with the Imperial Japanese Army.

"Good morning, Lieutenant," Kawaguchi said. "Enter. And you, Sergeant Makai."

Both men bowed deeply and slipped through the mosquito netting. Both came to attention and waited, rigid as support posts.

"You are familiar with a man called Decker, are you not?" Shimodo asked.

Although Makai's face remained impassive and he said nothing, there was a flash in his eyes. Hondo, for his part, deigned to chuckle.

"Oh, we know him, sirs," said the lieutenant, bitterness edging his tone. "We fought him at Vungana and were captured during the battle."

"Indeed?" Nakira asked, his brows going up.

"We escaped," Makai offered.

"Yes," said Kawaguchi. "And Decker yet lives."

Hondo frowned and cast a look at his sergeant. Again, Makai said nothing. Oka had to admire the man's stoicism. If he didn't know any better, he'd swear he was looking at a Bushido warrior… or a Samurai.

Hondo drew in a breath, uncertain of his position and what response he'd get. However, he simply said: "It was decided that slipping away with what intelligence we were able to gather was better than attempting to do mischief upon our exit."

"Really?" Oka asked and glanced at Makai. "Why is that? I presume you escaped during the night… no doubt a few American throats could have been cut in the process?"

"It was my suggestion, sir," Makai said tonelessly. "We knew not of the situation outside our cell. Had we murdered a man or two… and we were caught… we would likely be executed."

"Such is war," Nakira said flatly.

Makai glanced in his direction and yet his face still gave away nothing, "One or two dead Americans is but a pittance as compared with what might be done with gathered knowledge. Sir."

Oka nodded, "Understood."

"No doubt, however," Kawaguchi went on, "you two men would enjoy a chance to settle this particular score?"

"I would indeed, sir," Hondo said.

"And you, Sergeant?" Oka asked.

"I go where I am needed, sir."

"Tell me, Sergeant," Oka asked, a hint of a smile tugging at the corners of his mouth, "were you not informed that you were to stay back at the log bridge command post and gather a party? And that Lieutenant Hondo was to come alone?"

"The men have already been picked, sir," Makai said.

"In such a short time?" Nakira narrowed his eyes as he spoke. "How could this be, Sergeant?"

"The men," said Makai, meeting the officer's battering ram glare with a brick wall of impassivity, "had been assembled days ago for just such an order. The lieutenant believed it prudent to be prepared, sir."

Oka chuckled, "I advise you not to fence with this one, Same. He has seen many campaigns and understands what is required."

Nakira scowled. Shimodo allowed just a hint of a smile, as did Kawaguchi himself.

"Very good," said the general. "Then I have a mission for you, Lieutenant."

Every man there, including Hondo himself, detected the underlying and unspoken words. Although Hondo was the officer and would be placed in command, it was Makai on whom they were truly counting.

"I believe," continued Kawaguchi, "that Decker and his men attacked Mount Austin last night. Further, I believe that they are engaged in a long-range patrol deep into our territory. They will push west as far as their carried supplies will allow and report back to their base on the disposition of our forces."

"How far can that be?" Hondo asked.

"If they follow the highlands to the south," Shimodo replied, "perhaps as far as Cape Esperance. They could easily extend their range by foraging. And there *are* native settlements all over this side of the Matanikau River."

"Yet they cannot radio Henderson field," Makai observed. "Begging your pardon, sirs… ahh… or perhaps they can."

Hondo looked from one officer to the other and then to his

sergeant, "What do you mean? You're correct, Makai. They will not carry any long-range radio equipment."

Makai, without smiling, pointed overhead. Even as he did so, the faint sound of a radial engine buzzing past nearly made Oka break into laughter. It was so perfectly staged.

"Ah so…" Hondo nodded, trying to hide his embarrassment. "Overflights. Perhaps that is an advantage to us, sirs. We can observe *where* the Americans fly and perhaps track Decker's progress. That and scanning radio frequencies and monitoring their communications. Both the sergeant and I speak English."

"Just so," said Kawaguchi. "However, I have something slightly different in mind. Rather than having you *chase* Decker… I propose that you *intercept* him."

"We can transport you to Cape Esperance," Oka said. "We have a CP established there, of course. You can then follow the midlands south of the plains and eventually, run straight into Decker's force."

"And cut them to ribbons," Nakira added, showing just a hint of teeth in his smile.

"Precisely," Kawaguchi said and looked to Makai. "Are your hand-picked men ready to proceed, Sergeant?"

"Of course, General," Makai said. "We can have them here in minutes, provided we are given transportation."

"See to it," said Kawaguchi with a nod and just a hint of a smile. "Lieutenant, please sit and have a bite of breakfast with us. We can discuss strategy."

Summarily dismissed, Makai bowed and exited without a word or an expression. Oka smiled to himself, thinking that the squads who would be going out on this expedition was lucky to have the stoic sergeant leading them. As for their officer… he would reserve judgement.

GUADALCANAL – OCTOBER 3, 1942

"Let's halt for a break, men," Decker said, lifting off his boonie hat and mopping at his sweat-soaked face.

The team had broken camp at dawn and had proceeded west, northwest for more than five hours. The going, while easier than down in the densest jungle, was not particularly fast. Both Decker and Oaks estimated that they might have covered six or seven miles at best.

The terrain was similar to what was to the north, except that they were on something of a plateau between the true hills and mountains and the northern flatlands. There was still plenty of rainforest, but it appeared to have been scattered about haphazardly, in random patches. Between were often patches of open ground dotted here and there with hard woods and sometimes clearings filled with waist-high Kunai grass. In the past hour, the team had been traversing a sort of flat and almost arid patch of coral bordered on the right by a steep ridge nearly fifty feet high and to the left by dense jungle.

By then, the sun was nearly directly overhead, and the men were slowing down. The oppressive heat of the rainforest was diminished ever so slightly at their elevation and in open ground, but the direct sun's rays were still heating them mercilessly.

"Let's find some shade," Oaks said to the weary travelers. "Drink some water and we'll have a K-ration and some of that dried fruit."

"Then we gotta get Billy to dig us a latrine," Jones said and grinned.

"Your latrine's right over there, Jonesy," Gartrell jabbed a finger at the jungle. "Plenty of leaves to wipe with."

"Maybe we oughta look for some fruit trees," Treadway suggested as he and the rest of the Marines moved toward the jungle and a collection of rosewood trees intermingled with birds of paradise. "I mean… we're hoofin' it through banana land… where are the damned bananas?"

Decker snorted, "Coconuts, too. Haven't seen anything edible since we got up on this plateau."

The men settled in, finding what shade they could while staying far enough away from the broad leaves of the birds of paradise to avoid being bombarded by the palmetto bugs and other insects that congregated under the leaves and that fed on the water that saturated the plants. A chorus of ohs and ahs and groans indicated just how tired they already were.

Decker upended his canteen and drained half of what was left. The water was tepid and flat, but he gulped it down greedily, barely managing to restrain himself. He wiped his mouth and looked to his top, who was doing the exact same thing.

"Where's the next river, Guns?" Decker asked.

Oaks frowned and pulled out his map, "Best guess… we don't have good maps of this side of the Matanikau… maybe a mile ahead, maybe less. Probably a ravine there and a watercourse. You don't have to go far on this rock to find one, thankfully."

"All right then," Decker said, finding a bit of ground near Travis and Evans. He too emitted a long groan as he sat and grinned sheepishly. "How you holding up, Hank?"

Evans smiled and gnawed on a corner of the rock-hard chocolate bar that was laughably referred to as rations. So difficult to eat a man had to chew on it to soften it or shave slices off with a knife, the K-ration did pack a large number of calories. In the heat, humidity, and malodorous environment of most of Guadalcanal, this was critical to survival and for being able to function.

"I'm four-oh, sir," Evans said cheerfully. "Teddy patched me up great."

Decker wriggled out of his pack and dug through it until he found a small packet of dried figs and a K-ration of his own, "Good. Any trouble with that left arm?"

"Little sore, but it works, Major," Evans said.

"He virtually indestructible, sir," Travis offered. "Always them mild-mannered farm boy types what is tough as nails."

Decker grinned, "Good thing. Tell you what, fellas… we'll lounge here for an hour and then Charlie Mike. When we get to the next river, we'll drain these canteens, fill 'em up again, drain that, and fill 'em again. Replace some of these vital fluids. Anybody got any of that powdered lemonade?"

Lider, who sat a few feet away scoffed, "That battery acid? No thanks, Major. Rather drink halazone-flavored river water."

That drew laughs from the rest of the men. Decker looked over to Entwater, who had unclipped his walkie and extended the antenna. The Raider set the device in front of him and turned up the volume.

"You know what we need," Taggart offered from Lider's other side, "some kinda radio what scans through the freqs automatically. Then if we hear any Jap talk, we stop on that one and give it to Phil."

"Oh, you mean our Jap spy?" Lider teased.

"Hai," said Oaks. "I rika da flied lice. Ah so… asshole…"

That broke the men up and they all had to cover their mouths to stifle the guffaws. Decker smiled inwardly, glad to see his men were in good spirits.

"Nothin' like bein' stealthy, fellas," Gartrell jeered.

"Ain't no Japs round here, Bill," Jones surmised. "They down on the beach plottin' how to lose another battle to us."

That drew more laughter. As it died down, Decker cocked an ear, "You hear that?"

Everyone fell silent and listened. At first, all that could be heard were the incessant calls of parrots, parakeets, other songbirds, and the chittering of uncounted millions of insects. Yet out of their buzzing rose a distinct sort of hum that grew louder and closer.

"Aircraft," Jones said, pointing to the east.

"We need to cover?" Evans asked.

As if in answer, Entwater's radio crackled and a very American voice said, "*Bashful, Bashful, this is Doc. Do you copy, over?*"

Entwater grinned and held up his radio, but Decker shook his head. He was carrying the other unit and quickly extended its antenna, activating it.

"What freq, Teddy?"

"Fifteen, sir,"

"Doc, Doc, Bashful here," said Decker. "We read five by five, over."

"*Glad to hear your voice, Bashful,*" said the man, who sounded familiar to Decker. "*Heard about your little circus last night. Snow White is very pleased. Over.*"

By now the aircraft was visible. It flew past them, keeping low to the south and hugging the hills. It was perhaps two miles away and what could be seen through breaks in the trees was clearly the form of a Grumman F4F Wildcat.

"Roger that, Doc," Decker said. "Any word from Snow White, over?"

The Wildcat flew on, not even turning and circling. The pilot knew better. The last thing he wanted to do was indicate to the Japanese that there was something... *anything*... on the ground in which he was interested. Yet even low and moving at over 120 knots, the line of sight to the walkie would give the pilot several minutes of talk time. There was a brief pause as Decker and the pilot moved up five channels.

"*Negative, Bashful... how about you? Doin' okay? Need anything?*"

"Four-oh, Doc," Decker wanted to ask the pilot to give him a run down on what terrain was ahead, but again, that could be a mistake over an open channel. Instead, he just said, "For the time being, it's off to work we go. Over."

A pause and then: "*I read, Bashful. High-ho, high-ho. Out.*"

Decker collapsed his antenna and sighed, "Sure wish we could get a little more of a heads up… but one never knows when the Jap has his ears on."

Oaks snorted, "My money's on always."

After an hour's rest and what passed for lunch, the team took up the march once more. It felt good to rest, but everyone was now experiencing the dark side of taking a break. When you were tired and stopped, taking up the burden once more took twice the effort. At least at first.

Two hours later, however, they found the watercourse Oaks had speculated would be there. It was indeed a river, a rather fast-flowing one at that. The course cut its way down from the mountains, slashing a jagged gouge through the land and ending at a small waterfall as the cool water plunged off the plateau and into a far larger, far slower and muddier river below. This then cut its way through dense jungle toward the sea.

The trouble was that where the team stopped, the river ran through a shallow yet steep ravine. Said ravine was perhaps no more than thirty feet across and ten feet deep, but with its nearly sheer walls and roiling white water below, it might as well be the Kongo.

"It's *always* something on this goddamned rock," Dave Taggart grumbled as he kicked a pebble over the edge of the cliff. The small rock plunged into the frothing water below and vanished.

"Water's probably cold," Entwater offered.

"And clean," Gartrell added.

"And in a canyon with rapids at the bottom," Lider sighed. "How in hell we fill our canteens? Let alone get across?"

Decker pondered the problem for a time. To their right, there were plenty of hardwoods between them and the edge of the fifty-foot cliff face. To the left, more jungle obscured the hills to the south, although the foliage seemed slightly less tropical and a little more temperate now.

"We can lower the canteens down on ropes," Treadway said. "That's easy enough… if a bit time consuming."

"Caesar and the Germans…" Travis muttered.

"What?" Jonesy asked. "What Germans?"

Decker glanced at Travis, "Travis? You got an idea?"

Travis smiled a little sheepishly, "Well, sir… I was just thinkin' about how Julius Caesar dealt with them German tribes when he was in Gaul. In 55 BCE, he crossed the Rhine and invaded the territory of the Suebi. Germans be scared silly after that."

Everyone gawked at Travis, even Jones, who knew him better than anyone. Travis frowned at them.

"What?" he asked. "I like history. A *Black* man can't read?"

"Take it easy, Jimmy," Oaks soothed. "It's not that… just you never mentioned you were a history buff before."

Travis shrugged and scowled, "Well… don't nobody ever *ask* before."

Decker grinned, "I know something of Caesar's campaigns in Gaul, Jim. He built that timber bridge in what… ten days?"

"Nine," Travis nodded, "A simple but effective design, sir. You can do a lot with forty-thousand men."

"We only got twelve," Jones jibed. "We can't build no bridges, Jimmy."

"Shit… we only got twelve… but one be *me!*" Travis drawled and pointed at the nearby trees. "We got lumber. And we only need to get twelve men across, so we don't need a forty-foot-wide bridge. Half a dozen logs, laid side by side and lashed with vines. Then you pack mud into the cracks and boom! Foot bridge good enough to get across a thirty-foot ravine. So shove it, Jonesy."

Joens chuckled and Decker grinned, "Y'know… that's not a bad idea. Especially if we're gonna be followed up by more troops someday. Let's get to it. We've got the tools… Guns, I want two parties. Tree cutters and vine gatherers. Dave, Joe, you're with me. Everybody drain your canteens and pile them up over here by the edge. We'll see to filling them."

"How?" Taggart asked, shooting a grin at Treadway.

"I'm ready for anything, sir," Treadway said gamely.

"We're gonna lower Joe down on a rope and he'll fill 'em up for us," Decker said.

"Uhm… nuts to that… sir," Treadway appeared dubious.

"You'll be fine, Joey!" Taggart enthused. "It *ain't* that hot… our hands hardly slip at all on this climbing rope we got."

"Thought you were ready for anything, Corporal," Decker grinned.

"Me and my big mouth…" Treadway said as he shrugged out of his pack. "Ought to learn to keep my yapper shut…"

"See there?" Taggart slapped him on the shoulder. "Bein' a Raider is an educational experience."

Decker laughed, "Okay, fellas… drink up and let's get this shindig underway. Looks like a fine place to camp on the other side of the river. High-ho, high-ho…"

10

"How you doin' down there, Joey?" Taggart called down from the edge of the ravine where he and Decker held Treadways rope.

"Swell," Treadway said.

He was standing on top of a flat rock just at the edge of the ravine. Although the rock was several feet across, its surface was slick with water as the raging river swirled and boiled around it. There was no growth on the rock, but eons of water had polished it to a near glass-smooth texture and without the rope, Treadway would've tumbled into the rapids almost immediately.

"Just take it easy, Joe," Decker encouraged. "One canteen at a time. Fill 'er up and attach it to the other line. Nice and easy now…"

Treadway had already filled half of the team's twenty canteens. Each man carried two, giving him a gallon of water. In theory, a man needed no more than half a gallon per day to survive, but in the hot and humid climate of Guadalcanal, a whole gallon hardly lasted thirty-six hours.

Treadway squatted down, submerging the next canteen and

angling its mouth so that the water could flood in, and the air inside burble out. It was thirsty work, due only in part to the heat of the day. Just being around so much fresh and clean water made Treadway's mouth as dry as the Mohave.

Although it was hot down in the ravine, as the sun was still near its zenith, the light breeze that flowed down the little canyon was cool. The water he was filling from was fresh from the mountains and so cold that by the time he filled a canteen, Treadway's hands hurt. Yet it was a pleasant contrast from the boiling heat of the jungle above.

A shadow fell across the Raider. He looked up and emitted a little bleat of fright as something long and heavy flopped down almost directly overhead. He jerked backward and landed on his rump, immediately soaking the seat of his trousers and the ass end of his skivvies.

"Jesus!" Treadway shouted.

"Sorry, Joey!" Travis's dark, smiling face peered over the edge. "Just testin'."

"Well go test somewhere else, Jack!" Treadway grumped as he re-positioned himself. "About jumped outta my skin!"

Travis grinned and vanished. Even from ten feet down, Treadway could hear the laughter. He muttered something dark and vengeful before turning back to his task.

"What do you think, Julius?" Gartrell asked as he and Lider pulled the log back onto solid ground.

"Just about right," said Travis, who was in charge of the bridge project. "I'd say about fifty feet. Good solid base on either side. Let's get five more and we'll see how it is. Might want to go to eight. These poles pretty thin… and it's Gaias."

Travis's team, consisting of himself, Gartrell, Lider, Jones, and Entwater had discovered that most of the hardwood trees weren't straight enough to make good long poles. However, Jones had discovered a large stand of bamboo on the other side near the jungle and the men quickly set to work on them.

Several of the trees were easily more than long enough. At their base, they were nearly a foot across and about half that at the length Travis wanted. It was Entwater who supplied the method of cutting the very rigid bamboo down.

"I learned this when we were in Norambao visiting Jake Vouza's family," he explained. "You chop a hole in the base segment and then light a fire in there. The fire heats up and busts the segment open and fells the tree. We can cut the far end with hand axes, but this here is way too thick. Take all day."

So it had been done. The first bamboo log was felled within fifteen minutes and Lider and Jones went to work chopping off the skinny end. Meanwhile, Travis, Gartrell, and Entwater selected five more plants and set them to burning. Within an hour, they had half a dozen fifty-foot poles ready to go. By then Treadway and his full canteens had been pulled up, too.

"We gonna lay 'em head to foot," Travis explained to the men gathered around. "Now we got two choices. Lash 'em all together and slide the bridge over, or lay the poles out one at a time… then somebody got to go out and do the lashing."

Everyone frowned, including Decker. He reached down and hefted one end of the bamboo. It was heavy. It'd taken two men to carry the pole to the staging area.

"All six together has gotta weigh… a thousand pounds or more," Decker frowned. "I suppose we can slide the whole thing… but…"

"But it'll be a back-breaker," Lider offered.

"We can place 'em all and then drive in stakes on either side," Treadway suggested. "Get some hardwood and then use those as braces."

Travis nodded, "Yeah, be a good idea. Would want that anyway.

Let's get these lined up. I don't know about the mud, though… ain't much to make it up here."

"There is topsoil," Decker said. "And we have water."

"Yeah, can always send Joe back down for more," Taggart teased.

Treadway scowled but did not object.

Travis grinned, "Let's see what we got now."

Soon, the six poles were laid out, skinny end beside fat end so that they more or less made an even bridge across the ravine. A bridge about five feet across.

"Not bad," said Decker. "Be nice to have a handrail… but it's plenty wide enough for the dozen steps to get across. Still… the spaces between the logs could be treacherous."

"What the mud was for, sir," Travis said. "We can also use small rocks, pebbles, even leaves and junk to pack it and make a level deck."

Oaks emerged from the jungle with Evans, both men having draped a dozen finger-thick vines over their shoulders. They grinned when they saw the bamboo poles lying across the small canyon.

"The hunters have returned," said Oaks, hefting the heavy vines off his shoulders and letting them thump to the sandy ground.

"How long, Gunny?" Travis asked.

"Each one is about thirty feet," Evans said, gasping a little and mopping at his sweaty face. "Nice and flexible, too. Got ten."

"That enough?" Oaks asked, eyeing the construction project.

Jones and Gartrell approached with several pointed sticks in their hands. They smiled at the vine party and bent down, placing the stakes beside the bamboo and began pounding them in with a hammer and one large rock.

"I think so," said Travis, picking one vine up and examining it. "I'll frap these around the logs and when they dry out, they'll actually shrink, getting tighter. How Indians used to secure arrow heads to shafts. Using animal sinew soaked in water. You wrap it up and then when the sinew dries, it shrink and squeeze tight."

"Holy cow, Jimmy!" Evans beamed. "You oughta become an engineer. You really know your stuff."

Travis flushed a little and shrugged, "Aw… it ain't nothin'. Just an interest of mine. Besides… who gonna let an ignant darky get him a degree?"

"Me or I'll know the reason why," Decker said. "Talent should never go to waste, Jimmy. Hell, maybe you oughta switch to the Seabees."

Travis waved that off and got down on his hands and knees, carefully moving on top of the bamboo. When he was at the edge of the cliff, he lay down flat and passed the vine below the poles. It took a few tries, but he caught the bitter end and pulled until he had two equal lengths. He did it again, now having two parallel lashings. He still had more than six feet of bitter end. He could do a third frapping but instead, began weaving the two loose ends through the parallel wraps. Finally, he tugged them tight. He then used his knife to cut a slit in the vine and pushed the bitter end through, securing it.

"Not bad!" Oaks enthused. "Tight enough, Jimmy?"

"It'll do," said the impromptu engineer. "Y'all start gettin' filler and I'll do the rest. Pass me another couple of vines, huh, Hank."

Rather than going out a few feet and doing it again, Travis carefully made his way to the other side and created another frapping near the far edge. Now, the bridge was secure enough that its logs wouldn't roll away from one another and spill anyone into the river below.

By late afternoon, the bridge was complete. Travis had frapped it tightly and the rest of the men packed in stones, leaves, bits of clay they'd found in the trees, and homemade mud until there was a more or less flat and even deck to walk on. Then they made their way across, located a copse of teak trees and slung hammocks and rain covers.

"Phew," Taggart said as he sat with his back against a tree and sipped from his canteen. "That was different."

"A job well done," Oaks said.

"Hail Caesar!" Entwater, Treadway, and Evans exclaimed, hoisting their own canteens.

Travis's dark face flushed even darker, "Y'all quit pickin' on me… I just a humble darkie from North Cacalackie."

Decker laughed, "We're not, Travis. That was some fine work and some fine thinking. That bridge is solid, too. Anybody else comes along and they'll be able to use it. Only took us what… five hours? Not bad."

"I'm impressed," Gartrell offered with a smile. "And I'm just an ignant honky from Joe-guh."

"I know *that's* right! Now all we need is some Germans to scare," Jones said and everyone, including Gartrell, chuckled.

"No Germans… but plenty of Japs," Gartrell said.

"Speakin' of Japs," Oaks said. "What's our next move, Skipper?"

Decker sighed, "Well, we're not moving on today. We need the rest. However… there's still a couple of hours of light left. I wouldn't mind sending a couple of scouts down the ridge and into the jungle to the north a klick or two. Just to see what's what. Best guess I can make is that we're only a few miles west of the Matanikau."

"Hell… for all we know, we just built a bridge across it," Lider chuckled.

"Nah, we done passed it already," Gartrell said. "This here might be the one what goes by Kokumbona… or another'n. They only got about five hundred rivers on this island."

"Wish we could figger out code so that the airdales could give us the skinny," Oaks bemoaned.

"True enough… even some aerial photos would help," Decker

said, making notes on his hand-drawn map. "We're cutting new trails out here, sort of. Guess we're cartographers, too."

"Too bad we ain't got a sextant," Travis mused. "If we could figure our position, we could measure our progress better."

"Listen to ole Archimedes now!" Jones said and smiled at his friend. "Next he gonna invent us a water wheel or somethin'."

Everyone stared. Jones shrugged.

"Hey, I ain't no dummy, either," said the Marine. "I's can read, too."

That drew a laugh and Travis said, "With a sextant, we could get our exact latitude. Too bad we ain't got a barometer, too. Then we'd know our elevation. We could dit our numbers back to base and they could track our progress."

"So many inventions and so little time," Lider said. "Lucky we got some woodsmen in this team, though. Intuition and experience works, too."

"Has so far," Oaks commented.

Decker glanced at his watch, "All right, gentlemen… it is now seventeen hundred and twenty hours."

"That's a lot of hours," Lider deadpanned.

"Shut up, Charlie," Decker said.

"Aye-aye, sir… shuttin' up now, sir."

Decker rolled his eyes but couldn't hide his grin, "Anyway, by my reckoning, we've got an hour and a bit more of light left. Might be just enough time for a couple of energetic lads bucking for a promotion to do a quick scout to the north. One klick up, one klick back. Any volunteers?"

Groans and grumbles from all the men. However, without exception, each one raised their hands. Decker smiled.

"You fellas are a helluva bunch," he said with genuine admiration.

"Hank and me just cut vines all afternoon," Oaks piped up. "We'll go, ain't that right, Hank?"

"Sure, Gunny."

"And I filled canteens down in a nice cool ravine," Treadway said, showing a lopsided smile. "I'll go... Sergeant Taggart'd be happy to go with me, huh, Sarge?"

Taggart glowered at Treadway and then broke into a grin, "Sure, kid. Gimme a chance to teach you somethin'."

"Shit," Lider chimed in. "Joey *already* knows how to goldbrick. Even though he don't do it as much as you, Davie."

"And you can kiss my bright red rosey on Main Street, Charlie," Taggart pretended to grump.

"Gartrell, Entwater, you go with 'em and help them down the ridge face," Decker said. "Leave the ropes rigged. Both teams get to the base, go a hundred paces in opposite directions and then go north. Figure... twenty minutes out, twenty back, and then come back to the ascension point. If it gets dark, you should be able to find your way. Quick and quiet like."

"Should we take a radio, sir?" Taggart asked.

Decker nodded, "Yeah. Wish we had a third... but what can you do. On your way."

Five minutes later, Entwater and Gartrell secured one of the climbing ropes to a thick lignum vitae tree that had contrived to anchor itself half on and half over the edge of the coral ridge. The ridge appeared to be higher at that point, closer to a hundred feet than fifty. It wasn't a sheer cliff, however, but a steep slope perhaps twenty degrees off the vertical. A relatively easy descent and the climb back up would be less arduous.

"Good luck, fellas," Entwater said.

"Yeah, we'll be right here keepin' an ear out," Gartrell added. "If somethin' jumps off..."

"You'll hear it and won't be able to do a goddamned thing," Oaks said, "but you can report back to the skipper. All right, children... down we go."

∽

Although the sun was still above the horizon when the two teams paced out their separation, it wouldn't be for very much longer. And the jungle ate so much of the light that even before sunset a man could hardly see twenty feet in front of himself. However, both pairs of scouts moved relatively quickly through the brush. One kept his eye on the compass and the other acted as guide, his eyes and ears peeled as they weaved through the deep shadows and thin beams of light that poked through the foliage.

There was no real way to tell how far north they went. Counting steps over the length of a kilometer was simply not practical. Even using time didn't quite give anything like accuracy.

More than once, both Oaks and Taggart tried to count steps over the course of a minute and multiply. Yet they found that one minute's pace could be completely different than another's. So they resigned themselves to go until 1750 and then turn back.

At a quarter till six, both teams discovered that the entire point was moot. 200 yards or so apart as they were, they both emerged from a dense section of jungle where a narrow river, perhaps a hundred feet in width, cut a slash through the dense rainforest. The water course more or less followed the contours of the coast, flowing west, northwest effectively blocking further progress.

They knew this because both Evans and Treadway tossed a leaf into the water and tracked its leftward movement. Both teams accurately guessed that this was the same river over which they'd built their bamboo bridge earlier.

"*Blue, Red... Blue, Red...*" Oaks's voice crackled over the walkie at low volume.

"Red, Blue, we read. Over," Taggart said into his unit.

"*Have run into watercourse,*" Oaks reported. "*Unable to proceed. Your sitch, over?*"

Taggart snorted softly and caught Evans's eye before he replied:

"Roger that... same boat. However, have spotted enemy position on other bank. Possible scouting unit. Have identified six to ten targets. Over."

A long pause and then, *"Shit... Roger that, Blue. Time to get back to the ranch. Concur?"*

"Concur," said Taggart. "On our way. Out."

The sergeant slid the antenna down and clipped the walkie to his belt. He smiled at Evans and the two men turned to backtrack their course. As they did, the trees to their left rustled to life and three figures in khaki materialized out of the twilight.

Although short and slightly built as compared to the Americans, the bore at the end of the long Arisaka barrels yawned before the two stunned Marines like the pits of hell.

11

"All right, let's pack it in," Oaks said as he put his radio away. Treadway frowned and looked up the river. A gentle bend in the course prevented them from seeing Taggart's position, but he could imagine it all the same. Around that bend, there was possibly a squad of Japanese soldiers, and it made him uneasy.

"Gunny…" Treadway began but couldn't quite find his words.

Oaks looked at the young man, followed his line of sight and then nodded, "Yeah… I don't like it either. Still, Davie and Hank should already be headed back. Unless the Japs have a boat, they can't get across, so…"

"I've got a bad feeling, Gunny."

Oaks drew in a breath to try and dissuade the other Raider but stopped. He had the same feeling and out in the bush… in Indian country… a wise man did not ignore his instincts. Not ever.

"C'mon," said Oaks and started moving.

Hank Evans had turned to stone. Taggart didn't move a muscle either, of course. When you had three rifles pointed at you, you were wise to stay still.

Yet deep down, Hank knew that wasn't it. He was petrified… literally. He'd never been afraid of combat. Never flinched from a fight. He'd only been with the team for a few weeks, replacing another man who shared his name.

That Evans had died at Vungana. He'd been embroiled in hand-to-hand combat and he and his opponent had gone over the edge of the cliff and plunged 400 feet to their deaths. Yet even this admittedly spooky coincidence hadn't bothered Evans. Not really.

On the other hand, the fear of capture… the fear of being tortured by a vicious enemy… that well-wetted knife of terror had found its way into his deepest of places. Had lodged there, stewing and brewing and waiting to come alive. And now, as darkness crept over Guadalcanal, Henry Evans was face to face with a fear he now realized went deeper and burned hotter than he ever imagined.

Strangely, the three soldiers didn't move either. Evans still controlled enough of his thinking brain to wonder if they'd been as surprised as the Marines. If the three young soldiers, for none could be more than twenty, had accidentally stumbled into Evans and Taggart and were just as shocked and scared as Evans himself.

One of the Japs, the one in the middle, snapped out a string of commands in his own language. The words were harsh, clipped, and angry. Yet… did Evans detect a hint of fear in them? Nervousness at least?

Both Americans just stared at the dim figures before them and shook their heads in truthful incomprehension. One of the soldiers smiled and the effect set Evans's belly to twitching. He pointed with his rifle at the water and repeated his buddy's words.

"They gotta be touched, they think *we're* goin' for a swim…" Taggart said softly. "Fuck you, Tojo."

"Sarge…" Evans hissed.

The Japanese didn't understand Taggart's English any better than the Americans their own language. However, they *did* recognize Tojo and apparently understood Taggart's derisive tone. The soldier in the middle swore, or so it sounded, and jabbed his rifle barrel forward, bayonet and all.

"Now you've gone and done it, Sarge," Evans managed to say without his voice going as tremulous as his belly. "You the kind of guy sees a bear and can't resist poking it or what?"

"In kind of a pickle here, pal," Taggart said, smiling at the Japs as if that would appease them.

The center Japanese spoke again and shoved his blade forward further still, almost into Taggart's throat. He then gestured at the river and not even the dwindling twilight could hide the gleam of sadism in it.

"Bastards…" Evans whispered, images of suckling leeches and saltwater crocodiles and the horrifying deaths that had been describe to him by the others, Entwater especially dancing in his mind's eye. Strangely, even as he considered it, Evans found the prospect less frightening than the three soldiers leading him and Taggart back to their camp.

Evans saw Taggart nod, a big, exaggerated gesture and take a step backward. For a split second, Evans believed the older Raider was actually complying.

"Take a step back, Hank…" Taggart said quietly, still maintaining his smile. "On the count of three…"

Evans stepped back, putting a foot or two of distance between himself and the stabby end of the nearest Arisaka. He wanted to ask what was going to happen on three, but didn't dare.

"Two…" Taggart said quietly. "Three…"

Taggart crouched and launched himself forward, arcing his body beneath the levelled rifles and into the central Japanese soldier. Evans, reacting on instinct in spite of his shock, did the same. He ducked, sprang and hurled himself into the slight but sturdy body four feet in front of him.

The world went mad. Curses, surprised exclamations, and the sounds of rustling, struggling, and blows. Evans, fueled by the huge terror that had welled up in him, now turned into white-hot rage, lifted the smaller man off his feet and drove him backward into the trees. He slid his hands up and found the other man's throat, clamping down with desperate strength.

Evans was face to face with the enemy. Two huge brown eyes bulged out of a pale, terrified moon face. Instead of feeling empathy for the young soldier, his blatant expression of fright only enraged Evans further. After all, seconds before, he and his friends were having themselves a ball terrifying the Americans with what might be in the water.

There were no shots. Somewhere in the back of Evans's mind, he registered that, and it surprised him. Yet there was a good deal of swearing, both in English and Japanese. But not by his man.

"Now you go for a fuckin' swim, slopey Jim!' Taggart roared from somewhere and almost immediately, there was a tremendous splash behind Evans. Almost immediately following that, a shriek of terror.

"Hold it!" another American voice said and there was a single pistol shot.

"Hank!" somebody called out. "*Hank!*"

A pair of hands seized Evans and hauled him off the Japanese soldier. Phil Oaks's face swam into Evans's vision, and Evans was shaken.

"Hey! You got him, pal!" Oaks said sternly, locking gazes with the younger Marine. "You got him. Take it easy."

Evans blinked, "Gunny?"

Oaks smiled, "Yeah, we didn't like you two being over here with a bunch of Japs across the way, so we came runnin'. You all right?"

"I... how's Taggart?" Evans managed.

"As pretty as ever, Hank," Taggart said, coming over and clapping Evans on the shoulder. "Good work."

Treadway appeared next, "These two are dead. But that guy…"

Taggart scooped up one of the Arisakas, shouldered it, took careful aim and fired at the head of the man now swimming across the water. The crack of the shot echoed up and down the river. The man stopped abruptly and his head vanished below the rippling river.

"We better breeze on out, fellas," Oaks said, pointing across at the dark jungle on the other side of the river. "Think the natives are gettin' restless. Gather these rifles, ammo, and anything else useful. Let's move out."

William Gartrell stared out over the land stretching out before him. The sun had set, and full darkness held Guadalcanal in its iron fist. Gartrell, who'd grown up in the rural south, was no stranger to deep, dark nights. Even where he'd grown up, light pollution was mild. Yet when he and his pa or he and his friends went out into the wilderness on a camping or hunting trip… the depth of night and the enormity of the star-littered sky was dazzling and even a little frightening.

Guadalcanal was the same. There was no modern civilization there. No electric lights, save those at Henderson powered by the generators. Even those were few, as the airfield was careful about not making itself too easy a target for Japanese guns. Only now and then when planes had to be brought in after dark would runway lights or search lights be employed.

If there was any light at all on the island, it came from fires and torches. And in the region they were traversing, there was nothing. Just a vast, black slab only discernable from the sky due to the sprinkling of tiny points of light above.

So when a voice called out from the stygian blackness below, Gartrell nearly leapt out of his boots. He heard Entwater curse softly under his breath from the other side of the tree that anchored the climbing rope.

"Who goes there?" Entwater called out, albeit quietly.

"Just four lonely servicemen lookin' for comfort," came Dave Taggart's ghostly voice from a hundred feet below. "Any sexy broads up there?"

"I swear…" Gartrell snorted and couldn't help but laugh.

"You're late," Entwater teased. "You were supposed to be home before the streetlights came on."

"Ain't no streetlight anywhere," Oaks said. "We were held up."

A laugh from below and Taggart said, "And how."

Within minutes, the Raiders came up the line one at a time. Oaks was the last, and once he was up on the ridge, Entwater bent to untie the rope from the tree.

"Any word from the skipper?" Oaks asked Gartrell.

"Nah. Me and Teddy just been sittin' here twiddlin' our thumbs."

"Well, let's get back… we may or may not have a problem," Oaks said.

"What happened, Gunny?" asked Entwater as he began coiling the rope.

"Found a Jap patrol across a river about a klick north," Oaks explained. "And they'd sent a couple of boys out across the river. Not sure how. Waylaid Dave and Hank."

"And you got away?" Entwater asked, audibly impressed.

"Beat the tar out of 'em," Taggart chuckled. "Hank gave one the old Sicilian handshake."

"What's that?" asked Gartrell.

"Choked him to death," said Oaks.

"Damn…" Entwater muttered.

Back at camp, Oaks filled Decker in. The major listened,

grinned at the ballsy move of attacking three men with guns, and then shrugged, "Well, I doubt they'll be heading up here anytime soon. Be foolish to try and go after an enemy in this dark and without knowing our numbers. So let's set a watch and get some rest. First light we'll haul stakes and keep on truckin'. Good work, fellas. You okay, Hank?"

NORTHWESTERN COAST OF GUADALCANAL

Ata Hondo did not like boats. He joined the Army rather than the Navy specifically so he could avoid boats. A poor swimmer, the young lieutenant had never taken to the water. He secretly harbored fears of both drowning and being devoured by unseen beasts below the surface.

The war in the Pacific and his time on Guadalcanal had in no way diminished those concerns. Indeed, his fears and aversions were stronger than ever. After all… great ravenous reptiles lurked in the many rivers in the island's interior. He'd personally witnessed more than one soldier being eaten alive and had seen more taken when the monstrous things came to scavenge on the decaying flesh of those who did not survive a battle.

Then there was the ocean. Clear, turquoise waters that appeared so lovely and inviting… to others… yet hid uncounted hungry denizens. Again, Hondo had witnessed sharks attacking dead bodies floating in the surf. He'd seen these same sharks rise up and snatch living men as well. Tack onto that the horror stories told of men whose ships were blown out from under them only to be dropped into a horde of gnashing teeth and billowing blood…

So Hondo avoided the water as much as possible. However, when one fought a campaign in and among islands, even the Army had to bend to the practical. Water was the best way to move large numbers of men and materiel around the theater.

So there Hondo sat, stiff and unmoving in his canvas seat as the motor launch puttered along the coast. It was not a swift craft, perhaps only moving at eighteen or twenty kilometers per hour… no, knots. Boats used the nautical mile. Ten knots or so, then. Which meant a trip of between four and five hours.

Four or five hours being rocked back and forth. Four or five hours of being hit by flying spray. Hours of enduring the reek of men succumbing to sea sickness, their sour belly-spill sloshing about in the bilge. Perhaps worst of all… the indignity of being a source of amusement for the Navy sailors who operated the craft.

The sea was light, they said. Only a meter high at most. That might be true, but following the coast meant that the boat kept its flank to the incoming sea. And rolling side to side was the worst kind of motion for men not inured to the constant movement of wind and wave. So half of Hondo's men lie in the bottom of the boat, moaning pitifully while remnants of their vomit effused its mephitic reek in an almost calculated attempt to bring down the rest.

Hondo fell back on the only defense he had against the misery and the fear. He fell back on conversation with his inferior.

"I thought that the general ordered a dozen men, Sergeant," Hondo said to the bulkier shadow sitting beside him.

Makai, the stiff-necked cretin, seemed entirely unaffected by the motion of the boat, the cool breeze or the flying damp, "He did, sir. Yet when I began gathering volunteers, many more stepped forward. No doubt the desire for something to do and to get some revenge on the Ame-cohs drove this. Now we have nearly a full platoon's worth. Thirty-six to Decker's ten. Advantage Japan, sir."

Hondo snorted, "And if we're successful… those whose opinion matters will say that it was foregone. That we certainly *should* win… and the glory to be gained shall be diminished."

Hondo couldn't see Makai's expression in the dark. He was little better than a silhouette. Yet he could tell that the sergeant was looking directly at him. Studying him. With admiration? Contempt?

"Perhaps, sir," said the sergeant neutrally. "Yet true glory comes from doing one's duty. From serving the needs and requirements of the emperor."

It took effort for Hondo not to sneer. Imperial pride was all to the good, but true men of the world understood how things *really* worked. How promotions were earned when a man could coat himself in glory, rather than just being another obedient automaton who simply *did their duty*.

"True enough," Hondo lied. "Yet our people value valor and achievement, Sergeant. As I'm sure you well know."

"Hai…" Makai said softly and said nothing more.

"Lieutenant," the boat's pilot spoke out of the darkness, the cherry of his Golden Bat bouncing before his shadowed visage. "We near our destination, sir."

Grateful news to the miserable officer, "Good. How long?"

"I will make my turn into the beach momentarily," said the pilot. "Once the destroyer drops its load, we shall move in and run ashore. Once your men step onto the sand, sir, they will feel world's better, I assure you."

Hondo flinched, "Destroyer?"

"Yes, sir… two points off the port bow," the pilot said. "A rat transport. More unlucky souls to be doomed to this foul place."

Makai harrumphed but made no further observation. Hondo couldn't help but chuckle, "Indeed."

The pilot must have incredible eyes. Try as he might, the Army officer couldn't see the shape of a ship off the bow. Although he thought he could *smell* something. A brief shift in the wind allowed a carbony, burnt waft to tickle his nostrils.

Another reason to hate the sea… death could hide anywhere, even on its surface. Hondo shivered and waited. Soon enough, the boat was turned, and the sickening roll subsided into a gentler rise as waves rolled under the stern and rocked the boat gently. Soon, the craft crashed through the breakers and nosed up to the beach.

Before Hondo could say a word, Makai snapped out the orders that sent the men, even the sick, piling onto the bow ramp and even over the sides. Others handed down extra bags of equipment and supplies.

Finally, Hondo rose, "Thank you."

"Hai," said the pilot. "Good luck ashore, sir."

Better than going back out on the water in the middle of the night... Hondo thought.

Makai helped him over the bow and the lieutenant's boots splashed down in a few centimeters of water. Yet the solid, unmoving ground beneath his feet was welcome. He only wondered how long the phantom rolling would last before he gained his land legs once again.

12

GUADALCANAL
OCTOBER 5, 1942

On the fourth afternoon of their trek, Decker's team began seeing a diminishment of tropical fauna and more cloud forest foliage. Hardwood trees, pines, plenty of lush greenery but less of the sort that held and collected water and vines. They'd crossed two streams, one so small that it could be swung over on a rope. The other was wider but in a ravine with gently sloping sides and plenty of stones projecting from the moderate rapids. The men simply stepped across in pairs and made short work of it.

On that day, the team was picking their way through a forest. On their right, the plateau still ended abruptly at a steep coral slide that was now easily a hundred feet above the jungle below. On their left, beyond the trees, jagged walls of granite, steep slides, and craggy ravines cut into a steadily rising shelf that joined steep mountains perhaps a mile or two inland. Presently, Decker and his men entered a clear area near the banks of a modest river.

Unlike the previous water courses they'd found, this one was level with the ground. The fifty-foot or so river ran quickly enough to show relatively clear, but without being so swift that it boiled and rolled. The river came to the edge of the plateau and tumbled in a wide, silvery waterfall into a small lake below, where the river again followed its meandering course toward the sea.

Across the river more forest resumed after a wide stretch of open ground, perhaps another fifty feet, just like the side they were on. Perhaps two or three hundred yards inland, the river flowed out of a steep ravine a hundred, hundred fifty feet high.

"Let's call a halt, Top," Decker told Oaks, standing in the open and glancing around. "I want to examine this location a bit."

Oaks nodded, "A little cooler here. Five degrees, anyway. Take five, boys!"

The Raiders spread out, sluffing off their packs and finding spots to rest with their backs against the trees. Decker and Oaks did a quick stroll around the perimeter outside the trees and came back to the men.

"Smoke 'em if ya' got 'em, fellas," Decker said. "Fill up on water, too. Got a good source here. Running but not racing and fairly clear."

"Major, you see them cliffs up there?" Taggart pointed to the ravine and the walls of granite a few hundred yards to the south.

"Can't hardly miss 'em, Dave," Decker grinned and lit himself a Lucky Strike.

Lider chuckled and Taggart said, "Well, to the left of the ravine, a little back… there's a sort of… tuft of trees."

"Yeah…" Decker said, turning and looking where Taggart was pointing and then he tumbled to what the sergeant was getting at. "Oh… I see. If we can see them, they must be on a higher elevation…"

"Maybe a good OP, sir," Entwater added.

"This whole place might make a good base, sir," Oaks said. "Got fairly open ground, a cliff to the north, cliffs to the south, and a solid watercourse. Plus multiple avenues of escape."

"And maybe a good high observation post," Decker added,

scratching at his chin. "Now if we can find a way down into the plains... and up to those trees of Taggart's... yeah, this might be a helluva location for a coast watcher station or even enough to support a company or at least a couple of platoons. Where do you figure we are, Phil?"

Oaks unfolded his map, which was beginning to look the worse for wear. Decker did the same and smiled. They oriented their maps to the north and compared.

"I'd say we've come... between thirty and forty klicks," Oaks said.

Decker nodded, "My guestimate is about thirty-five. That puts us about halfway to Cape Esperance. Now how far inland we are... that's hard to say."

Oaks frowned and stared out over the plains, "Well, we're maybe a hundred feet up and I can't see the ocean. That means it's at least a dozen miles away. Mount Austin is only about half that... so it seems like the more west we go, the more inland we're going, too."

Decker nodded, "Probably why we haven't seen a single Jap patrol since that little run in the other night. We can double check that with the next overflight."

"Wouldn't be a bad place to make camp, sir," Travis offered and flicked an ash onto the mossy ground.

"No, it wouldn't, Chief engineer," Decker grinned. "Got plenty of wood here, and lots of deadfalls we could use as firewood, if we chose. Looks like more variety of trees and stuff across the river... think you could do us up another bridge, Jimmy?"

Travis frowned, looked about him and drew on his Pall Mall, "Well... not like the last one. River's just too wide. But I bet we could rig up a floating log bridge, sir. Need more vines and stuff, though. r a good supply of rope."

"Wish we had real tools," Jones put in. "Saws, hammers and like that."

"We got saws and hammers," Gartrell said. "How we done the bamboo."

"Yeah… but small, portable stuff," Travis said. "With good carpentry tools and such, we could really do us a fort here."

"Fort Travis," Entwater smiled.

"There's some pretty big teak trees," Evans said. "Some rosewoods… a few palms, too. And some others… like those over there, not sure what they are."

"Casuarina," Decker said. "Problem is, it'd take us a year to cut down any of these big boys."

"We don't need to make somethin' permanent, though," Treadway said. "Just tie some logs together and anchor 'em on either shore, right? Maybe it won't last years… but who cares?"

Travis nodded, "Yeah, that the best we can do with what we've got. Just a foot bridge."

"Then again, maybe this water's only a foot deep, so we don't need one," Oaks said.

Travis frowned, glanced at the river and shook his head, "We can test that, Gunny… but you ever hear the sayin'… still waters run deep? Just by lookin', I can tell that water be three, four feet at least and probably deeper in the middle."

Decker smiled, "Okay, here's what we're gonna do. Treadway and Gartrell, you're with me. We're gonna scout up those cliffs to the south and find Taggart's OP. Top, you and Entwater find us a way down into the northern jungle. Rig us a climbing rope. Taggart, you're in charge here. Get a camp set up and work on cutting logs for a floating bridge. Travis is in charge of that. If you need vines, Travis, the seven of you can pick a party to go down into the jungle and haul some up. I'll take a radio and leave one with Taggart. Before that, though… let's crack open a can of beanie weenies and live, huh?"

It took nearly an hour, but Decker and his party eventually found a way up the rock faces. At least to the next level. They wound their way to the cliffs by following the river and then followed the basalt walls eastward for perhaps 200 yards. There they found a section of the plateau that had collapsed, perhaps from structural imperfections or perhaps an earthquake.

A section of the hundred-foot wall had crumbled, leaving a fairly gentle ramp a few dozen yards across and well over a hundred yards deep. They had to be careful going up, stepping over and around boulders and carefully avoiding loose piles of scree, but they made it to the next plateau without incident.

Decker paused and they all wiped their faces and sipped from their canteens. Gartrell looked back to where they came from and smiled.

"Hey, I can see my house from here," he said.

Treadway chuckled, "Yeah, there's the river… can't see our guys, though."

"No… trees are in the way," Decker said. "Still… I think I might be able to see the ocean now."

Treadway pointed past more piles of boulders and intermittent trees, "Look there, sir. There're the sarge's trees. Looks like a stand of them on top of that outcropping… maybe three hundred yards?"

Decker nodded and began walking on the flattish ground between the cliffs and the next rise, "Yeah… looks pretty steep, too. Gonna be tough to get up there."

"That Vungana village is 400 feet above the river, sir," Gartrell said. "And they got them a path all the way up the cliff."

"We'll see," said Decker.

Soon they came to the base of the outcropping. The trees in question were another hundred feet or so overhead and were clustered together at the end of a narrow finger of rock that jutted out from a sheer cliff a quarter mile away. Being that close, Decker wanted up at any cost.

"We could toss a grappling hook," Decker said. "Climb up. Kind of rough, but..."

Gartrell frowned at the geology for a long moment and finally said, "I don't see no trail... but it could be these faces aren't as steep all around. Just ten or fifteen degrees off the vertical and it makes the climb twice as easy."

"You done some rock climbing, Bill?" Treadway asked. "In Georgia?"

"Naw... well, you go into the mountains, and you might," Gartrell said. "But there's better rocks in Tennessee. Done some hiking up there. Plus me and Travis climbed a face on Santa Isabella."

"Oh yeah..." Treadway mused. "When we attacked that Jap OP..."

"All right," said Decker. "Let's split up and circle this finger. See if we can find—"

From the northeast, a low, steady buzzing asserted itself over the sounds of insects and avian life below. Decker yanked his radio off his belt and extended the antenna. In a few minutes, the buzzing became the sound of an aircraft's engine, and a small dot appeared low over the jungle.

"You two go on," Decker said. "I'll check in with our pals up there."

Treadway and Gartrell saluted and split up, one going to either side of the fifty-yard-wide end of the granite finger. Decker watched the plane and waited.

"Bashful, Bashful... this is Doc, do you copy?"

Again, Decker thought he recognized the voice, "Doc, Bashful here. I read. Hey... your voice sounds familiar."

A laugh over the channel and the dot began to take on a distinct shape as it drifted closer, *"Captain Marion Karl, at your service, sir."*

A breech of protocol, but even if the Japanese just happened to be listening, it would mean little to them. Decker smiled and said, "Thought so. How we doin' this afternoon, Doc?"

"*You're alone, far as I can tell. Little dryer today, huh?*"

That was code for informing Decker that he was further inland. The major thumbed the switch, "Seems so. Gotta get to work in the mine, ya' know."

A pause and then, "*Oh yeah? Any luck?*"

"Maybe… but it's gonna take some effort."

More code. Decker had just informed Karl that they'd found a potential base. He'd also let him know that there was a need for an airdrop. Karl banked left and made a lazy loop, never coming too close to Decker's position. The next part would be tricky.

"*Would love to help, Bashful… but I left my shovel back with Snow White. Hope that's all right?*"

Karl's circle had taken him past Decker and toward the mountains. The Raider eyeballed it, paused for a few seconds and then said, "That's all right, Doc."

Immediately Karl banked to starboard. Decker wanted to simply tell him to follow the river, but either through an application of skill or luck, Karl figured it out. He flew along the river, tracking its path right toward the camp. Decker grinned when he was nearly overhead and spoke again.

"Thanks for checking in, Doc… tell Sleepy we say hello," Decker said, indicating when Karl was directly over the camp. "My regards to Snow White."

"*That's a Rodge, Bashful… talk to you tomorrow… if not sooner. Doc over and out.*"

Decker grinned and slid the antenna down. If he'd read that right, then there was a chance that by tomorrow, or even overnight, Henderson would drop a care package nearby. Of course, it'd be rather difficult in the dark, at least pinpointing their location. They'd have to figure out how to light a small signal fire that would be visible from the air but not the Japs lower down in the plains.

"Sir!" Gartrell jogged up, panting and smiling. "I found it. Good climbing spot! Already tossed a grapnel and we can get up to the trees whenever you're ready, sir."

Decker nodded, "Good work. Where's Joe…?"

Treadway jogged up, also panting, "No joy, sir… all vertical on this side."

"I found a spot," Gartrell said.

Treadway frowned a little and shrugged, "Are we goin' up, sir?"

"That we are, Joe," said Decker. "Lead the way, Gartrell."

Travis watched as Jones and Lider carried a freshly cut log from out of the forest and set it beside the half dozen others waiting by the edge of the river. The log's ends were rough, having been hacked apart with hand axes. However, the log was five feet long and about half as thick. Travis smiled.

"This one okay, Julius?" Lider quipped.

"Keep 'em comin', fellas," Travis said, immediately going to work with his axe, stripping the bark and chiseling a two-inch wide, two-inch deep track encircling the log near both ends.

"We gonna need twenty-five of these," Jones huffed, sipping from his canteen. "And we got *seven*…"

Travis grinned at him, "Probably closer to thirty, brother. Plus we need four sharp poles we can pound into the ground. Two on each side. Act as anchors so the bridge don't float off."

"Boy…" Evans huffed as he and Taggart brought log number eight. "I'd give five bucks to go swimmin' in that river…"

"With all these crocs around?" Entwater emerged from the trees with several vines draped around his neck.

Oaks came next, shaking his head, "Oh, for God's sake, Teddy… you and your damned crocs. It never ends with this guy, fellas… don't go in the river, there's crocs… check your bedroll at night… might be crocs… open that can of spam slow now… could be a *croc* hidin' in there!"

Everyone laughed, except Entwater of course. He scowled and threw his vines to the ground, "How many Japs we seen eaten by them things, Gunny. Two, three, four? You wanna swim with 'em, be my guest… least it'd keep my balls from being busted."

"Nah, that wouldn't do nothin', Ted," Jones said. "No croc would eat the gunny. Too mean."

"We might eat *him*, though," Oaks said, grinning. "Like that time we went out on our first patrol. Remember that, Jimmy? You shot one of them things and we cooked him up. Pretty damned good really. Tasted like chicken."

"Swamp chicken," Jones laughed.

"Anyway," Evans said. "No crocs up here, Ted. They're down there where the water's slower and along the coast. Nice and clean up here. Wouldn't mind a bath, that's for sure."

"Neither would the rest of us," Travis quipped as he piled more bark beside the logs. "Don't mind you done took a bath, that is."

"*Blue, Red… Blue, Red… do you read, over?*"

Oaks pulled the radio from his belt and held it up, "Go ahead, Red. Found the treasure?"

"*Roger that, Blue… good as gold. Made contact with Doc, also. Now it's off to work we go. High-ho, high-ho.*"

"Acknowledged. Blue out," Oaks slid the antenna closed, conserving the radio's battery. "Skipper found a way up and now they're inbound."

"Good," Lider sat on the log Taggart and Evans had just brought in. "Maybe they can take a turn cuttin' up these damned trees. Goddamned hard piece of work."

"Why we get the big bucks, Charlie," Taggart sat beside his fellow sergeant with an audible groan.

Travis set his axe down and pushed his fists into his back, bending and stretching and peering at the sun, now three-quarters of the way across the sky, "How many vines you fellas get?"

"A dozen," Oaks said. "About twenty feet long each. Was a bear gettin' 'em up the cliff."

"Good…" said Travis, calculating. "That's enough to do four logs… what I wouldn't give for some good, half-inch nylon rope. Hell… two fifty-foot lengths of half-inch chain and a box of six-inch nails would do even better."

"Will it work?" Taggart asked, pointing at the pile of vines and the logs, most of which were bare of bark. Their sappy yellow interiors glistening in the sun.

"Oh sure… for a while," Travis said. "Couple months, maybe. But sooner or later, bugs, weather… all sorts of stuff be eatin' on this wood and them vines."

"Couple of months… this campaign will be over, one way or another," Entwater opined.

"Think so, General McArthur?" Lider teased.

Entwater shrugged, "My guess. Japs'll hold out for a while… but if the rumors of another big push at the field are true… and if they fail…"

Evans nodded, "Too many failures and too many resources expended against an entrenched enemy, right?"

"Hope you're right…" Taggart muttered.

"Makes sense," Oaks said. "Come Christmas, either we'll be pushed back, or it'll be all over for the Jap. What with the Army promising to send in a regiment in the next week or so. That happens… we'll have way more guys. Don't mean it'll be easy… but a lot harder for the Jap."

"Then what, I wonder?" Jones asked, plopping onto the ground. "The Corps packs us up and ships us off where?"

Oaks chuckled, "Damned if I know. Way above my pay grade. But maybe we move closer to Rabaul… maybe we hit New

Guinea… dunno. But we gotta push Tojo back to his doorstep, that's for certain."

"Well, we ain't gonna do it jawin' all day," Travis said, smiling at his friends. "Better get to work before the skipper finds us all sittin' here gold-brickin'."

"Give a guy a little power and look what happens," Lider said to Jones.

"That's true," said Jones, flashing a big white smile. "Can't give no darkie power, Sarge… he run you White boys ragged if he do."

"I *heard* that…" Travis drawled.

13

It was just after zero-one-hundred when the gentle tropical night was broken by a distant buzzing. Lider and Evans, who were assigned the midnight to three watch, hurried through the cluster of slung hammocks, emitting a warbling whistle that... in theory... resembled one of Guadalcanal's night birds.

"Plane?" Decker asked sleepily.

"Yes, sir, I think so," Lider said.

"Get to the drop zone," Decker ordered as he rolled out of his bedding. "I'll gather the party. You got lights?"

Both men held up their red-filtered flashlights. Decker nodded and waved them off.

The best place to receive aerial deliveries, Decker had determined, was the open ground between the trees and the cliffs to the south. Not far from the outcropping on which they were to set up their observation post. The ground was open enough that even at night, the aircraft should be able to hit it from a hundred feet up.

"Sounds like they're over the mountains, Sarge," Evans noted as the two of them reached open ground.

"Probably comin' in from the south so's the Jap don't see 'em,"

Lider said. "You stay here, I'll take the other side. Lights on and straight up, for now."

Every man on the team knew this drop would be tricky. There had been no way to arrange exact procedures. No markers could be set out to outline the drop zone and no radio communications could be risked. The Marines had to hope that Captain Karl had adequately described the terrain and that the pilots had sharp eyes.

"Sounds like an R4D," Evans called to Lider fifty yards away as softly as he could. "Not a Dauntless."

Lider frowned. He wasn't an expert on airplanes but knew some by sight. As the aircraft drew closer, he thought that Evans might be right. The pitch of the engine was lower and there might even be two.

"Here they come!" Lider whisper shouted. "Point the lights and blink 'em!"

The two men aimed their lights at the sky and the sound of the approaching plane. The night was mostly clear, and thousands of tiny diamonds twinkled above them, dominated by the fat, lopsided smile of a silvery moon.

The two men switched their lights on and off, searching the dark sky for any sign of the plane. It was close, that much was clear based on the low throb of the radial engines. Lider was almost ready to believe the ship had missed them when something large and black suddenly blotted out the moon and the stars and whooshed by so close overhead the sergeant would swear he felt the wind of its passing.

The aircraft banked away to the south again, throttling up and rapidly exfiltrating the area. Evans pointed with his light and Lider saw several lumpy somethings fluttering down between him and the stars.

A moment later, as the hum of the cargo plane was swallowed by the calls of Guadalcanal's night fauna, three heavy objects thumped and slid on the gravelly, mossy ground.

"Got 'em!" Evans said, running a few yards toward the middle of the clear land. "Damn near perfect, Sarge!"

Lider joined the other Raider and shined his beam on what had come down. There were three canvas bundles, several feet long and nearly two feet on a side. Attached were parachutes of red and green and not blue, indicating ammunition and rations but no water. Transporting water wasn't generally necessary on Guadalcanal.

More Raiders emerged from the woods, still blinking away sleep as they joined the two guards. Silently, the men went to work. Several detached the chutes and folded them while three pairs grabbed each of the bundles to carry them back to the camp.

"Nice," Oaks mentioned as they all tromped through the woods to the bivouac area. "Three A4s. Hope somebody thought this through."

Decker chuckled, "I'm sure they did, Guns. Of course, considering the supply sitch at Henderson, we're probably lucky in whatever presents Santa brought."

The packages were stored near the hammocks and the parachutes placed on top. Decker ordered the men to return to their hammocks and that the goodies could be examined in the morning when there was light.

It was only after the remaining eight men bedded down once more and Lider moved off to his post to watch the eastern approach that Evans began to worry. He stood by the row of logs everyone had prepared for the bridge that day and studied the dark river before him and the much darker forest beyond.

Several nights earlier, he and Taggart were nearly captured by Japanese soldiers. Only through bold action and luck had they escaped. Evans couldn't help but ponder what would've happened if they hadn't. What would the Japanese have done to them?

If anything, his close call with becoming a prisoner of war had only intensified his fear. The young farm boy turned Marine Raider simply couldn't understand it. He had no fear of combat…

or at least, no more than anyone else. He supposed you just got used to it. Used to the fear, the adrenaline surge, and even the exaltation of winning. That was normal for fighting men, he thought.

Yet the idea of being held prisoner and possibly tortured… was like a yawning black pit in his soul. A pit filled with every frightening possibility an imaginative young man could conceive. Hell, he'd heard the stories. Heard Jacob Vouza's account of being captured, beaten, deprived of water, tied to an ant pile… stuck with bayonets just for fun…

Perhaps, Evans tried to reason, it wasn't so much the individual horrors but the whole idea itself. Being robbed of your freedom… robbed of your identity and your dignity… humiliated and treated as sub-human…

Geez… maybe he ought to talk to a shrink. He wished he could talk to Decker or Oaks about it… yet he was afraid he'd be labeled a coward or a sissy. So who could he talk to? Jonesy and Travis seemed to understand… maybe it was because they were Black?

After all… Black people had been slaves in America before the Civil War. Robbed of *their* freedom and dignity. Even afterward… even up until that very day… many Whites treated them as sub-human. Not fit to eat at the same counter or use the same John. How must that make them feel?

"Hey, Hank, how you doin'?"

Evans flinched and just kept himself from whirling around. So absorbed was he in his own thoughts, so lulled by the steady but sleepy sounds of Guadalcanal night had he been that he hadn't heard Jones step up to him.

"Uhm… good morning, Jonesy…" he mumbled, glad it was too dark for the other man to see how foolish he must look.

Jones flashed a white smile in the dark, "Sorry, brother. Didn't mean to startle ya. You okay? You look white… whiter than usual, I mean."

Evans managed a small chuckle, "Just... thinkin' is all. You my relief?"

"Zero-three-hundred," Jones said. "Me and old Bessy here'll keep them Japs worried. You gotta get some rest or Santa won't come."

Evans snorted, "He already did. Say, Jonesy..."

"Yeah?"

"Nothin'... forget it."

Evans turned to go but a gentle hand on his shoulder stopped him. Softly Jones said: "Hey, Hank... we a team. We's all brothers here. You got somethin' on your mind... got somethin' you want to get off your chest... feel free, all I'm sayin'. You still bothered by the other night, huh?"

"Maybe you oughta be a head shrinker, Jonesy," Evans said, smiling now himself.

"It be one of the powers we darkies got."

Evans snorted, "Thanks, Jonesy... it's nothing, though."

Jones nodded and patted the other man again, "Okay, Hank. Offer still stands, though. Nighty night."

"Sir! Sir!" the insistent voice and incessant shaking brought Hondo to a reluctant wakefulness.

He blinked and tried to focus on the shadowy form before him, "What... what is it, private? You had better not have awakened me for nothing."

"No, Lieutenant... Sergeant Makai wishes to speak with you. He says it's urgent, sir."

Grumbling and cursing in Japanese as well as English, Hondo rolled out of his hammock and stretched, "Take me to him."

A moment later, the private led his commander into a small clearing in the semi-tropical forest. Makai stood there, spotlighted in a pale shaft of moonlight. Appearing more ghostly than living. He just stood, stiff as a statue with his head cocked. It gave Hondo a mild shiver.

"Sergeant," Hondo grumbled. "What is—"

Makai held up a hand and then a finger to his lips. Softly, he said, "Do you not hear that, sir?"

"I hear nothing," Hondo snapped and was about to berate the man for waking him when it was not his watch and then stopped.

He did indeed hear something now. Something other than the incessant chitter of insects, squawk of the damned birds, and other sounds he could not identify and wasn't sure he wanted to. There was a humming. A monotonous buzzing that appeared to be growing louder and sounded as if it was coming from the east.

"Is that... an airplane engine?" Hondo asked.

"Two engines, sir," Makai said. "Two *American* engines if I do not mistake."

"At *night?*"

"It's there," said Makai, not stating the obvious that it was foolish to debate what was plainly true. "I find it... interesting, sir. I estimate the aircraft is... perhaps ten or fifteen kilometers along our path."

"But it's moving."

"Circling now... yes, I think it's circling... now moving off again."

Hondo was not yet wise enough, if he ever would be, to appreciate rather than resent Makai's greater experience. The older man's length of service and seemingly endless well of knowledge irked Hondo. More times than not, the officer felt like a rank amateur beside the seasoned soldier and the effect was mildly shameful and emasculating. Of course, he couldn't show this... not obviously... but the resentment glowed warmly all the same.

One thing Hondo loathed most of all was how Makai often failed to volunteer information. Forcing the younger officer to ask for it. Hondo wondered if the sergeant did it on purpose. To subtly let Hondo know who was really in charge. To put the officer in what Makai felt was his proper place.

"The purpose?" the lieutenant asked sternly.

"No way to know… it could be reconnaissance," Makai replied. "Yet at this hour… that seems unlikely. My best guess would be a supply drop."

"Decker…" Hondo muttered. "He's extending his patrol or…"

"Or his team is setting up a more permanent command post," Makai finished. "And the airbase has used the cover of darkness to slip in some materiel."

Hondo thought for a moment, "And they are more than a day's march… perhaps two… giving Decker enough time to set up his CP before we locate him and take it from him. Excellent. Let the Americans do the hard labor, and we shall simply… relieve them of their burden."

"Yes, sir," said the sergeant, his even tone betraying nothing of his feeling on the matter.

"Very well," said Hondo, pulling himself erect. "You were right to inform me. Now I shall return to sleep."

"Yes, sir."

Just after first light, the men rose and stowed their hammocks. Although they left them tied to the trees with their packs, as the plan was to stay at the location until some of the work Decker wanted done was complete.

The major had the red parachute soaked in the river and then strung up between four trees with heavy canopy. Once serving as something of a low cover, Decker allowed Entwater and Treadway to build a fire ring and small fire to heat up some of their rations.

The wet chute would serve to capture the smoke, and the smoke would also serve to smudge out the chute's red coloring.

"All right, let's see what old Saint Nick brought us," Decker said. "Phil, Taggart, inventory those three containers. Travis, how much more time for your bridge?"

Travis glanced at the edge of the river where sixteen logs had already been stripped and notched. He rubbed his chin a moment and said, "I need ten more, sir. If I can get them this morning… I should be able to lash them together and extend the bridge to the far bank. All we need to do then is pound in the stakes over there, tie it up, and we done. Say… late afternoon?"

"Good," said Decker. "Then you can have every man here for that work. At least to get the logs cut. Then I want to go up to that outcrop again and set up a more permanent OP. Depending on how today goes… we might send out a couple of patrols later. Certainly tomorrow."

"This one's ordnance, Skipper!" Taggart enthused as he opened one of the cylindrical canvas cases. "Looks like some explosives… might be 400 or 500 rounds for the Springfields… and they included a dozen mags for each BAR and Thompson. Oh… and I think… holy cow! There's a bundle of tools in here, too! Real ones, sir."

Travis moved over to take a look, "Shovels, picks, axes… and a two-man tree saw, sir! That'll speed things up."

"Got rations in here, sir," Oaks said as he and Gartrell opened another package. "Couple hundred pounds of canned food, K-rations, water purification tabs… and some medical supplies."

"This'n's got socks and skivvies," Jones chuckled as Evans helped him open the last container. "Oh, and maybe some BDUs, sir… camos, too!"

"Look at this," Evans hauled out an armload of white coils. "Rope. Several gauges, Major!"

Travis beamed, "Oh, if I could have some of that…"

"Extra walkie!" Jones said. "And some batteries."

"Good, very good," Decker grinned. "Let's get those bundles stored in the trees."

"Gimme that saw," Lider said. "C'mon, Hank. You and me will get to cuttin'. If you think that arm will stand it."

Evans smiled, "It'll do the job, Sarge."

Decker smiled, "Jonesy, let's you and me put together a ditty bag. Dozen cans of food, that green parachute, and two of the Jap weapons we snitched. What ammo have we got for them?"

"We got six rifles, sir," Taggart replied. "A dozen stripper clips for 'em and four ammo pouches."

"Not bad…" Decker tapped at his chin for a moment. "We'll take two rifles, two clips and a pouch. Jonesy and I will set up a rough OP up on the finger. Don't suppose there are any extra canteens?"

Oaks, Taggart, and Jones shook their heads.

Decker shrugged, "In the meantime, Travis, you have every man here for your bridge detail… except the gunny. He'll be watchman. Jonesy and I should be back in an hour or two. Let's see the work done, men."

Later, as the two Marines hauled up their bundle using the climbing rope, Decker turned to Jones, "So Jonesy… things seem to be okay with you and Gartrell these days, huh?"

Jones untied the knot from the ditty bag they'd rigged, "Oh yes, sir… started out rough, but me and Jimmy got him around."

Decker smiled and hoisted one side of the bag as the two Raiders moved along the narrow finger of rock toward the tree-covered promontory, "Good. Can't have any bullshit in a unit like this. We're too close and need each other too much."

"Sure is right, sir."

"So…" Decker wasn't one to pry but there was something he needed to know. "Is it me, Jonesy… or has Hank Evans been a little… off these last few days?"

Jones glanced sidelong at his CO and cocked an eyebrow, "You seen that, Skipper?"

Decker grinned, "These oak leaves give me powers, Marine."

Jones chuckled, "I ain't sure sir… and I don't wanna talk outta school about another man's… whatever."

"Understood," Decker said, treading carefully. "And I wouldn't ask you to betray a confidence, Jonesy. But… if there's something you've noticed… something bothering him or what have you… I'd like to know. Like to know if I should talk to him about it."

Jones frowned. He *did* have more than an inkling about what bee had found its way into Evans's bonnet. Yet some of that came from personal conversation and some from observation.

The two men made their way into a stand of pines and teak. The trees were sparse, but their branches entwined overhead to give a fairly good cover from aerial observation. Beyond this roughly fifty-foot diameter roundish bulge at the end of the granite finger, the land dropped off and gave onto a vast panorama of the northern plains of Guadalcanal.

Decker drew in a breath and set the bag down. He turned to his Marine, "Jones… Ed… my concern is for the unit. For the safety of my men. And yes, for Evans personally. If it's something you two exchanged man to man…"

Jones shook his head, "Sir… I think he worried about being taken prisoner. That thing the other night… well, he a bit shaken by it."

Decker nodded, "Okay… because otherwise, he's proven to be damned near fearless. I'll have a word with him, see if he'll talk about it without me prying… or letting him know we talked."

Jones smiled, "Thanks, sir. Think that'd be good."

"In the meantime," Decker said, pointing at a line of clouds moving in from the southeast, "we might get a spell of rain. Let's rig this chute for some cover in the center of these trees and then take a gander out over the land out there. See if we can't spot Tojo and see what kinda shenanigans he's up to."

14

KOKUMBONA

OCTOBER 6, 1942

There was little fanfare of course. Kawaguchi and Oka were warned of their coming, naturally, and lined up an honor detail to greet the new arrivals. Yet there was no band, no trumpeting, nor even any flag waving usually associated when a lieutenant general and a major general arrived on the front lines.

Secretly, Kawaguchi could not have been more pleased. He seethed over his loss at Henderson several weeks before and at how little he'd been able to accomplish since. Not that it had been a total waste. The route of the Marines the previous week had in itself been a strategic victory.

Yet it wasn't enough. Not nearly enough compared with the thousands who'd died in battle, of their wounds and of disease since. All one had to do to know exactly how HQ felt about it was to watch the line of light tanks, and who it was riding in the Type-95 Curogane scout car in their midst.

Kawaguchi, who stood beside Oka at the end of the double line of soldiers at attention, glanced at the colonel sidelong. Oka appeared pinched and unhappy. That nearly caused Kawaguchi to smile. Both men knew what was coming, but for his part,

Kawaguchi swore that he would not show even a hint of the shame and rage boiling inside himself.

He allowed himself just a brief smile when he saw the two generals riding into camp. Kawaguchi, a major general himself, had walked in. As had Oka, for that matter.

Presently, the tanks broke off and were directed to their parking zone. The four-wheel-drive car, Japan's answer to the American Willys Jeep, rolled to a stop. Oka called out an order for attention and to present arms.

"Welcome to Kokumbona, General Maruyama," Kawaguchi said formally, giving a proper salute. "And to you, General Nasu. I'm sure you both remember Colonel Oka, who recently played a major role in repelling an American push across the Matanikau River."

The two generals got nimbly from the car and saluted and returned the bows. Nasu was a lean man, reminding Kawaguchi of Oka somewhat. Nasu appeared reserved and polite, only nodding but saying no more. Maruyama, on the other hand, was bulkier, shorter, and his broad face was trending toward pudginess.

Too much time in the rear enjoying plentiful supplies… let him see how it is in hell for a change, Kawaguchi maundered.

"Gentlemen, Maruyama began, his dark eyes crawling over the officers, men, and the village. Kawaguchi accurately detected disdain in their fathomless depths. "This campaign has dragged on far too long. It has been marred by failure and loss. Even our victories have been hollow. That is now ended. It is time we showed the Americans what a *properly* led fighting force from Imperial Japan can do."

Kawaguchi saw Oka flinch. He regretted it, for the colonel had not been on the cursed island for long. Only a few days fewer than Kawaguchi himself. For his part, Kawaguchi showed no emotion. Maruyama had always enjoyed the sound of his own voice, and it was no surprise that he would take the opportunity to rub salt into Kawaguchi's wounds.

It was unfortunate, however, that his words would also sting others who did not deserve them. And what did it matter anyway? Kawaguchi also knew what was to come next.

"General Kawaguchi, you are hereby relieved of your responsibilities on Guadalcanal," Maruyama said, meeting Kawaguchi's eye and then looking away again. "As are you and your men, Colonel Oka. You will make your way to Cape Esperance where you will be evacuated back to Rabaul. There to receive further orders. Your time is passed, your chance squandered. Now *we* will lead these brave Imperial soldiers to victory."

Kawaguchi smiled then and it was as warm and friendly as a ravening shark, "Big words… for a man who's been resting in comfort for so long. I think you will find that you have much to learn… *sir*."

Maruyama flashed his own teeth and stepped closer, "But you will not be the one to teach me, *General* Kawaguchi."

"No," said Kawaguchi, still smiling, "this rock will. And I suspect it is going to be a very hard lesson."

"You wish failure on us?" Nasu asked.

Kawaguchi shook his head, "That would be dishonorable. It would be wrong… for our men and our empire. I wish you both luck. As much as there is… you will need it. Permission to depart, sir?"

Maruyama's eyes blazed, "The sooner the better."

HENDERSON FIELD

Edson, Puller, and Lieutenant Colonel Herman Hanneken, commander of the battalion from the Seventh Marine Regiment, had set up a command post between the Lunga River and the Matanikau. They moved all five battalions over and had them bivouac along the left bank of the Lunga. Ready to go but not too close to potential Japanese movements.

In the command post tent, Edson, Puller, Hanneken, along with Bill Whaling and their seconds had gathered to discuss the next day's operation. The command tent thrummed with tension. Not simply from impending battle but also riding on the back of a failure barely two weeks old.

By then, everyone knew that when the men from Puller's regiment were trapped on hill 84 at Point Cruz, Edson had refused to send more men after them. Puller had run off, commandeered a Higgins boat, and organized a rescue mission. It was rumored that the two old friends still had some heat smoldering between them.

"Gentlemen," Edson, the highest-ranking officer and in nominal command began. "As we all know, our last attempt at this failed. We all suffered, from Mount Austin to the sand spit to the men sent ashore at Point Cruz. Thanks to Colonel Puller's dogged persistence, many of those men were saved… and for my part, I'm grateful. As you all know, I refused to send more men into the situation… and I know that didn't and perhaps doesn't sit well with Chesty."

Puller had just filled and lit his pipe. He watched his old comrade speak, gray tendrils of smoke appearing to waft around Red Mike's face as he did so. At Edson's last words, Puller smiled thinly.

"It was a helluva day," Puller said. "And I understand why Merritt refused. I'm not one to hold a grudge, Merritt. I'm just glad you didn't try to stop me."

Edson, a usually collected, cool… almost cold… man, allowed a thin smile, "Wouldn't have even tried, Lou. I knew if anybody could get those Marines back… it'd be you. That all said, however… and that air cleared… it's time to focus on *this* push."

"Frankly we've got more men and more support," Hanneken stated. He was a heavy man of medium height who had a tendency to scratch at the backs of his hands. As if they itched to be wrapped around a weapon. That was the only time he *didn't* fiddle with them. And a helluva lot more intel thanks to Bill's scouts, too."

Edson's XO, Lt. Colonel Lou Walt, nodded solemnly, "HQ is coordinating artillery and aerial bombardment for the push. It won't be like last time."

"No, it will not," Edson said. "Nobody's running across open ground against dug in positions, that's for goddamned sure."

"Are we to establish a permanent position when we're successful, Colonel?" Hanneken asked.

Edson frowned and glanced down at the map, "Honestly... I don't know. Probably not. We know that the Jap is assembling a major force for an attack on Henderson in the next few weeks. Intel also says that General Hyakutake will be here in the next few days, and he's to lead it."

"Idea is to deny the Jap safe passage across the Matanikau near our perimeter," Puller offered. "Make him think twice before trying to march his troops east anywhere within a few miles of the coast."

Edson nodded, "Yes, I'd say that's right, Lou. Problem with establishing a position there is that there's no natural barrier. Here, we have the Teneru on one side of the base and the Lunga on the other. A little buffer in between and the Matanikau. But west of the Matanikau, we're in Indian country and exposed. But that doesn't mean we can't make *them* forget the idea of using the ground, too. Because with a successful push, we prove to the Jap that we can come and get him by land, from the air and with artillery."

"So what's the plan, Merritt?" Puller asked.

Edson pointed to his map and tapped the mouth of the river, "I'm taking two battalions here, to the damned sandspit. Can't seem to get away from the damned thing... Henderson will shell the other side and we'll be well armed and manned. At the same time, Herm takes his battalion with Bill accompanying him across the One Log Bridge and heads north. Goal is to trap the Japs on the other side of the sandspit between the Seventh Reg and the sea. That's when we'll lay on the pressure from our side. Lou, you and Bill take your men in behind Herm and push northwest to this area here... a deep, wooded ravine behind Point Cruz."

Puller nodded, "Hit the reserves and keep them from engaging you and cut off their line of retreat as well. I like it."

"It looks good on paper," Edson said. "But we all know how this goes. Adapt, improvise, and overcome. Any questions?"

"Backup?" Hanneken asked.

"I've got what's left of my First Raiders on standby," Edson said. "Christ... there's only about two companies worth, but they're ready to come in either at the bridge or the spit. I'm keeping them here because of Bill's recommendations. Bill?"

Colonel Whaling stepped forward, "My scout teams have seen a lot of activity. Especially near the bridge and the spit... but in between, too. Men and vehicles gathering. I believe there might be a limited number boating across the river to a point a few hundred yards south of the spit. Not quite sure why... but we suspect they're either a forward artillery unit or a reserve."

"What ever happened at Mount Austin?" Puller asked. He'd fought a battle there not long ago.

Edson smiled again, "Al Decker happened. There was a Jap platoon there, Lou. Pretty ballsy after the pasting you gave them a few weeks back. Al and his men surprised them with a night attack. Killed most of them, although a few ran off. Then they razed the camp. It'll probably be re-used unless *we* can establish a position there. Trouble is that the Old Man is more focused on keeping the perimeter than expanding for the time being."

"Can't say I blame him," Hanneken said. "Considering Bloody Ridge and what the Jap is planning next."

Edson nodded, "Yes... and if tomorrow's foray is successful, Hyakutake will have to march his assault force south far enough that the Matanikau is just a stream to ford. But then he'll have to cut his way west and will try to hit us from the south again."

Walt snorted, "That went so well last time for Kawaguchi, why not try it again, huh?"

Edson nodded but did not smile, "Hyakutake will have three or four times the number of men. If he does come that way, it's gonna make Bloody Ridge look like a training exercise. All right, we've got our orders, and we've got our plan. Please brief your men and see that they're well rested. We move at first light."

NEAR DECKER'S OBSERVATION POST

"Holy sheep shit… I sure do hate this fuckin' place," Charlie Lider growled as he narrowly avoided having a tarantula fall on him as he pushed aside a loose branch. The annoyed arachnid landed, flexed its hairy legs and lifted itself up, glared at Lider for a long moment and then scurried off into the underbrush.

Joe Treadway snickered from behind him and Phil Oaks, on point, half turned and cracked a crooked smile. He held a finger to his lips.

Lider grumbled something under his breath and the three men pushed further into the jungle. Their goal was close, it seemed, as there appeared to be a break in the foliage ahead. Five more minutes and they emerged onto the bank of the same river that flowed past the camp on the plateau above.

"Lot bigger down here," Oaks mused quietly. "Hundred yards wide here at least. Let's take five and see if anybody's around."

"I could sure go for a smoke…" Lider mused.

Treadway smiled, "Go ahead… probably no Japs around. Why worry?"

Oaks chuckled, "Me too, Charlie… hey, you see that… just around the bend there. Is that a clearing?"

Treadway stepped to the water's edge, glanced up and down the river for a few seconds and then peered to where Oaks had indicated. He frowned and nodded, stepping back the half dozen paces to the tree line.

"I think so, Gunny," Treadway reported. "Maybe a village?"

"You want we should check it out?" Lider asked.

Oaks shrugged, "Be worth a look. Not sure I want to talk to anybody, though. About the only people these islanders see over here nowadays got slanted eyes. Probably report us. Still… worth givin' it the old once over."

The three scouts followed the right bank for a few dozen yards and came to a break in the rainforest. A trail had been cut or tramped, and it appeared to follow the river and lead toward the village. Treadway took point and the three men moved carefully and quietly down the trail.

The canopy overhead was a bit thinner, but like most of the jungle on the island, still dense enough to block out much of the light. Inky shadows were occasionally broken by small patches of brilliance or just areas of colorless gloom. All about them, insects chittered, birds sang, and humidity wrapped them in its damp cloak.

All about them, the very atmosphere was thick with unseen life and the tension of potential unseen enemies. The density of Guadalcanal's jungle made it possible for men to hide mere feet away and never be noticed. It was an unpleasant and stressful thought that never left any man's mind for long… if he was wise.

That's why when Treadway froze in his tracks and held up his fist… and then immediately yanked his 1911 from his holster… and crouched low, both Lider and Oaks followed suit. The two sergeants crab-walked up to the third man and hunkered down close.

"What?" Oaks whispered.

"Listen…" Treadway hissed and pointed with his pistol barrel down the path.

Perhaps fifteen or twenty yards ahead, the gloom was being beaten into submission by dappled rays of sun punching through the foliage. The path bent a bit to the left and more sun painted the brush around the corner.

"End of the trail?" Lider asked. "What are we listening for?"

Oaks frowned. It was hard to separate any distinct noise when one was surrounded by so much living biomass. He opened his mouth to ask Treadway what it was and then paused, cocking his head.

"Is... is it the buzzing?" Oaks asked.

Treadway nodded. Lider cocked an ear and then heard it too. A faint, low buzzing that he couldn't quite locate.

"Plane?" Treadway asked.

Oaks scowled, "Dunno... it's not changing at all... let's get closer to the village. Maybe some open ground will help."

"Shit... hope it ain't a giant wasp nest or somethin'," Lider said.

Both Treadway and Oaks turned and glared at him. Neither had thought of that, but it certainly made sense. Oaks harrumphed and moved up, stepping carefully but steadily forward.

The Raiders rounded the bend. The jungle did break not long after, opening into a wide clearing dominated by a semi-circle of thatched huts constructed on short poles. Typical Guadalcanal style. To the right was a small field where once some sort of crop had been planted. Now, though, it was nothing more than a blackened and charred ruin.

The buzzing drowned out all other sounds, still steady and almost monotonous. It was the only sound in the village. No voices spoke nor did the background of the jungle offer much in the way of a mask.

Oaks pointed to the far-left hut, the one closest to the river. The three men jogged over, heads swiveling and ears peeled. Yet all they heard was the steady buzz, like an electrical power line with a steady short.

Oaks was the first to see and jerked to a halt as horror seized him in its icy talons. Involuntarily, he brought up his gun hand to his mouth, as if to stem the rising tide of his gorge.

"Oh... oh my sweet Jesus..." Lider gasped.

"What...?" was all Treadway could manage.

Piled in a heap near a communal fire pit was a jumbled, misshapen pile of rags and flesh. What remained of perhaps twenty bodies had been tossed together into an untidy heap and was a long way toward complete decay.

Bloody rags partially covered gray, desiccated flesh out of which brownish fluid dripped and congealed in the dirt. Jagged ends of bleaching bones stuck out like pins haphazardly jammed into a decomposing cushion. Above this hideous display, a dark cloud hung, roiling and morphing with each passing moment. A gruesome cloud that pulsed and thrummed with terrible vitality.

Yet it was not a cloud... at least not of the traditional variety. Every few seconds, part of the cloud would thicken and blacken and cover a portion of one of the bodies. A living cone of flies lit upon a fresh morsel and then would dissolve once more as yet another feeding colony took its turn.

Treadway turned and a column of bile, water, and canned beans jetted onto the ground at his feet. Lider's gorge rose and he turned to let go and froze once more, a scream of sheer horror stopped only by the volcanic explosion of his lunch geysering from his open mouth.

"Holy... holy... holy..." Oaks couldn't finish his expression of horror as he too beheld what had struck Lider dumb.

The pile of rotten corpses wasn't the only thing upon which the millions of flies were feasting. To the right, on the other side of the fire ring, a new and somehow even more grotesque horror had been perpetrated.

There were six men, or what had been men. Four were tied to a drying rack constructed of bamboo reeds. Two others had been impaled, thick bamboo having been driven into their anuses and erupted from their chests and coated in dried gore. The men were Japanese. The Marines could tell because their bloated faces had the round shape and slanted eyes of the Asian. There was no other indication from below the neck, however. Not even that they were men.

For the skin from the neck down had been flayed, leaving grayish meat and beige bone to bake in the sun. And it was on this that uncounted insects lighted, roosted, laid eggs, and feasted in a mind-numbing tableau that defied description.

Oaks was desperate to look away, wanted to quell the surging in his belly, but he couldn't... The macabre scene held him hypnotized. Finally, after half a dozen tries, he found his voice.

"Joey... call this in," Oaks croaked. "Let's... let's step behind this hut..."

"Who did this?" Lider whispered, afraid to raise his voice because he might draw the attention of whatever nightmare was in charge of the charnel scene.

"I... at first glance I'd have said the Japs killed the villagers," Oaks licked his lips and swallowed hard. "But... but who slaughtered those soldiers?"

"I ain't sure I want to know," Lider said. He gulped several mouthfuls from his canteen, swished, spit, and then swallowed a few more.

"Skipper's been apprised, Gunny," Treadway said, his voice not entirely steady. "He's ordered us to come in."

"Thank God..." Lider said, turning to go.

Oaks cast one last glance at the carnage and shivered. Long after they were out of range, that ghastly humming still rang in his ears. All the way back to camp, he couldn't shake the feeling that something terrible knew they'd come... and now trained its evil eye on them.

15

FORT TRAVIS

OCTOBER 6, 1942

Al Decker was pleased with the progress he and his men had made on their little camp over the past few days. The bridge across the river was complete and working perfectly. In honor of his work, Decker has labeled the location Fort Travis.

The high OP on the outcropping was set up with extra food and a couple of canteens. Additionally, several Arisaka rifles had been placed there just in case.

The observation post had a horizon view of almost sixteen miles. It was more than enough to see Iron Bottom Sound and any activity there. Most of that, of course, was American. At night, it was simply too far and too dark to see Japanese destroyers moving beyond the shore. However, during the day, Japanese movements were observable, to a degree. Decker and anyone posted there had noted some vehicles and men moving along the coast road, although the lower perspective didn't give anything like the view from Vungana.

At the camp itself, the men had set to work building a bamboo structure in the center of the trees. Then they used the parachute to cover the roof and create a dry place to sleep. They also arranged a thatched roof cover for supplies. Beyond that, the men had felled more trees and assembled a log wall on the western side of the cluster of trees that made up the post. It was close enough to the edge of the tree line so that the structure wouldn't be obvious to any nosy Jap pilot who might happen to fly by. There were plans to make another log break the next day to cover the eastern approach, too.

That afternoon, Decker and the men who weren't out scouting had taken a few minutes to wash their clothes in the river along with their own sweaty, dusty bodies. In the warm sun of the island, the utilities dried quickly, and Decker was just pulling his back on when Oaks and his two scouts came out of the wood near the edge of the drop off.

"Major!" Oaks hurried over, came to attention and saluted. Treadway and Lider did the same.

Decker narrowed his eyes at them. The three men all shared the same odd, haunted look and Decker did not like it, "Welcome back, fellas… something wrong? Do we have company?"

Oaks glanced at his two scouts and then at the activity along the water, "Why don't you two guys go get washed up, too. I'll fill in the major… if that's okay with you, sir."

Decker nodded, "Certainly. Gonna be sundown in an hour or so. Get your BDUs done first, they should dry before dark."

With a flourish of "aye-aye, sirs," Lider and Treadway dashed off. To Decker they appeared relieved, as if they wanted no part of what the gunny was about to say.

"Phil… what's on?" Decker asked. "You look like you could use a belt."

Oaks snorted, "Maybe two… sir… we found a village. About five klicks north, along the river. Small place, maybe twenty, thirty people… and the Japs have been there."

The hairs on the back of Decker's neck danced and he frowned, "Burned?"

Oaks drained the last few inches from his canteen and sighed, "Crops were. Japs probably picked them clean and set them ablaze... the bastards. But... Christ... they slaughtered those villagers. To a man, woman, or child. Piled their bodies and left them to rot."

"My God..." Decker said. "Goddamned *butchers*..."

"That ain't the worst of it," Oaks visibly shuddered. "No, that ain't quite right... that wasn't the *last* of the horrors. There were half a dozen Japs there. The ones that probably did the deed. But sir... somebody had... they'd..."

"Just spit it out, man," Decker urged, seeing how shaken the gunnery sergeant was and not liking it one bit.

Oaks blanched slightly and he drew in a steadying breath. When he spoke, his voice was low and sepulchral, "Someone... killed them. But... but they hung them on a scaffold and two were... impaled. And then whoever it was they... they skinned them from the neck down."

Decker stared, the hideous image dancing through his mind, "Oh my... who...?"

Oaks shook his head, "No signs of whoever it was. They sure weren't a fan of Japs, though."

"Islanders," Decker said. "Question is... would they be on our side... or try to pull the same gag on us?"

Oaks shrugged, "No way to know. We're already being vigilant... but maybe we should increase the night guard to three instead of two."

Decker harrumphed, "Christ... what I wouldn't give for at least a platoon's worth of men. But you're right, Top. This place is pretty defensible. Got a river on the west, northwest, a cliff on the northern side, and another south, and then more right behind it. The only approach that's wide open is the direction we came from.

Even if any Japs come from the west, they gotta cross the river in single file over Jimmy's bridge and then deal with the barricade. Brother… if we had the men we could really do something here. All right, it's getting late. We'll increase the guard and do some more scouting tomorrow. Probably start heading back day after. Who knows what other crazy shit is happening near the perimeter?"

"What about the village?" Oaks asked.

Decker flapped a hand in the air, "Hopefully the islanders that killed the Japs did so in retribution and aren't just on a spree to take out any non-islanders. But we'll keep a weather eye open, as our buddy Anvil Art would say."

Hondo had chosen to make camp along a narrow stream that was fed by a short waterfall running over the edge of a series of coral and granite ridges. The camp was an open area that may once have been a village. Although no structures remained and the two or three open hectares of land were dominated by kunai grass, it was odd for an open patch this size to be left untouched by the surrounding jungle.

For his part, Makai wasn't quite as pleased about the location. Yes, they had a water source, but they had only one natural barrier. Additionally, there were a variety of trails that had been cut through the rainforest near the clearing and along the stream, which widened as it marched more than fifteen kilometers to the sea. However, with some effort and a controlled burn, much of the kunai grass was removed and the men set to work setting up tents, a thatched pavilion and ammo dump. Assisting them were more than two dozen slaves, some islanders, and some Chinese and Korean workers pressed into service.

"My goal here, Sergeant," Hondo explained as the sun set and darkness began its inexorable and rapid march from the east, "is to recommend to command that this location be manned by a company-sized unit. A permanent command and observation post to guard this sector and prevent what we believe Decker is attempting. Infiltration from our rear… or flank."

On the surface of it, Makai saw the logic. However, he also knew… far more than the officers would have guessed… what was being planned for the next two weeks or so.

General Hyakutake was on his way and once on Guadalcanal, would assemble the soldiers and march them to the airfield in a massive assault. Should they be successful, then no remote outposts would be required. Should the attack fail… or even achieve a stalemate… then the outlook for Japanese success on Guadalcanal would be grim at best.

"Of course, sir," Makai said, spooning a bite of rice and fish from his mess kit. One advantage of the small unit, the sergeant was acting as Hondo's second and ate as well as his officer.

"For now, it should do," Hondo went on, sipping from a bottle of sake he'd somehow managed to locate before the platoon set out. "Our scouts should be in, and I am hopeful, Sergeant. We've seen American aircraft patrolling several times. A good sign… for locating our quarry, that is. My instincts tell me we're close… I can *feel* him, Makai… my very bones tingle with the nearness of my revenge."

Makai only nodded. For his part, he thought Hondo was being more than a little melodramatic. They were soldiers. Decker and his men were soldiers. They were at war and in war, soldiers fought. It was nothing to take personally.

"I pray you are correct, sir," Makai said. "This environment is hard on the men. Hot, humid, biting insects… disease… a successful battle is just what the men require to bolster their spirits."

Hondo allowed a chuckle, "Mine too, Makai."

"Sergeant! Sergeant!" one of the guards on duty near the stream called out even as he led two figures out of the approaching gloom to the fire where Makai and Hondo sat. "Oh… Lieutenant! Sir, Soaring Eagle One has just arrived with news."

Makai allowed *himself* a smile. The scouts enjoyed choosing code names. A bit melodramatic, but an enthusiastic scout was better than a reluctant one. When the sergeant turned to his officer, he was careful to remove any hint of amusement.

Hondo's face stiffened into hard lines and Makai could see anger dancing behind the flames that flickered in his eyes. The officer hadn't liked that the guard was calling for Makai and not him. Of course, that was the chain of command… yet the young officer's ego had still been pricked. Makai avoided frowning.

"What is your report?" Hondo asked as the three men came to attention and bowed.

"Sir," said the middleman, the leader of the two-man team. "We… that is, the private and I…"

It was then that Makai noticed the pallor on the two scouts' faces. The men stood near the fire, their eyes haunted and their stance as rigid as tent poles.

"Corporal," Makai said firmly but not unkindly. "Gather your thoughts and take a breath so that you may provide the lieutenant with a professional report. Have some water if you need it. Are you all right? Were you attacked?"

"You may return to your post," Hondo told the guard. He was impatient to hear but did not countermand Makai. "At ease, men."

They both drank greedily from their canteens and seemed to relax a bit. Although to Makai they still appeared more at attention than ease.

"Sir," the corporal went on calmly, "we discovered a village, perhaps six kilometers to the west along the right bank of a sizable river. Much broader and deeper than this stream. We found a dead log and the private fashioned paddles, so we went across."

Makai smiled, "Initiative. This is good."

"Continue," Hondo barely managed not to snap, but he cast a cutty-eyed look in Makai's direction.

"The village was small and evidently our troops had found it sometime in the past," the corporal went on. "Many bodies were piled near the center… and… and sir…"

"What *is* it man?" Hondo's patience was crumbling rapidly.

The private hung his head but the corporal managed to meet the lieutenant and sergeant's gazes, "There were six of our men there… soldiers… and they had been killed and… and desecrated, sir."

"Desecrated?" Makai asked. "Explain."

The corporal wiped at his brow, "They had been killed… somehow… and their bodies hung up or impaled and skinned from the neck down. Sir… Sergeant… it was… it was *terrible*…"

"*Decker*…" Hondo growled, his face flushing with fury.

Makai didn't think so. In spite of the silly propaganda the common soldier was provided, he knew better. He'd seen Americans fight and deal with wounded and dead. He and Hondo had been prisoners of Decker not long before and had not been mistreated.

On the other hand, Makai had also seen wounded Japanese pretend to be dead and then attack American medical corpsmen coming to their aid.

"Anything else?" Hondo asked.

"No, sir…" said the corporal. He apparently expected more.

"Then you are dismissed," Makai said. "Refill your water and get a meal. Good work."

Bows were made and the men melted into the shadows of the tropical night. For many long moments, there was nothing said. Only the crackle of the fire and the distant chitterings and hootings of the island's nocturnal life surrounded the two men.

"The Ame-cohs are getting desperate," Hondo said and actually chuckled.

Makai, not for the first time, wished that he could belt the precocious greenhorn. Instead, he said, "I do not believe so, sir. What was described appears to be both a retaliation and a warning. I would say that the deed was perpetrated by natives."

Hondo appeared to mull this over, "As retribution for our attack on their village. And to leave a message. A warning that we're not invulnerable? Is this your thinking, Sergeant?"

Makai nodded, "It is, Lieutenant… and we should remain even more vigilant."

Hondo scoffed, "What we *should* do is sweep this island clean of its *filth*, Sergeant! Who do these animals think they are? It's bad enough we must deal with Americans. At least they understand modern ways and know how to *wash*. These filthy kokujin are little better than the things that scrabble in their diseased jungles."

Makai did not want to debate the idea nor explore it. He only nodded and said, "In the meantime… they know their land and pose a danger. Perhaps we might increase the guard, sir?"

Hondo sighed, "We have forty men here… and our servants. If you feel the need, Sergeant, then add an additional man or two. I leave such matters up to you."

Another chorus of greetings and excited exclamations broke out to the south end of the clearing. Hondo smiled grimly and pointed.

"And I leave it up to you to instruct our men on how to maintain discipline and not create excess *noise*, Sergeant," Hondo shook his head. "Why not just call the round eyes and give them our coordinates?"

Makai frowned, "Hai…"

Two more men materialized out of the darkness and bowed low. Yet another pair of scouts with a report.

"You have a report, Corporal?" Makai prompted.

"Yes, Sergeant… Lieutenant," said the man. Makai knew him to be a level-headed and well-seasoned soldier who'd also seen action in the last Seino-Japanese war. "We have located the Americans, sir."

That wiped the smug look off the young officer's face. He leaned in and speared the corporal with narrowed eyes, "Are you certain? Where? How? Did they identify you?"

"We were nearly discovered, sir," the corporal went on evenly. "We went up onto the ridge and moved eastward. Approximately two kilometers away, we detected noise in the trees. The jungle up there is thinner and contains more temperate vegetation. We concealed ourselves and waited. Shortly thereafter, three American soldiers appeared and passed us by."

"They did not see you?" Makai asked.

The private shook his head and the corporal said, "No, Sergeant. We waited patiently and perhaps an hour later, they appeared again, moving in the opposite direction. We came out of our concealment and followed. I allowed Private Betai to go ahead. He is a skilled woodsman."

"That so, Private?" Makai asked.

The private bowed low, "Hai, Sergeant. I spent some years in the Philippines before the war. With a logging company. I learned the ways of the forest and jungles."

"And what did this knowledge provide you tonight?" Hondo asked impatiently.

"I was able to track the Yankees, sir," the private went on, not entirely able to conceal his pride. "After several kilometers, we came to a river that flows out of the highlands. The Americans have built a log bridge and have set up something of a camp."

"Indeed?" Makai asked, clearly pleased. "How far?"

"Perhaps… five kilometers, Sergeant," said the private. "Measuring distance is difficult here… but no more than four hours walk to maintain a level of stealth."

The corporal nodded, "Going up there is easier than down in these jungles, sir. Also, we counted perhaps… eight men, although they moved in and out of the trees and so forth, so it was difficult to get an exact figure."

"And they had… kokujin among them!" the private declared, his disgusted tone suggesting that he'd as much as seen the Marines engaged in a homosexual orgy.

Hondo harrumphed, "Yes… the Ame-cohs know nothing of propriety. However, we know that *must* be Decker. Do we not, Sergeant?"

Makai nodded, "Indeed, sir. Anything else, men?"

There wasn't and the two soldiers were dismissed. The two remaining men stared into the fire, both of their minds turning over the information they'd received.

"So… we have them," Hondo said, his teeth flashing with lurid firelight.

"We could attack before dawn, sir," Makai suggested. "Move the men into position overnight?"

Hondo considered this for a long moment, "Yes… but I think we will wait, Sergeant. Give the round-eyes one more day to become complacent. Post sentries up on the ridge and near that river. But not too close. No closer than two kilometers from Decker. We want only to keep an eye on them. However, let those men know that if any American gets close… they are to eliminate them."

"That could give us away, sir."

Hondo chuckled, "Perhaps… but they know that they are in our territory. And if I'm correct, Decker has but few men. Losing one or two will be disastrous. Before sunset tomorrow, we will move, leaving only a fire team to guard the camp and our slaves. An hour or two after dark… we attack. And then, perhaps… we'll have *two* outposts, eh?"

Makai nodded, "It shall be done, sir. Yet I do have one suggestion, if I may?"

Hondo scowled, "And that is?"

"That we send a squad to the east. Tonight. They can follow the ridge and cross that river. Just as our first scouting team did.

Indeed, if they find the river and move north, they can cross near the village, using the corporal's log boat. Then they march another two kilometers east and turn south, back to the ridge."

Hondo frowned and then slowly nodded, "They can camp there and get up onto the plateau before we attack. Come in from Decker's rear? Yes… yes… that is a logical plan, Sergeant. In fact… it's so good, I would like you to lead them. It's not something I'd trust to just anyone."

"Of course, sir."

"Excellent. Then it's settled. Talk to the squad leaders tonight and pick several pairs of scouts. It will be a long night… but you'll have time to rest. Tomorrow night… we pluck this American thorn from the emperor's side."

Makai rose and bowed. He melted into the night and did not even feel the anger he ought to. Nothing Hondo did surprised him anymore. And although the arrogant little shit was no doubt trying to punish Makai for his presumption… the sergeant would make certain that it would be *he* who provided the linchpin for victory.

Or at least did not suffer the shame of defeat.

16

KOKUMBONA

0500, OCTOBER 7, 1942

"Good morning, General Nasu," General Maruyama said as the other man entered his command hut. "I hope you slept well?"

Nasu nodded, "Yes, sir. A bit warm, but that was expected."

Maruyama allowed a small smile, "It will get considerably warmer today… certainly for the Americans. Come, familiarize yourself with this map."

The regimental commander stepped forward. An aide handed him a cup of tea and Nasu gazed down at the map. It was a portion of the island around the Matanikau River and Point Cruz. It also included the Lunga River to the east.

Maruyama had already placed several X's and O's on the map at strategic points near the river on both sides. Nasu understood immediately and nodded his approval.

"I want your fourth Infantry to take these positions," Maruyama explained. "One battalion here… and here. First Battalion will station itself at this point, at the sand spit. Then you will send three companies across the river to establish a forward position on the opposite side… perhaps… 300 to 400 meters south of the river mouth. I suspect that the Americans will make a try for the mouth of the river, as they did two weeks ago."

"And were pushed back," Nasu said, smiling.

Maruyama grunted, "Barely. One thing that I have noticed after reading all of the reports from this island is that from Ichiki's first attack at the Teneru to Kawaguchi's disaster south of the airfield and even to the two previous engagements along this accursed river… it was too little men, too little support."

Nasu nodded in agreement. However, what he did not say was that those troops had poor intelligence, poor logistical support and too few men. It was easy to criticize from afar, yet Nasu knew that what HQ thought and what was true on the front lines were worlds apart.

Nasu knew that Maruyama was fully aware of this. No one rose to high rank without having suffered their fair share of difficulties dealing with ignorant planners' battle strategy. It was always the same. Here is a nearly impossible goal for you to achieve with less.

Yet Maruyama's jaundiced eye toward Kawaguchi and their evident rivalry either blinded him to this or simply didn't matter. Maruyama was set on showing Kawaguchi up. Nasu only hoped that this desire was not so great that he lost sight of the true goals here. And… that when Hyakutake showed up, he didn't walk into a disaster.

"These forward companies will be supplied with artillery," Maruyama went on. "From that position, they can blast right through the Marine perimeter, harassing them until we have swelled our ranks to full strength. Command initially estimated five to six thousand Marines here… but that estimate has been increased. We believe there are easily twice that many. It's my understanding that General Hyakutake intends to wait until we have twenty thousand men on this rock before moving in and overwhelming the Americans and retaking *our* airbase."

"Ambitious," Nasu observed.

Maruyama nodded, "This is why your troops are being stationed here. To ensure that the Americans cannot establish positions near the Matanikau and hinder our operations."

"Sir, what of the companies near the One Log Bridge?" Nasu asked. "They've been holding that for some time."

Maruyama nodded, "Many of them were Kawaguchi and Oka's men and have been withdrawn. There is still a force there, but we must focus our efforts toward the mouth of the river. We know that several battalions have moved west of the Lunga, and an attack is likely today or tomorrow. If the men at the bridge encounter trouble, we'll send in reinforcements. General… I wish you to take command of the Fourth Infantry's activities today. See that your men are placed and well led."

Nasu bowed, "Hai. It will be done, sir."

2ND AND 7TH MARREG – BETWEEN MATANIKAU AND LUNGA RIVERS

As the sun rose, its heat penetrated the jungle and began boiling away the dew into rafts of steam. Everywhere, tendrils of wispy vapor floated into the air, combining and thickening into a mist that would, for at least an hour, make it impossible to see more than 200 feet in any direction.

It was the perfect cover for a couple of scouts to get close to their objective and see exactly what was going on. Sergeant John Basilone and Marlin "Whitey' Groft had been chosen for this detail because, as temporary part of Whaling's scouts, they'd been in the vicinity recently.

Just a few days earlier, they'd met with Al Decker's team and scoped the Japs along the Matanikau at the One Log Bridge. They were surprised, therefore, when they crept in close enough to see that things had dramatically changed.

"I don't get it, Sarge," Groft muttered as they settled onto a low hill to the southeast of the bridge. "Where'd they go?"

Basilone propped himself up on his elbows and peered through his binoculars. Where there had been a substantial forward bivouac just a few days earlier, now there was hardly a platoon's worth of men stationed on the east side of the bridge. He couldn't see the other side of the river, thanks to the mist. Just a spectral shape of the jungle beyond the water.

"I dunno, Whitey…" Basilone said. "Maybe they were pulled back… maybe they know there's three battalions about to roll over 'em… but if so, then these poor slanty-eyed buggers didn't get the memo."

"They might got more on the other side, though," Groft mused.

"Most likely," Basilone said. "But whatever the case… we gotta secure this position for tomorrow's push. Gimme the blower."

Groft shifted and pulled the walkie-talkie from his belt and handed it across. Basilone exchanged the radio for the binoculars and pulled up the antenna.

"Charlie, Charlie, Sugar-1 do you read, over?" the sergeant asked.

A crackle of low-volume static and then Colonel Whaling himself replied, "*Sugar-1, Charlie… we read. What's your status, over?*"

"Have reached objective, Charlie," Basilone reported. "Enemy numbers appear greatly diminished. Morning mist prevents Obo second target. Over."

A long pause and then Whaling came back, "*Sugar-1… understood. Can you estimate numbers on Obo-1? Over.*"

"Platoon strength, far as we can determine, Charlie… not sure where they all went. Observations from five days ago indicated a company. Over."

"*Understood, Sugar-1. Maintain position. Will contact you in thirty mikes. Out.*"

"What'll we do till then?" Groft asked with a crooked smile.

Basilone slid the antenna down, glanced at his wristwatch and grinned, "Gimme a fifty cal and I'd show ya'."

Thirty minutes later, Basilone activated his radio again. He was asked if he and Groft were in a secure position off the beaten path. Basilone indicated that they were. They were then commanded to stay put and that a section was on the way to clear out the riffraff.

Not long after, the main trail leading from the bridge to the west, the trails perpendicular along the river and slightly inland exploded with roaring Marines. Dozens of grenades, propelled by M1 launchers fitted to Springfield rifles arced out of the trees in a shower of soaring, flashing and thundering death. Rifles erupted and sent a hail of lead into the Japanese camp. Seemingly from nowhere, a trio of men burst from the jungle, set something heavy and black down on three spidery legs and opened fire, the M2 "Ma Deuce" .50 caliber machine gun blasting everything it touched into slivers, splinters, and pulverized bloody meat.

The Japanese, surprised as they were, mounted a defense. As admirably quick as they were, it was short-lived and hopeless. Men died by the handful and the three Nambu nests were hardly manned before heavy fire cut the men to ribbons.

Within fifteen minutes, all resistance had been neutralized and not a single enemy soldier made it across the bridge. By this time, the sun was well up and the mist had cleared. Although there was occasional fire from across the river, it was sporadic and quickly suppressed. Not long after, a platoon from the Seventh was sent over to sweep what had once been a substantial Japanese position.

"Well," said Chesty Puller as he stood near the east bank of the Matanikau and watched the proceedings on the other side. "That was easy."

Hanneken stood beside him and frowned, "Don't tempt the fates, Lou."

Puller chuckled, "You weren't with us two weeks ago, Herm. We had artillery fire reigning down over there. We had a section of SBDs drop a load of eggs on those slanty-eyed sons of bitches… and they still kept us from pushing over."

"Sort of makes you wonder, doesn't it, sir?" Whaling asked as he stepped up.

"How's that, Bill?" Hanneken asked.

"Where they went and why," Puller said.

Whaling nodded, "Last report was that there was at least half a battalion here. Now what? Maybe two platoons all in all? Maybe a company? Where'd they all go?"

"And *why*…" Hanneken said.

Puller lit his pipe, "Well, gents… for today, that's not our problem. We'll camp here for the night, rotate men at platoon strength on the other side as guards and push across in the morning. Love to go now… but we gotta give Fifth time to strike. Goddamned Japs have been reported floating men across on rafts and boats since before dawn."

"Permission to send a couple of my scouting units out to scope what's ahead, Colonel?" asked whaling.

"Granted and good thinking, Bill," Puller said, narrowing his eyes. "Just you wait, Tojo… because there's a Marine green wreckin' machine and it's on the way…"

5TH MARINES

"Forward scouts report at least two companies of Japs set up near the sandspit, Colonel!" Corporal Walter Burack said as he jogged up to Edson, who stood between the columns of his two battalions backed up by a company of half-track mounted 75mm guns.

To Burack, Edson somehow looked gigantic standing there with Major Louis Walt beside him and surrounded by several thousand men. In spite of his smallish stature, Edson had gained a reputation as a combat giant on Guadalcanal. The battle of Lunga

Ridge had been an astonishing victory, with Edson defeating a force more than five times his own strength. The ridge had been renamed Edson's Ridge in honor of this achievement. The rumor mill even had it that the full-bird colonel was getting The Button for it.

"Trying to move in on our front porch, eh?" Edson asked but without humor.

"They got balls, sir, you gotta give 'em that," Walt said, and he *was* trying for humor.

Edson harrumphed, "Let's see if we can't knock a few of them off."

"We're ready, sir," Walt said.

"All right," said Edson. "I want first bat to move right, hugging the shoreline and making for our side of the spit. Second bat moves a hundred yards south, straight into the Jap's right flank. There's a ridge up ahead. Not a big one, maybe twenty, thirty feet. I'm going up there and gettin' the guns set up. We'll sweep the field and then break the columns into companies. Form lines and swap out. Once we've got them pinned and panicked… we charge. I want these devils running across the spit and trying to swim for it. Everyone got that?"

The individual company commanders, ranged in a line near the admin staff nodded and gave a chorus of "aye-aye, sirs."

Edson nodded, offered a tight smile and gave the order, "Move out!"

A roar rose as every man whooped and hollered and began their orderly march. They had a few hundred yards to go and there was time for Edson to issue more orders.

"Corporal, make the call," Edson said as he too began marching ahead of the halftracks and their platoon of riflemen fire support.

Beside Burack, a private wore the backpack radio and handed the corporal the handset, "All set, Corporal B."

Burack smiled at the young man and thumbed the transmit

button, "Mother Goose, Mother Goose, Little Red Riding Hood. Do you copy, over?"

"We read five by five, Riding Hood. Go ahead."

"Mother Goose, we are on the way to grandma's house," Burack reported.

"Copy, Riding Hood… are you clear?"

"That's a Rodge, Mother Goose. You may begin. Riding Hood standing by. Over."

From the west, a thunderous roll boomed over the land. One might have at first mistaken it for thunder, except that there were a dozen individual thunderclaps, and they came in almost perfect separation so that there was no mistaking what they were.

Overhead, shells screamed through the air, arcing over the Marines and down, delivering death from above in 155mm packages.

The trees and low ridge ahead blocked the view of what happened, but it wasn't necessary. The ground shook as artillery shells as large as any six-inch naval round plunged out of the sky, blasting craters in the earth, coral and killing Japanese soldiers by the dozen on both sides of the river. Explosive trauma followed by jagged hunks of rock tore into fragile human flesh and left little room for cover.

Although the Japanese had time to dig in a little, it wasn't easy on such low ground. What foxholes they had were knee-deep in water and mud or simply shallow divots carved out of hard rock. Here and there, dead tree trunks and stones were used as barriers, but this offered little protection from falling artillery.

After three volleys, the shelling ceased but didn't leave the enemy time to relax. From out to sea, a mechanical buzz rapidly grew into a mechanical roar as two sections of dive bombers drove in from the sea, low and menacing. In groups of two, they came in low and dropped 500-pound bombs in the scattered enemy forces, further scattering the and piling up the dead.

By then, Edson and the gun division had reached the ridge. The forty men of the platoon ranged ahead, racing up the hill and into the medium-thick jungle, rifles crackling to clear the way for the command staff.

"Burack!" Edson shouted over the din of weapons fire and shouting men. "Call it in!"

Burack and his radioman were ready. The corporal snatched the handset and shouted into it, "Mother Goose! Mother Goose! Little Red Riding Hood is almost to the cottage, over!"

"*Acknowledged, Riding Hood! Give granny a big kiss from us, huh? Mother Goose out!*"

As if by magic, the thunder ceased. Although the shelling was enormously loud, its absence hardly left the world quiet. In its place was the cacophony of an impending infantry action. Birds screeched from the foliage, men shouted, whooped and cursed and, at least for the moment, bolt-action rifles crackled in controlled volleys as the leading platoon of the half-track company made way for the heavy weapons. Those mounted guns growled up behind them, rumbling and huffing diesel fumes like mythical dragons hungry to descend on a medieval village.

"Clear!" a man shouted from the top of the ridge.

Edson quickened his pace. He and Walt, along with Burack and his radioman, hurried up the shallow slope. Behind them, the guns spread and out found their paths. To the left and right, a hundred yards apart, hundreds and hundreds of Marines swarmed toward the river like giant green ants. Already, several fifty cal units were setting up along the ridge at what would be the ends of the 75mm firing line.

Burack's heart raced and his whole body tingled with excitement. He'd seen combat before, but this was the first time he'd been in a major battalion-strength scrap. Seeing thousands of men racing to battle, friendly ordnance falling from the sky and eight rolling guns driving up a hill made his blood run swiftly!

When he got to the top and saw what lay before him, Burack's jaw dropped open. Although there was plenty of jungle and some uneven ground, making it hard to tell exactly where the enemy was, some could be seen. Smoking craters coughed streamers of dust and grit into the air over a line the size of three football fields. To the right, small black figures could be seen trying to organize a defense in the relatively open ground near the sand spit that separated the Matanikau from the ocean. Although open, that ground offered some cover from stands of mangroves between the sea and the river and tiny light khaki dots zipped around there, standing out like tiny bugs against the dark green-black of the mangroves.

The young corporal's excitement dimmed somewhat when the enemy began to fight back. Not simply satisfied to sit complacently and get slaughtered, the Japanese company's and the men that remained set up a withering return fire, including Arisakas, automatic weapons and light mortars. Now bullets zipped to and fro like angry bees, thunking into trees, hissing through leaves and occasionally, finding American flesh in which to burrow. 50mm shells hurled through the air, sometimes exploding harmlessly above ground, sometimes digging into the dirt so deep they only managed to send up dusty cones of ejecta. Now and then, however, they exploded near enough to cut Marines up with hot shrapnel.

The Japanese were shouting, roaring Banzai chants along with American shouts of anger, fear, and barked orders. Now though, there was the occasional cry of pain and a frantic, "I'm hit!" as the battle ramped up in pitch.

As if this weren't enough, Japanese light artillery placed on the far side of the river answered the American challenge and lent their voice to the feeble knee mortars with their own more substantial roar. Although the river mouth was too wide for machine gun fire or even rifles to hit anything effectively, it was a short run for even small artillery. Japanese shells arced across and smashed into the American lines, mostly being absorbed by trees and sand, but once in a while, a lucky shot would blast a man into crimson jelly. Or one would land near a fire team and explode, ripping into their flesh with jagged, razor-sharp shrapnel. Every scream, every howl of pain jabbed into Burack's belly.

"Halftrack section one, concentrate on the spit!" Edson shouted at his aide. "Section two aim for the Jap artillery across the river! I want those damned guns *silenced*, Corporal!"

It took Burack several seconds to realize that his colonel was addressing him. He shook his head, pushed the sounds of dying or wounded men out of his mind and focused.

"Yes, sir!" Burack shouted and began working his radio.

Soon another radioman joined the command post and Burack had his hands full coordinating orders and information between all of the units engaged in the battle. Within minutes, he hardly noticed what was going on, so focused on making certain that all information flowing to and from Edson got where it was supposed to and that there were no mistakes.

However, when Burack had to deliver messages to Edson, who switched between scoping the battlefield with his binoculars, snapping off shots with his own Springfield… and hitting almost every time… and using a walkie-talkie to speak directly to company commanders, his fog of concentration broke and once more the battle surged up around him. At no point, or so it seemed, did a Japanese bullet not whistle past or whine off something close by. As on Lunga Ridge, Edson stood tall, watching, shooting and shouting with absolute indifference to the flying death all about him. Burack was nothing short of astonished.

"*Charlie Peter! Charlie Peter! Bat-1 actual, do you copy?*"

Edson had heard and glanced over, offering a wry smile to Burack, "Sounds important, Corporal."

Burack flushed, "Yes, sir… Bat-1, Charlie Peter. We read you, over."

"*Have secured our side of the spit, Charlie Peter!*" and excited young voice shouted. "*Actual requests permission to send Able and Baker across to ferret out stragglers in the mangroves. Over!*"

Edson couldn't help but chuckle, "Some men will do anything for a promotion. Burack, give me the talker."

Burack handed the set over and exchanged a quick smile with the radioman.

"Bat-1, Charlie Peter Actual… do not pursue. Repeat, do not pursue," Edson ordered. "Hold position and stay vigilant. We're not out of the woods yet. Still have substantial enemy forces south of you. And now that the fracas has broken… suspect enemy commander will send in reinforcements. Standby. Out."

That's when Burack noticed that the raucous gunfire to the north had nearly died down to nothing. It was hard to tell over the volleys from the big 75mm cannons arrayed to his left and right, but between blasts, he did notice that it seemed quieter near the beach.

"No, we're not done here yet, Burack," Edson said, as if reading his mind. "There's still a couple of companies out there, hiding, and biding their time. We're going to have to flush them out. Call back to HQ and ask after Colonel Griffith."

Burack did and was informed that the First Raider commander had been medically evacced the day before. Edson frowned at that, for both personal and professional reasons. Griffith and those men had been his not long ago, and from nearly 900 men who'd first landed on Tulagi, the First Raider unit had barely 200 men left. But they were still the best counterinsurgents he had.

"Sir," Walt stepped up. "If you want to have them sent in… I'll take command."

Edson nodded, "Good man, Lou. Keep in mind, though, I'm sending them into the Jap area to flush the bastards out. It's bound to get nasty."

Walt flashed his CO a quick grin, "I didn't just come here for the surfing and good chow, sir."

Edson allowed a small smile, "Good man. Permission to go back and get them ready. I want them here by sundown. Burack… tell second bat to do what they can to contain the Japs, but do not move in. That ground 400 yards south of the spit is full of jungle, ridges, and tidal pools. Before we move in force, I want to know *exactly* where they are."

"Have we got them on the ropes, Colonel?" Burack asked.

Edson frowned and shook his head, "Oh no, son. This is only the first round. We haven't even gotten to the hard parts yet."

17
FORT TRAVIS
OCTOBER 7, 1942

Al Decker stood on the edge of the granite finger frowning at the landscape arrayed before him. In truth, he was frowning at what he *couldn't* see, rather than what he did.

The sun was low in the west and from the east, a staccato thunder rolled across the miles, starting and stopping and being joined by smaller rumbles. And although the sky was not completely clear, it was partly cloudy and there was no rain in sight.

There was a battle going on in the general direction of Henderson. Perhaps twenty miles and more away, Decker's fellow Marines were embroiled in a life and death struggle. And here he sat, far away and in relative comfort as men on both sides fought and died. His frown deepened into a scowl.

"Major," Edgar Jones spoke from back in the trees. So engrossed was Decker in his thoughts that he didn't hear the surprise in the man's voice. "Major! You have a visitor, sir."

Decker broke himself free of his frustrating reverie and turned around, "Visitor? Jonesy, what…?"

From the trees, a slim, lithe figure emerged dressed in simple trousers, boots, and tunic. The loose-fitting clothing did not entirely hide the good figure beneath and the long hair pulled into a braid revealed a lovely brown face that wore a devilish smile.

"Lana!" Decker blurted, just stopping himself from lunging for her like a lovesick schoolboy. He grinned from ear to ear and walked up to her, hands extended. "Lana… my God… what in hell are you *doing* out here?"

Jones's smile could've lit a room. He nodded respectfully and moved to take up the observation position, giving the two a bit of privacy. Lana came into Decker's arms and the two held each other with desperate longing.

"I feel like I haven't seen you in months," said the American, his voice thick with emotion.

Lana turned her face up and they kissed, "It's hardly been more than two weeks, Albert."

"A lifetime," he grinned.

Lana's big brown eyes met his and her smile was as sweet as Carnation milk, "I know… you seem well. I'm glad."

"Same," said Decker. "But… what…?"

She pulled back a little and took on a more serious expression, "It's my island, Albert. I live here."

He chuckled, "Not this far out you don't. What gives?"

Lana drew in a breath, "I'm scouting. I'm leading a party of a dozen men. We're trying to ascertain the disposition of enemy units west of the Matanikau."

Decker smiled, "Listen to you. You sound like a Raider."

"I am, for all intents and purposes," she said. "We've been in the bush now for over two weeks. My goal is to report back to the airfield and Martin as well. We have found… some disturbing things, Albert."

Decker's belly dropped like an elevator loosed from its cables. His eyes bulged and it took several tries for him to ask: "The… the village… you…"

Lana nodded solemnly, "We discovered the Japanese scouts after they'd slaughtered those people. They were still there… eating the food, lounging around… they *murdered* them, Albert. Thirty innocent people! They slaughtered them to a man, woman, and child… of course, the women were last…"

"Oh my God…" Decker's voice was little more than a whisper. "And then you… you…"

"Yes," Lana's own voice was suddenly edged in steel. "We returned the favor and left them as a message for the next group of Naponapo who wandered by. We wanted to let these yellow *bastards* know that they are not as safe as they believe themselves to be. That *we* are everywhere. That *we* may *strike* from anywhere! You have been shocked in the past, my love, by my willingness and ability to kill. Perhaps after being here and seeing all that you have… you understand why."

"I do," said Decker softly.

Lana drew in a calming breath and the hard set of her face softened into a thin smile, "I'm sorry, my love… I didn't mean to distress you."

Decker smiled, "This is a war."

"And it is yet underway," Lana explained. "Aside from the joy of being reunited, Albert, I've come here to give you a warning. You are being targeted by a Japanese platoon. They are camped a few klicks from here and are planning to attack after sundown."

Decker gaped, "They've scouted us?"

Lana nodded, "And we them. The commander is none other than your friend Ata Hondo."

"Holy Christ…" Decker muttered. "Coming from the west, I imagine?"

Lana nodded, "Most of them. However, the sergeant… Makai? Yes, Makai is leading a party around to strike from your rear."

"Well… we have some cover down there in the trees… and the

floating bridge is a choke point on that side… we might be able to handle a three to one numerical disparity."

"Two to one," Lana said. "I've positioned my men in strategic locations. Once the Japs attack… they will also."

Decker frowned and took to pacing. He didn't like it, especially not the idea of his lover being in the fray. His American sensibilities were difficult to ignore, in spite of all he'd seen on Guadalcanal.

"What's their armament?" he asked instead of demanding that she stay up on the OP where it was safe.

Lana smiled, as if she'd just read his mind, "All have spears and knives. Four men are equipped with, and proficient with, Arisaka rifles. If you have an extra Arisaka… you usually collect them… I would appreciate it and as many rounds as you can spare."

"Spears and knives…" Decker muttered, running a hand through his sweaty hair. "Christ, Lana…"

"These are expert hunters," Lana said, her voice stern. "Experts at tracking and moving through the jungle unseen and unheard. More than once we have tracked you on your journey here. Do not fear, Albert. They are ready, willing, and able. As am I."

This last declaration was made as she locked gazes with him. The intensity in those large brown orbs set up a cocktail of mixed emotions in Decker. Fear for her, pride in her, and no small amount of desire in him.

"There is no time," Lana whispered, running her fingertips across his chest. "Not for argument and not for… more pleasant things, my love. We must prepare. When we are victorious… well, there will be cause to celebrate. Come, time grows short…"

Ata Hondo was already tired. The five kilometers between his camp and Decker's was a long way during a hot Guadalcanal afternoon.

On top of that, a short climb had been required, further taxing his stamina.

Of course, the platoon commander couldn't admit this to his men. Certainly not. If they had to slog it out, then their commander must do so as well and appear even less fatigued than they.

Perhaps that was the worst part of being an officer? The play acting that was required.

A series of low whistles floated to Hondo from out of the trees ahead. Shortly thereafter, two men materialized, strode forward, and saluted.

"Sir, we are near," said the senior of the two scouts. "The enemy camp is less than 200 meters away. There is a small river but the Ame-cohs have built a floating bridge across."

Hondo frowned, "How large is this bridge? Could you determine if it was secure?"

The second scout nodded, "Wide enough for a single-file crossing, sir. I got as close as I dared and the structure appears sound. The river is perhaps no more than ten to fifteen meters across in any case."

"You were not spotted?" Hondo asked tightly.

"No, sir," said the senior man. "Indeed… the camp appears deserted. I believe we saw one or two men through the trees… but there is little activity. We should be able to get the entire force across before they can mount a significant defense."

Hondo scowled, "Thank you, Corporal. When I desire a tactical analysis, I shall ask for one. Describe the base."

"Mostly a stand of hardwood trees and some brush between the edge of the ridge and the granite cliffs to the south," the corporal said. "However, the Marines have laid several deadfalls across the western edge of the trees to act as a sort of palisade. Not unlike what we had done at Mount Austin, sir. Beyond this, I cannot say. Whatever else they may have done must be in the thicket."

"Very well," said Hondo, casting a glance over his shoulder and seeing that the sun was half-buried in the jungle to the west. "You will guide us, Corporal. You and the private gather four more men. When we attack, you will spearhead the push, establish a position on the far side of the bridge and offer cover for the rest of us. When and if fighting begins, it should alert Sergeant Makai to begin his push. We must be cautious… the opportunity for friendly fire is high."

The corporal's face flashed with something for the briefest of moments before he wrangled it into stiff neutrality once more. Inwardly, Hondo was pleased. No doubt the man was not thrilled at leading the assault with only five other men on his fire team.

Serves the presumptive fool right, Hondo mused.

"We are ready, sir," said the corporal.

"Then let us proceed. No doubt you have chosen a spot near the line for the men to shed their packs and lighten their loads before combat?"

Hondo was mildly displeased when the corporal bowed and said: "Of course, sir."

"Then we move out," Hondo growled.

It took until the sun had disappeared and twilight had just begun to set its claws into the world before the corporal stopped the men in a rough clearing just out of sight of the river. Over the entire length of the march, Hondo had reviewed, altered, and refined his plan of attack.

With the corporal leading his fire team across, this left Hondo with exactly four fire teams. Among these sixteen men, he had four armed with the type-89 grenade thrower in addition to their rifles. He had eight dedicated riflemen and a team with two type 100 sub-machine guns. The other two men had Arisakas but also carried extra 30 round curved box magazines for the smgs. For his part, Hondo carried only his Nambu pistol and a cheap but serviceably sharp Katana blade at his side. There was a rifle for him as well, but based on scouting reports, the lieutenant knew that the battle to come would be close quarters and he preferred to be more mobile.

His plan was simple and elegant. The corporal would go first, crossing the bridge and setting up using the Americans' own log wall as cover. Then the smg team would join them as the two rifle teams lined up on the western side of the river to provide covering and sniper fire. The mortarmen would also spread out and send in volleys of grenades with Hondo at the center of these four teams to direct. Once the position was secure, everyone would move across, and the rifle teams would conduct a sweep until the objective was secured.

Hondo did not believe that the camp was empty. Either the scouts had not seen the Marines, or they were off someplace. There was, of course, a third possibility.

That Decker knew he was coming. Whether that was true or not, it would not save the Ame-coh from getting his just desserts.

Presently, the men were arranged. The corporal who'd led the scout had his team assembled and waiting for the word. Above, the sky had gone a deep indigo, and full dark would be upon Guadalcanal in minutes.

Hondo glanced at his wristwatch and nodded, "Five minutes and we move. Silent and carefully until we take formation. Corporal, you may proceed now at your discretion."

"Hai," said the corporal with a bow. He signaled to his men, and they quickly vanished into the trees.

Minutes later, Hondo moved after them, the two rifle teams flanking him and the smg team directly behind. Behind them, a few paces back, the four knee mortar men waited until their commander was nearly out of sight in the thickening blackness of the jungle.

They may or may not have heard it. The faint rustling from the foliage, the ghostly crackle of bare feet on dust, gravel and dying leaves… yet if they had, then the soldiers either didn't react at all or had no time.

A surge of fright was the last thing the four Japanese soldiers experienced as dark figures materialized behind them, dark brown hands clamped over their mouths and razor-sharp blades, at least one of which had once belonged to one of their countrymen, were slid expertly into chest cavities.

The Asian soldiers were eased quietly to the Earth. Their weapons were left for the time being. Without a word or a sound, the four assassins melted back into the darkness from which they'd come.

THE BAIT

Henry Evans cursed his luck. The choice had been fair, but lady luck had chosen to give him a swift kick in the ass.

Then again, he tried reminding himself, Edgar Jones had it just as bad, as it was he and Evans who'd drawn the short sticks. The short sticks that volunteered them to remain in the Raider's camp and draw the Japanese in… while the rest of them, red and blue teams, hid and waited to ambush the approaching enemy platoon from either flank.

Now the time had come. The sun had set, and dusk had turned to twilight and twilight to night. All the preparations were completed and now all that remained was to wait… wait while the fuse burned down to the inevitable explosion.

The Marines had spent the day removing all of their supplies from the camp. Food, water, and ammo. Backpacks, canisters, and parachutes. Now all that remained were a few downed logs to act as barriers and two men. Two men whose job it was to be seen so that Hondo and his soldiers would believe the entire squad was there.

"Full dark," Jonesy said as he sidled up to Evans and the tree on which he leaned. "You okay, Hank?"

"Sure, Jonesy," Evans lied. "You?"

"Right as rain."

Evans was not alright, however. His one true fear, that of being captured, had grown large and shaggy after dark. He and Jones were exposed, alone, and it was entirely possible that when the attack began, they would be cut down or captured. Evans would rather it be the former. He had no death wish… but the thought of bamboo shoots being shoved under his nails… of thousands of ants tearing at his flesh… of razor-sharp blades digging into his body…

There they were. Shadowy figures emerged from the darkness on the other side of the river. Dark figures, not wearing the light khaki that the Japs usually preferred but dark green. Green that might as well be black on that tense night.

A fist of arctic ice seized Evans's belly and sent ripples of fear racing through his entire form. The Japs were spreading into a line… but not all of them. A column of men was separating… running… crossing the bridge!

Evans brought his Springfield up, sighted in and even as he pulled the trigger, heard Jones swear from his hiding spot five yards away. The warning came too late, however. The rifle boomed as its .30 caliber round shattered through the sound barrier and zipped over the fifty yards to the river.

One of the soldiers, perhaps the third in line, cried out and tumbled sideways and into the flowing water. Immediately, his body floated away, moving slowly but ever so slightly faster as it neared the hundred-foot cataract that would deliver it to the larger river below… and perhaps the waiting jaws of a crocodile.

There were curses, shouts, and the world erupted as multiple Arisaka rifles crackled in a rippling volley that tore the night open. On their heels the staccato chatter of several automatic weapons added their howl to the war cry.

The jig was up for sure.

"Shit!" Jones growled. "You done it now, Hank!"

"I…" Evans tried to explain that his fears had gotten the better of him. That the roaring monster of fright had taken over and that *it* had killed that enemy soldier. But how could he explain?

"Somebody had to do it, brother," Jones actually chuckled. "C'mon, time we backpedaled… here they come!"

The five remaining men of the first to cross the bridge hunkered low and ran the rest of the way, diving down and using the Raiders' own log wall for cover. As they did so, dozens of rounds flew through the night over the top of the log. 8mm type 100 bullets and 7.7mm Arisaka rounds hissed through leaves, thunked into tree trunks, and turned much of the camp into a cloud of flying splinters.

"Go, go, go!" Jones shouted, moving to the east and trying to keep the trunks between him and the enemy.

Evans followed suit, getting low and melting into the darkness. Occasionally, one or the other man… once at the same time… would turn and snap off a quick shot. They didn't expect to hit anything, just to keep the Japs believing they had surprised more than just two men.

BLUE TEAM

"Looks like somebody lit the fuse…" Phil Oaks said, gripping his Thompson tightly.

"Do we go, Gunny?" Gartrell hissed.

"Not yet, keep your shorts on!" Oaks growled. "We gotta give the slants a chance to get into the kill zone."

"But it's early," Taggart insisted from down the line.

"First to go in battle is the frickin' plan…" Entwater grumbled.

Oaks's four-man team was stationed almost at the edge of the cliff near where they'd rigged the climbing rope. The cliff's edge was only fifty yards or so from the center of the camp, and the sounds of battle were crystal clear.

There was a slight difference in the sound that an Arisaka and a 1903 Springfield made when fired. It was slight, but after many months of hearing it, the Raiders could differentiate between the two. In addition, the type 100 light Nambu sub-machine gun certainly sounded different than the Thompson, whose .45 caliber round was nearly twice the size of the 8mm round the light smg fired.

Of course, the shouts and curses in Japanese certainly left nothing to the imagination. More than a dozen men were throwing up a considerable racket as they moved in from the east. Oaks only hoped that Evans and Jones were able to slip away before they were overwhelmed. He also hoped that Lana's people knew enough to stay out of the line of fire.

The plan was simple enough. The bait, that being Evans and Jones, were to show up enough so that the japs would believe they'd caught the Raiders unaware. Blue team was arrayed along the camp's right flank and Decker and his red team were huddled in the cliffs and boulders to the south. When the attack began and the Japs were most certainly in the camp, then a two-pronged attack would take place.

And it would be left to Lana's hunters to stop or at least hold up Makai's squad from sneaking up from the rear while the two teams of Raiders dealt with the frontal assault.

It was a good plan… but as Entwater had so rightly pointed out… real life rarely followed the script. The gunnery sergeant bit his lip, patted his trusty Chicago typewriter and drew in a breath.

"Time's up, boys!" he announced and then in a roar that must've carried for miles, shouted: "*CHARGE!*"

18

It wasn't until Hondo heard the American voice off to the left shouting for a charge that he discovered that his mortar team hadn't opened fire. His riflemen and automatic weapons teams were in place and the corporal's team had made it across the bridge with but one loss. Now they were hunkered down behind the American log break and the 50mm shells or type-91 grenades should have begun arcing through the night to deliver their deadly potential.

"You!" Hondo grabbed one of the ammo servers for the SMG team. "Retrace our steps and find out where the mortar team has gone! Quickly!"

Rifles cracked from the left, one of which sounded like a heavy sub-machine gun. Hondo knew the Americans liked their Thompson, which threw a big .45 caliber round. Poor over long range but at short range, the big slug was devastating. They were moving forward from the edge of the ridge… moving toward the center of Decker's camp… three of them? No… four… then where were the rest?

A little frigid pit took shape in Hondo's belly. There was

something wrong here… something that smacked of a well-laid plan… no, a well laid *trap!*

Decker had known he was coming. That was the only explanation! He'd left a few men in the trees to draw Hondo's platoon in and then would flank them from the left… and possibly the right?

A good plan, the Japanese lieutenant had to admit. However, Decker had not accounted for the fact that he, Hondo, could be clever as well. He had his own backup. A squad of men moving in from the east with Makai at its head. They would catch the arrogant Ame-cohs in a crossfire as well.

In the meantime, however, Hondo and his dozen men were exposed, lined up along the trees on their side of the river. He'd need to move more men forward to counter the Americans' move.

But where were the mortar men?

"Sir… sir!" the young private he'd sent burst from the trees, his moon face ashen and shining with brilliant fright.

"Report!" Hondo snapped, having no time nor patience for foolishness.

"The mortar men… they're… they've been killed, sir," the young man held up a type-89 launcher and bandolier as if to prove his claim. "Stabbed… throats cut… I don't understand, sir!"

At first, Hondo didn't either. Who could've… then the images described by his scouts the previous night swam into hideous focus behind his eyes. Images of half a dozen Japanese soldiers impaled and flayed to the bone… and he knew. And the realization swelled the peach pit in his belly into a medicine ball of horror.

"Give me that!" he grabbed the mortar. "Take your other ammo server and retrieve as much of their munitions as you can."

The young man balked, his face an open mask of fear, "But… sir…"

"Go!" Hondo roared. "Or I'll cut your throat *myself!*"

Hondo watched to make sure that the two men scampered off

and then knelt. He placed the mortar on the ground, loaded a grenade, and aimed. He smiled and pulled the trigger.

The mortar thumped as the grenade was propelled over the river, his line of men and into the trees, where it promptly exploded. He had no idea if he'd hit anything, but he had certainly given the Americans pause.

"Team one! Covering fire!" shouted the Lieutenant and then waved an arm at the five men to his left. "Team two, forward and reinforce. Private Sekuza, accompany! Quickly!"

This time, Hondo loaded in a 50mm shell and sent it into the camp, slightly to the left. If anything, it would keep the American fire team from making progress and allow he and his men to leapfrog across the river and move in, using their numbers to sweep the little camp clear of marines.

From off to the right and higher up, perhaps 200 yards away, a pinprick flash caught the lieutenant's eye. He puzzled over this for a second before understanding bloomed as a white-hot flash and crackling rumble twenty yards to his right removed all doubt.

The Americans had a grenade thrower as well. And theirs was set up on the high ground to the south.

In the meantime, the four riflemen and the private with his type-100 Nambu bolted across the log bridge, running hunched over and sliding none too gently to the earth behind the log wall, where the corporal and his men were upright, sending two and three shot volleys into the dark trees. They were answered by American shots, but as yet, neither side had homed in on each other.

Hondo bent to his task, pulling a second grenade out. He loaded it and aimed the mortar in the general direction from which the American grenade launcher's flash had come. The launcher could hurl a type-91 grenade just over 200 meters. It might be just enough. If he could get the range, then Hondo would send in the larger and longer-ranged 50mm shell. That would teach the arrogant Yankees to fool with *him!*

The launcher thumped and the grenade sailed off into the night. Seconds later, it exploded far off against the blackness of the cliffs and mountains beyond. Hondo couldn't tell if he hit anything, but he watched.

Sure enough, a second flash that was just a bit to the left of where he'd aimed and slightly higher. The lieutenant's triumphant smile evaporated when the American grenade landed fifteen meters away… and almost directly behind him.

"Team three, all of you… move up now!" shouted the lieutenant.

The damned Ame-cohs were homing in on *him* as well. Two shots from the same position were enough. Cursing, Hondo slid in a shell, adjusted the azimuth and angle and fired again, sending his last shell into the darkness. He didn't wait to see where it fell… and he didn't wait for his men behind him to re-emerge from the trees. The screams that accompanied the last American grenade told him all he needed to know.

And as if that weren't enough, there was a mysterious and deadly enemy at his back. Hondo left the mortar and the empty bandolier and ran for the bridge.

RED TEAM

"Red, Blue, Eagle… enemy units are on the move, over."

Al Decker hunkered down behind a pile of rubble not far from the second cliff. On the next plateau Lana and Treadway stood atop the OP evidently exchanging explosive rounds with the Japs near the river. Flanking him were Charlie Lider and James Travis. Red team was small, due to the fact that Evans was still with Jones.

Yet Decker's team was armed with automatic weapons. Both he and Travis carried a Thompson and Lider one of the unit's BARs. If push came to shove, the three of them could lay down severe withering fire while the rest of the six Raiders on the ground could catch the enemy in a crossfire. And that included Oaks's Thompson and Jones's with the other BAR.

Above, Treadway had their M1 grenade thrower and Lana was armed with an Arisaka. They had a bird's eye view of the camp, although darkness made picking out individual target's problematic. However, Treadway could easily make out the river and bridge, and his report reflected that.

Not for the first time, Decker wished he had more men. Even a platoon would dramatically increase his effectiveness and firepower. Of course, if he did have a whole platoon of Raiders, they'd probably be back at Henderson or at the Matanikau fighting on the line. Nothing wrong with that, but Decker's team had grown very proficient at guerrilla warfare over the past few months and the major had to admit he enjoyed it, perils and all.

Decker unclipped his radio and pressed the button, "Eagle, Red... Roger that. Blue, proceed objective Baker. Eagle, continue egging. Over."

"*Eagle acknowledge...*"

"*Red acknowledge...*"

From ahead and to the right, from what would be the far side of the grove of trees in which the camp had been set up, a twittering whistle arose above the din of random shots. Decker smiled and nudged Travis, who let loose with a shrill horse whistle. Two seconds later, he let out another and the three men ducked low, peeking up over their rocks and trying to see into the shadows in and around the trees.

No more than five seconds passed when two of those shadows broke free and took on the form of two men. The men ran almost directly toward Red team's hidey-hole.

"Sir!" Jones called out. "Jones and Evans!"

"Good work, fellas!" Decker said. "You all right?"

The two Raiders slid in behind their comrades, panting and heaving. Both men received pats from the other three.

"Phew…" Jones huffed. "Was gettin' hairy in there, sir."

"Yeah… thought we were… gonna get wiped out, Major," Evans panted.

The sound of the shooting had changed. Where seconds ago, two distinct groups were firing, now it was only one, from forward and left. Oaks and his party had already taken off to the east. Having done their job of letting the Japs know they were flanked, Oaks rushed to meet Makai's rear attack and head them off at the proverbial pass. Now the way was open for Decker to engage without the fear of hitting his own men.

It was several seconds before the Japanese realized no one was firing back. Except for Treadway, of course, who lobbed grenades down on the near side of the bridge and Lana's Arisaka cracking in the darkness above.

"You boys need a breather?" Lider asked.

Both Jones and Evans had their canteens to their mouths and were gulping greedily. Evans stopped first and grinned sheepishly.

"Uhm… sorry, sir…"

Decker chuckled, "No need, PFC. But we're gonna need to move in on Hondo's position. From the sounds of it, he's got four fire teams or better and they're on our side of the bridge. We gotta move in and throw some crossfire."

"We ready, sir," Jones said gamely. "Ain't that right, Hank?"

Evans, thankful to be out of the direct line of fire and with the potential for capture diminished, smiled, "Oh, yes, sir. Let's wipe 'em out!"

Decker grinned and held up his radio, "Eagle, Red… cease fire. Red moving in. Over."

"Now everybody stay low and move single file," Lider said as he rose. "We goin' in on the left, try to move close to the log wall. We can use the trees as cover and retreat. Nice and quiet like!"

Decker stood, stepping out in front, "Fall in and double-time it, men!"

Red team leapt from hiding and ran toward where several Japanese riflemen were still tossing cover fire into the trees. There were only a few dozen yards of open ground, and they crossed quickly. As they reached the tree line, the men split up into pairs based on weaponry.

Decker and Travis went left while Lider and Jones right. Evans stayed in the center, with orders to push forward from tree to tree, keeping low and picking off any Japanese targets he could find.

After splitting, the four automatic weapons came into action, peppering the Japanese positions with a hailstorm of lead quickly answered by another.

Evans was suddenly alone and felt the weight of it upon him. Although Lider and Jones couldn't be more than ten yards to his right and Decker a little more to his left, in the dark of the trees and with so much noise roaring from every direction, Hank Evans found himself staring into the darkness and was dismayed to find the demon that dwelled just under the surface of his soul staring back at him.

Gritting his teeth and slinging his rifle, Evans pulled his .45 and moved into that darkness. Certainly, he was worried about a stray round finding him… yet the idea that at any moment, a Jap could materialize out of the darkness and take him prisoner was by far worse… even though logically he knew the odds of that were miniscule.

Mustering his considerable courage, the farm boy from the Midwest moved forward, intent on delivering death to anyone who opposed him.

Hondo knew they had to move forward. Over the wall and into the trees proper. The men who'd been hitting his force from the left had gone. That much was clear. Yet now, from the right, multiple automatic weapons blazed. They were coming from nearly ninety degrees, which meant that the attackers were trying to get in close to the wall and use it to move in and slaughter his men.

"Right!" Hondo shouted. "Teams two and three, direct your fire! Team four move in and get close. Team one, standby to penetrate into the trees!"

Although fairly effective, the wall made from downed trees and deadfalls was showing signs of wear by then. In the darkness, great swaths of bare wood shown through where bark or mold had been scoured by many bullets blasting into the organic barrier. That and more than one of the American grenades landed close enough to blast a portion of the wall's right side to little more than a pile of kindling.

Hondo was oppressed by the overwhelming need to act quickly. He also wondered where in the name of the ancestors Makai was. He should be getting close by that time.

Another part of the lieutenant's mind kept turning to the forest on the opposite side of the river. The foliage from which he and his men had come, and where six of them lay slaughtered by angry islanders. Islanders who must still be out there but who, for their own unfathomable reasons, had not shown themselves again.

Why?

That question nagged at Hondo, yet the incessant fire of rifles and automatic weapons kept him from exploring the idea in depth. Instead, he moved forward and took up with his remaining men.

"Get ready," he commanded. "Once our right flank has engaged… we enter the Ame-coh camp proper!"

As if on cue, a dozen weapons roared out, brilliant flashes and tracers zipping through the forest and brush in both directions. Hondo paused to watch, and his belly knotted itself.

Four shadows broke from cover, the barrels of their automatic weapons flaring like tiny dragons' mouths. This relentless fusillade tore across the log wall and into the eight riflemen and ended any hopes of a flanking maneuver on the Americans. Hondo's fear roared up inside him, a guttural cry of fright and rage that nearly drove him backward and into the river.

"Attack!" he shouted, inwardly amazed that he wasn't shrieking like a woman. "Attack! Move in and take cover *now!*"

It was remarkably dark inside the stand of trees. Perhaps no more than thirty or forty yards on a side, the interior of what the Americans had chosen as their camp was a study in shadow occasionally broken by dim shafts of moonlight. The men broke once inside, fanning out and trying to find cover while getting deep enough into the gloom to be able to turn back on the Americans and attack.

With shocking swiftness, Hondo realized that he'd lost his men. All of them. There was a clear area in the trees where Decker had removed some ground brush for the actual camp, but it was still dark. Hondo could hear rustling and movement in and among the trees and through the ground cover, but it was chaotic… erratic and to mocked him from everywhere at once.

With a spike of sudden horror jabbing into his belly, Hondo found himself alone. Alone and exposed and with at least four or five bloodthirsty Americans hunting for him and his men. His plan had completely unraveled, and he now found himself vulnerable and in near total darkness.

Panic was there… lurking in the stygian depths of his mind, its heavy bulk rippling Hondo's mental surface. With gritted teeth and by concentrating on his anger and need for revenge, he kept the beast at bay… but only just.

He *should* stop. He *should* establish a position and wait things out. See who came by. Eventually, his men would circle back, their pre-planned escape route back the way they'd come.

When Hondo bounced off the trunk of an invisible tree and spun hard to his right, he stifled a grunt and finally stopped. Then his panic came for him as he understood that he'd lost his bearings. He didn't know which way to go and the rustlings and occasional shots in the dark offered no assistance.

Cursing and hanging onto his self-control by fingernails, the Japanese lieutenant took several tentative steps forward, his pistol at the ready and his other hand stretched out before him like a blind man. He thought he saw a thin beam of light ahead… a ghostly finger of moonlight dancing with tiny motes. He'd move that way and use the light to consult his compass, regain his bearings, and then shout for his men to join him. Yes, it would alert the Amecohs… but he would be waiting in the dark for *them*.

His foot struck something, and Hondo went sprawling. His Nambu pistol flew from his grasp and landed in a nearby bush. He struck the ground hard and emitted a little cry as some of his fear squeezed out.

Then something hit him again. A moving something that landed on his back and put a knee in its center.

"Turn to stone, Tojo," a voice said from the darkness. "You speak English?"

Hondo bucked and writhed, trying to throw the heavier man off. He received a short, hard blow from the man's heel to his left cheek for his troubles. He lay still, hoping that he would get a chance to grab for his sword.

"I said do you speak English, Slanty Joe?"

Hondo gritted his teeth and replied in Japanese. He hoped this would satisfy the Marine.

Then there came *another* Japanese voice, almost right beside them. A thump, a grunt, and a frantic shuffling and rustling.

"Sir! I have him!" said the scout corporal who'd been the first across the bridge.

Hondo rolled onto his haunches and blinked. All he saw was a faint shadow that might have been two men. Grinning, he fumbled in the brush until his fingers found the cold steel of his pistol.

"Excellent, Corporal," Hondo said. "What of the rest of—"

A throaty crackling roar as multiple automatic weapons let loose. This cacophony was joined by the screams of fright and agony as many men were cut down. Hondo's heart leapt into his throat and sped up to a rapid thundering.

The corporal's answer was unnecessary, "Gone, sir."

Hondo moved forward and saw the general shape of one man standing over another, perhaps on his knees. With impotent rage burning in his heart, the lieutenant lashed out with his barrel, smashing it across the face of the young Marine who'd tackled him.

"Then at least we have this filthy round-eye," Hondo said in English. "And when Makai arrives… our men will be revenged. Come, Corporal, let's get out of his way."

Sergeant Makai was uneasy. He and his squad were close to the American encampment now. The nearly incessant shooting and shouting was proof enough of that. He had perhaps a hundred, hundred fifty meters to go.

Yet something nagged at him. The images described by the scouts of the slaughtered soldiers in the native village. Those islanders had enough skill and numbers to surprise and destroy a six-man patrol. A well-armed Japanese patrol.

And it took no stretch of the imagination to believe that those same islanders had either joined up with Decker or were in the area, prowling the night for more Naponapo to cut down.

Yes, Makai had a dozen men including himself… but he was also moving in semi-open ground. In order to make time, he was staying at the edge of the tree line between the denser foliage and the southern granite walls and ravines. When he thought he was close enough, he and his men would penetrate deeper into the woods and flush out the Marines as they found them. All the while hoping that Hondo had the good sense to stay out of the kill zone.

Based on what he was hearing ahead, though, Makai had little faith in Hondo. Not that this was unusual, of course. The man was a damned fool as far as he was concerned.

Makai held up a fist and the men stopped. They gathered close around and he leaned in.

"Corporal Kaji," Makai said to his most senior noncom. "Take half the men and continue as planned. I'll take the rest and go north toward the ridge line. We'll proceed together and catch the round-eyes in a crossfire."

"When do we charge, Sergeant?" asked Kaji.

"When either of us makes visual contact with the American camp," Makai said. "He shouts Banzai and opens fire. The other team will follow suit. Move forward and we will meet somewhere in the center of the trees. This crossfire should flush out and potentially eliminate any Americans hiding within."

"What of the others, Sergeant?" another man asked.

Makai sighed, "Based on what I am hearing… things have gone awry. They will doubtless be retreating across the bridge and regrouping. Once we arrive, they will be able to come back in and support us. This is why the crossfire. It should leave the bridge and log wall unhit. Come, we are no more than a hundred meters away. Seven minutes and no more. Proceed."

The men split and vanished. Makai moved due north, wishing to make contact with the cliff as soon as possible. If his suspicions were correct, then it was possible that Decker had been warned about Makai's group. They would expect a direct attack from the east. At least this way, some element of surprise might be maintained.

There most certainly *was* a surprise, on all sides.

Makai and his men had hardly gone thirty meters when they

came to a relatively clear section of the forest at the exact same moment that Phil Oaks and his blue team did. The two groups of men gawked at each other for several seconds, the shock broken only when a blood-curdling battle cry rose thirty or forty meters to the south.

"Back!" Makai roared out, throwing himself backward and sweeping the legs of one of his men as he did so.

"Down!" Phil Oaks roared, leaping back and rolling behind the trunk of a tree, peeping out from the other side and leading with his Thompson's barrel.

Both sides fired at once. Arisakas cracked, Springfields crackled, and Oaks's Tommy gun bellowed its .45 caliber roar, the strobe of the muzzle flash lighting up the forty or fifty feet between the two groups of soldiers.

Both Oaks and Makai tried to keep an ear on what was happening to the south. Shouts, curses, and screams of pain rose along with random crackles of weapons' fire. Yet that didn't last long. Whatever was going on over there was rapidly devolving into a melee. A melee with half a dozen Japanese having been jumped by at least as many natives. Some of the shouts were in neither English nor Japanese.

"We gotta push forward, Gunny!" Taggart shouted.

Half a dozen rounds zipped past, hissing and thunking just over the prone Marines's head. Gartrell chuckled in spite of himself.

"You first, Sarge!" said the Raider.

"There's six of them!" Entwater said. "I've been counting shots."

"To four of us," Oaks grumbled even as his Thompson's bolt locked open. He cursed and ejected the magazine and fumbled in another.

"With that coffee grinder you got, Gunny, it ought to be even!" Gartrell offered.

Oaks cursed and charged his weapon, "We gotta move! Right five yards, stay low and cover! I'll cover you three. Ready… go, go!"

Oaks leaned out from the other side of his chewed-up tree and began pumping heavy rounds in the direction of the Japanese muzzle flashes. Using quick, three-round bursts, Oaks was able to maintain enough covering fire to give his marines a few seconds to move into a new position. Still, even with good fire discipline and a second or two between bursts, the men only had ten seconds to move. Then Oaks had to roll back behind cover and plug in another magazine… and he only had a few left.

Makai was faced with the same conundrum to the east. It would be possible, with time, to work around and closer… but there was the matter of the rest of Decker's men ahead. By the sounds of the firing westward, the outcome of Hondo's push seemed certain. He was losing and would have to retreat soon. Then Decker could reinforce his men and beat Makai's team into bloody pulp.

Then there was the matter of the six men now embroiled with what must be natives. They'd been surprised in the dark and had only gotten off a few shots before probably having to engage in hand-to-hand combat. And if the sergeant was right… those screams were those of *his* men.

Faced with these facts and with the safety of his five remaining men, the Japanese sergeant could make only one decision. He must retreat and melt into the dark, making as much time as he could back to where they'd climbed up the coral ridge. Anything else was pure suicide.

"Private Aga… you're with me. We lay down salvo fire and the rest of you retreat! As planned!" said Makai, regret dripping from his tone.

"But Sergeant—"

"Now!" Makai barked.

Four soldiers melted back into the forest. As they did, first Makai and then Aga sent a round downrange. One, two… one, two…

"Are they slacking their fire, Gunny?" Entwater asked.

Oaks looked to his right and the darkness that concealed his men. Entwater's voice seemed to have come from nowhere.

Oaks listened. Two rifles… perhaps five yards apart… left and then right. Left and then right…

"They're buggin' out!" Oaks declared. "Let 'em have it and give 'em reason, boys!"

Three Springfields snapped and Oaks laid down a spray of heavy rounds at the invisible enemy. After ten seconds he called for a cease fire.

The Raiders waited.

Silence… of a kind… dropped over the forest.

Silence ahead and silence to the right…

When multiple dark forms materialized from the woods to the right, chattering in excited pigeon, Oaks knew they'd driven Makai and his men off for good.

"Naponapo, e come, e go e sleep long time!" one hunter said, his smile brilliant in the moonlight.

Oaks began to laugh.

Evans's heart thundered in his ears. His fear was huge, and it was a contest between it and fury as to what would finally take over.

The two Japs somehow found the log wall. One held Evans's arm and the other pressed a gun barrel to his side. The message was clear and Evans's fear, which he'd tried to convince himself was irrational, was now a cold, hard reality.

He'd been captured.

He'd been captured and by some miracle, the two slants were getting away with it. The rest of the Raiders were now in the camp, ferreting out the Japs and taking them out. The two Japs were at the bridge and hustling him across… and nobody saw a damned thing!

Each footfall on the wobbly logs was one more step toward the realization of Evans's fears. For a brief instant, he entertained throwing himself into the river. He could sink down and swim away… and end up tumbling over a hundred-foot waterfall.

Or maybe he could get all three of them into the water. At least then he'd have a chance… and if nothing else, he could drag the two enemy soldiers down with him…

Something hard hammered him in the gut just under the ribcage. Evans's breath whooshed out and a dull, wetted dagger of pain stabbed into his diaphragm. It was as if one of the men had read his mind and made sure he didn't have the air or strength to fight just then.

Evans could feel it, the sour, acidic burn of panic rising inside him. He hated it, fought against it and the sting of shame that accompanied it was almost more than he could take.

He was a Marine… a *Raider*, goddammit! He couldn't panic just because he'd been captured… he couldn't lose his very manhood at the prospect of what the Nips might do! For Christ… stop being a baby and *do* something about it!

But what?

What could he do against two men with weapons?

You could fight, a voice said from inside. You might not win… but you can make damned sure these bastards don't!

Yet his other voice, the panicked one that was mortally terrified of being tortured by the enemy as a P.O.W. had plenty to say too.

Don't fight… stay cool… do what they say and maybe… maybe it won't be so bad…

They were in the woods again. Moving past shadowy forms lying dead on the forest floor. Evans couldn't see much, but he could tell that they'd been Japanese soldiers.

Soldiers sent to kill him and his friends… just men. As mortal and fragile as anyone. Probably with their own fears, too…

"No!" Evans shouted, allowing his fury to stamp out the growing blaze of panic.

He would *not* go quietly! He wouldn't be led to the slaughter like a docile cow... fuck that shit!

Evans exploded, wrenching himself sideways and hurling one of the men into the brush. A fist swung around in an attempt to punch his ticket, but the blow went wide, hitting the American in his solidly muscled chest. Roaring with rage and allowing his panic to vent out as anger, Evans kicked out, planting his boot into the man's gut and hurling him into the *brush*, too.

Part of Evans's traumatized psyche screamed for him to run... but he wouldn't. He couldn't. He was *not* going to let fear rule him. He wouldn't just run away like a coward.

No... these slopes wanted a fight, then he'd give them one!

Rustling from the bushes, shouts, thumping footfalls... and Evans couldn't find his targets. Both soldiers had vanished into the darkness.

"Come out, you slanty-eyed sons of bitches!" Evans shouted, his words and his anger beating back the fear and filling his body with sizzling adrenaline and fighting madness.

Figures emerged then. Four of them. Dark, silent, and as tall or taller than the American. After a brief moment of shock, Evans understood.

"Naponapo e belonga woods... makem longtime e come soon, you savvy?" one of the dark men asked and showed a broad and surprisingly white grin.

Evans laughed. He laughed so hard tears spilled over his eyes, "I got no idea, Chum... but thanks all the same!"

19
MATANIKAU RIVER VALLEY
OCTOBER 8, 1942

"Well don't this just beat all," Merrit "Red Mike" Edson declared from under the canopy of his command tent overlooking the river. "Pouring cats and dogs out there. Can't hardly see a hundred yards into this slop."

"Gonna make the second and seventh's push near impossible today," Lou Walt observed.

Edson grunted, "Maybe… although it'd be a good time to get in deep while the Japs have a hard time seeing or moving, too."

"My concern," Walt said, "are those Japs we've got pinned down on our side of the river. They're dug in pretty good, but I'll bet dollars to navy beans they try and break out."

Edson nodded, "Use this weather as cover. Look at the river and the banks. Already got a mist growing. I've had first bat set up a double apron barbed wire barrier near the spit. Just in case any optimists try to make a break for it. Got fifty cals arranged on both sides."

Walt looked at his watch, "Still… almost sixteen hundred and we ain't heard a peep all day. Permission to take the Raiders in and surround the Japs, sir. If they do try to break, we'll be there to make 'em regret it."

Edson smiled wanly, "Good old Raiders… my boys… permission granted, Lou. Burack, accompany the Major. You'll be our liaison. Take your radioman with you. Good luck, men."

"But Corporal B… it's pourin' out there," the radioman whispered.

Burack grinned at him, "Be the first good shower you had in weeks, PFC!"

It wasn't long before Walt and the Raiders got into position. The Japanese were sequestered on a low hill surrounded by dense mangroves. There were a series of coral ripples to the west and south, which made it difficult to move large numbers of men. The enemy couldn't have chosen a better spot to set up a forward observation post, but the only way they had out was either directly across the water or north to the spit and across.

Walt and his Raiders took advantage of that and set up a perimeter at the most likely point. Several platoons were sent to the ripples as well, just in case. By his estimate, Walt figured there to be approximately a company and a half. Perhaps 150 men gathered in the mangroves.

The Japanese had tried more than once to break out. But their efforts on the previous afternoon, overnight and that morning had been met with heavy resistance from the fifth regiment. However, with the storm raging and mist rising, Walt suspected that they would take advantage of the natural cover and come out swinging.

Walt and Burack stood together near the center. The world had gone mostly quiet, save the rumble of the heavy rains pouring onto the island. Tensions were high and men taut with expectation. Everyone was soaked to the bone but hardly noticed, so keyed up had they become.

At 1630, dense smoke began pouring out from the mangroves. Even with the rain, the breeze spread the gray fog, and it rolled down the hill, partially obscuring the trees. Then dozens of small objects flew out of the mangrove forest, bursting into individual puffs of smoke.

"Get ready, boys! Here the bastards come!" Walt roared.

The proverbial floodgates burst and the Japanese came roaring into battle. More grenades flew, throwing up dirt and flying water and shrapnel. Behind this screen, the Japanese poured out of their hiding place. They came twenty abreast and with automatic weapons blazing.

The attack was fierce and although the Raiders were ready, they hadn't expected such a fierce push. Men dove to the ground, rifles crackled, and machine guns opened fire, their throaty chatter joining with the lighter weapons of the enemy until a man could hardly hear the patter of raindrops.

Forward and left, Sergeant Ore Marion and his .50 caliber machine gun squad suddenly found themselves being overrun. Not just by soldiers but by a gaggle of officers as well. The officers and men rushed the Raiders, cries of Banzai in their throats, fire in their eyes and with razor-sharp Katanas slicing through the damp air.

"Bayonets!" Marion roared. "Meet 'em, boys! Meet 'em!"

The men did, admirably so, but the first wave of Japs was too much for them. The officers waded in, their swords arcing through the rain and into the yielding flesh of young Marines. Behind them and to their sides, soldiers drove in with bayonets, the sharp blades seeking any vulnerable flesh they could find.

Marion was shocked to his core. It was mayhem of the first class… and he knew he had to do something. Shoving one of his men at the .50 cal, he shouted orders to open fire and to watch out for their fellows.

Then he drove in, Springfield cracking and his own fixed bayonet gleaming with occasional reflected lightning. An officer was drawing back to swing his blade at a young Raider who'd attempted to intercept him. The Marine had slipped and fallen to his knees.

The kid was trying to bring the barrel of his rifle up to ward off the snarling officer's blow.

Marion could see that it would not do. With a roar of fury in his throat, he drove forward, driving his bayonet through the officer's forearm and wheeling the shocked man around. Marion lashed out, plowing his boot into the Jap's gut and heaving him off his feet. With a jerk and a snarl, Marion yanked his blade free, aimed it at the officer's throat and plunged it in, the steel sinking into yellow flesh that erupted in a fountain crimson gore.

Marion didn't wait. He saw another section of Japs coming in and emptied the rest of his stripper clip into them. He then drove in with his bayonet, even as the heavy machine gun behind him ripped into a line of Japs trying to race past toward the sand spit.

Fifty yards away, Walt himself was embroiled in hand to hand with a Japanese soldier and his officer. Walt had contrived to knock the deadly sword from the officer's hand even as the soldier came in with a combat knife. Walt threw himself sideways, twisting and wheeling out of the way. Yet the blade still found cloth and flesh, tearing a gouge in the major's bicep that welled up with warm blood. Howling with pain and rage, the Marine officer swung his rifle and lunged forward, driving his bayonet right into the temple of the soldier.

The Jap danced and convulsed, dying on his feet and dragging Walt's weapon out of his hands as he fell. With growing horror, Walt discovered that he was now face to face with the Japanese officer. The man, younger than Walt, grinned savagely, his face streaming with rain and his eyes wild… and his Nambu pistol barrel yawning before the major like a train tunnel. There was perhaps a second, maybe two, before the gun would discharge and Walt's life would end in a brilliant flash and searing agony. In that brief moment, the two men's eyes met and held one another, each filled with the harsh and unforgiving reflections of war.

Until a green-clad body slammed into the Japanese officer,

tumbling it and the enemy to the ground. There was a yelp of surprise, a grunt and a dull thud as the pistol went off. The shot seemed almost gentle amid the shooting, screaming and thundering weather.

The officer lay on his back, rainwater filling his lifeless eyes as he stared upward at nothing. A Marine issue KA-bar handle protruding from his chest. The green shape rolled off the man he'd tackled and onto his back, staring up at Walt with a pale face filled with agony... and so young...

It was Corporal Burack, Edson's aide.

Walt fell to his knees in the mud and swallowed hard. Burack's rain-soaked utilities were stained even darker as dark heart's blood soaked onto his chest.

"Sir... you... all right?" asked the corporal, his voice raspy with pain.

Walt's eyes ran with water and the image of the young man blurred. The major couldn't be sure if it was rain or tears.

"Burack... Walter... you... you saved my life, son..." Walt croaked.

Burack managed a bloody smile, "Oughta be worth a three-day pass, huh, sir? Impress the girls back at... someplace... with my purple heart...?"

"You got it," Walt smiled and watched as the light died from the corporal's eyes.

Burack was number twelve to be counted among the Raiders that day.

Later, when the report came in to Edson's HQ, he turned away and hid his own tears. Burack had been a good kid... like Winehouse... and so many other young men who'd never enjoy the rest of their lives. Edson wept and his men saw and were moved.

Along the barbed wire barricade, Sergeant Frank Guidone directed his squad and their machine gun. One by one and sometimes in pairs, they cut down Japanese soldiers making a mad dash for the sand spit. A few did make it, but many of them, either frightened beyond reason or overly optimistic, tried to push through the barricade and became caught.

"Gah-lee, Sarge!" one of the ammo servers blurted. "Look at them Japs in the wire…"

"Yeah…" Guidone said stonily. "Really busted 'em up, didn't it? Serves the yellow buggers right. Here come more, pay attention now."

Although the fighting was fierce, it lasted only forty-five minutes. When it was over, a dozen Marines lay dead, and fifty-nine Japanese had joined them. The rest had either gotten away or surrendered. Upon inspecting the dead, the Raiders found that the Japanese packs contained extra food, clothing and even shoes. These were new men to the island, and not the worn-down soldiers of Kawaguchi's force. This only confirmed what command already knew… the Japs were assembling for a massive attack.

ONE LOG BRIDGE, OCTOBER 9, 1942

After conferring more than once on the previous rainy day, Puller, Hanneken, and Whaling decided that while moving during the storm might give them an advantage, it was equally possible that it would give the Japs one, too. After all, if the Japanese leadership had any brains at all… and there was no doubt that they did… then they would prepare for just such a move.

No, they decided, better to wait until good conditions when the full strength of three battalions could be utilized. That's why just as dawn broke on the ninth, Puller led his two battalions from second regiment across the bridge, quickly eliminating any foolish resistance that might be waiting there. Hanneken and his seventh bat followed with Whaling and his scouts… the smallest group… to come last.

The plan was simple. The three groups would split and move

north with Whaling hugging the Matanikau, Hanneken moving up the center and Puller on the left flank. The first two groups would push to the western end of the sand spit and eliminate what Japanese forces were dug in there. Puller would move in behind them and prevent their escaping toward point Cruz. There would be no small measures on this push. With more than 3,000 men at their command, the three commanders made an impressive and deadly show of force.

Surprisingly, neither Whaling nor even Hanneken ran into very much resistance. Occasionally, a Jap sniper would take a potshot at the Americans, or a small patrol would attempt to engage from an advantageous position such as a dense bit of jungle or ridge. However, such efforts were met with overwhelming and deadly force.

It took no more than a couple of hours, therefore, for Whaling and Hanneken to reach their objectives. There they hunkered down, arranged themselves and made short work of the Japanese that had claimed the western side of the Matanikau valley for quite some time.

Puller's two battalions also had little trouble on their march. They were able to move quickly thanks to some native help that Puller had arranged through Martin Clemens. Up until the war had started, Clemens and the Solomon Islands protectorate had made wide use of islanders as carriers. Men and women who would help with moving supplies and gear as well as with other chores.

Now with the Protectorate functionally dissolved and money no longer an option, other forms of currency had been found and utilized for such efforts. With several hundred Melanesian porters assisting, Puller's force could bring more food, water and ammunition. Each porter agreed to the job for the nominal price of one twist of tobacco per person per day. As Puller was an avid pipe smoker, along with many other men at Henderson... and thankfully tobacco in both leaf and cigarette form was always a part of the supply shipment... there was plenty to go around.

Presently, Puller came to a hill that overlooked Point Cruz. From that position, the colonel could just see Sealark Channel and even the smoke rising from the exchange taking place between the Japanese, Whaling and Hanneken to the east. And there was something else, too... something that drew Puller's attention and tugged hard on a personal desire for payback.

To his left and front, a ravine cut its way toward the sea, although its northeastern end was not open but a twenty-yard-tall cliff, as were the other two of the four sides of what was effectively a shallow box canyon dug out of the coral.

Inside this wooded ravine, an entire battalion of Nasu's men was spread out and awaiting orders. It would turn out to be Nasu's second battalion, fourth regiment.

Puller organized his men. Rifle companies and machine gun squads to cover the entire valley. Before ordering them to open fire, he called back to Henderson and was connected to Colonel Pedro Vallejo's artillery battalion.

"*Able-1, Able-1, this is Mother Goose. What've you got for me, Lou?*" Vallejo's cheerful voice said over the radio set.

"Mother Goose, Able-1... have sighted entire jig Baker and would appreciate it if you softened them up a bit," Puller replied. "Approximately three klicks west of Matanikau sand spit. Estimate... 500 yards north. Be obliged if you'd send in a range smoker."

"*Understood, Able-1... standby... shot out,*" Vallejo said even as a distant clap of thunder echoed over the low northern ground of the island.

A few seconds later, something arced in, whistling as it fell and struck a few hundred yards away. Puller smiled and raised the handset.

"Mother Goose, Able-1... not bad. Up five and left seven."

Another shell arced in. By this time, the Japanese down in the ravine were beginning to get the picture. Voices rose in alarm and officers and sergeants shouted curses and orders. The second shell struck almost dead center into a thick grove of hardwoods in the ravine.

"Good line!" Puller shouted. "Two degree spread east-west… one degree north south! Fire for effect, Mother Goose!"

More thunderclaps this time. Deeper, heavier, and more menacing. As explosive 155mm shells flew through the afternoon sky, Puller ordered his own mortars to begin lobbing shells into the ravine.

Panic had set in for the Japanese now. Hundreds of men scattered, running in every direction as big artillery shells splashed down, blasting trees, gouging craters in the earth and sending dozens of men to an early grave. From above on the ridge line, Puller's smaller mortars dropped in, scattering more men and cutting off their retreat to the mouth of the ravine.

"Sir! They're goin' for the far wall!" someone shouted.

"Machine gunners… cut 'em down!" Puller hollered. "We've set up a machine for devastation, men! Now let's put her to some good use!"

The slaughter was just that. A horrifying loss of enemy life with hardly a shot fired in return. The Japanese couldn't fight through the artillery barrage. And even when it stopped, second reg's own mortars kept the pressure on. In panic, the Japanese tried to scale the far wall, scrambling up and out of the ravine, only to be cut down by withering streamers of .50 caliber Browning M2 fire.

In little over an hour, the battle… to be generous… was over. Some Japanese did escape, but it amounted to little. When the smoke cleared, Puller himself led a company of Marines into the canyon to assess the results. And even though he himself had ordered it, Puller was shocked and appalled by what they'd found.

Nearly 600 Japanese soldiers were counted. Almost the entire battalion. Perhaps ninety percent of the men who'd been waiting in that ravine to strike at any American push had been wiped from the Earth.

Just like what Lou Walt and the Raiders had discovered on the previous day, the Marines of Puller's command found many soldiers with full packs. In addition, however, they found two items of significance. Every man carried with him a propaganda leaflet. There was also an order, carried evidently by the battalion commander, which was brought to Puller.

Puller read over the two bits of intel and whistled. Once back on the hill, he gathered his men around so that they could hear some of what their enemy thought.

"The first thing I want to share is an order carried by the commander," Puller began. "It should illustrate to you men just what we're up against… ahem… From now on, the occupation of Guadalcanal Island is under the observation of the whole world. Do not expect to return, not even one man, if the occupation is not successful. Everyone must remember the honor of the emperor. Fear no enemy, yield to no material matters. Show the strong points of steel and even rocks and advance valiantly and ferociously."

Murmurs, whispers, and curses floated among the men as they listened. Finally, they threw up a cheer and offered a response that was rather less than respectful.

Puller smiled and went on, "I couldn't agree more, men. These Japs… they're young men fighting just as you are. Yet in some ways, they're very different from us. Their government, their leaders, lie to them and incite them to brutality. Hear now what they are told about you… The Americans on this island are not ordinary troops, but Marines. A special force, recruited from jails and insane asylums for blood lust. There is no honorable death for their prisoners. Their arms are cut off, they're staked on the airfield and run over with steam rollers. Escaped Japanese prisoners also said that Marines were men who killed their mothers or fathers."

Silence fell then. The Marines considered what they'd heard. In the end, though, they offered the same sentiment. Not so much to the brave young men who lay below, but to the men who'd sent them there. Men who sat back in Tokyo safe and fat and happy.

Within the hour, Vandegrift ordered all units to return to base. They had accomplished what they'd set out to do. However, maintaining such a large force out of and away from the perimeter was not what the Old Man was after.

However, neither General Maruyama nor Hyakutake would ever order large numbers of men to occupy the Matanikau valley again. It was simply too draining on an already strained supply chain. So the Marines marched back to Henderson and were at camp before the suns set on that day… except for Edson's men, of course. They stayed in their position just in case.

EPILOGUE
MOUTH OF THE MATANIKAU

Colonel Edson stood alone on a ridge; hands clasped behind his back. Before him, the men of his Fifth Regiment were just finishing up laying the last row of mines on the sandspit. Another section had rigged an array of lights and a generator so that neither by night nor by day could any Japanese sneak across the river again.

No one spoke to him, not even Lou Walt, who'd dismissed the Raiders and had once more taken up his position as Edson's XO. Walt had known his commander long enough to know when he wanted solitude.

Edson was in mourning. Mourning for all the men that had been lost as well as those he knew personally. Edson was not a man who showed emotion easily and would prefer his space when he was feeling low.

A messenger ran up to Walt with a slip of paper in his hand. The young Marine cast a furtive glance at Edson's back before speaking in a low register, "Major… message from HQ. Colonel Puller, Hanneken, and Whaling have returned to the perimeter, sir.

Also, intel overflights have not detected any new Jap movement beyond Kokumbona, sir."

"Very well, thank you, Private," Walt said. "The colonel will be glad to hear that. Means what we did here... what we did before, too... wasn't for nothing."

"Good to know, sir," said the young man and dashed off to the CP once more.

"Lou," said Edson, without turning. "You're right."

Walt turned and saw Edson's shoulders heave up and down and then he turned around and stepped closer. "As painful as it can be sometimes... what we're doing here matters. Matters for us, for our station and for our nation. We must never forget that."

"No, sir."

Edson allowed a small smile.

FORT TRAVIS

"That's the last of 'em, sir," Oaks said as he strolled up to Decker and Lana standing by what remained of the log wall. "Least the ones in the camp. Might be a few more west... but Lana's scouts say they're far enough away that the island will deal with 'em."

Decker watched as the last two Japanese soldiers, stripped of munitions and supplies, floated down the river toward the waterfall. First one and then another pitched over the edge... a gruesome flume ride to what lay below. And what lay below, sooner or later, would be a plentiful bounty for the ancient carnivorous reptiles that dwelt in the lowlands.

"How many?" Decker asked.

Oaks frowned. "Thirty, sir."

"There were thirty-eight," Lana said. "We tracked them and counted them more than once."

"And neither Hondo nor Makai was among the dead," Oaks added.

"Which means," said Decker, lighting a cigarette and drawing deeply, "that we'll meet them again. I have no doubt of that."

"At least it isn't dull, Albert," Lana smiled.

"So are we staying, sir?" Oaks asked.

Decker shook his head. "No… we'll spend the rest of the day fortifying here, though. Marty Clemens will want to use this place. Then we're headed back. Should be able to reach the base in a couple of days. No doubt there's more to do… although who knows what other crazy shit they'll think up for us."

Oaks turned to Lana, "You and your people saved our bacon, lady."

Lana grinned and stood on tiptoe to kiss the big gunnery sergeant, "When you're good at something, Philip… you keep at it."

The three of them laughed and it felt damned good.

NEAR CAPE ESPERANCE – 2100

Although grateful to be on dry land once more and to have made it through Iron Bottom Sound without his ship having been torpedoed… General Harukichi Hyakutake almost immediately disliked Guadalcanal. Even hours after sunset, the place was still hot, humid and insects had begun to devil him almost since setting boot to sand.

It would take time to disembark the 1,100 men who'd accompanied the general down on their squadron of destroyers. Time to get them and their gear ashore, time to retrieve the supply canisters floating onto the beach and time to greet the men who were departing in their stead. This was something Hyakutake was eager to do. He wanted to see them… see the results of the past month. Most of all, however, he wanted to lay eyes on Kawaguchi.

What the new station commander found, however, was both unexpected and horrifying. A large number of Kawaguchi's and

Oka's men were assembled and awaiting transport. Men who'd been on the accursed island for no more than a month, and yet who appeared as if they'd just spent a decade in hell itself.

Hyakutake strode past the paraded men, struggling to control his face. The sight of these battered, ill, and downtrodden soldiers was enough to put any man off his stride.

Hyakutake saw men who, even if they could still boast a complete uniform, were gaunt, hollow-eyed, and haggard. Many of them could only lay claim to scraps of clothing. Scraps that revealed wasted, half-starved bodies. On dozens of men… perhaps hundreds, the general could see rows of ribs standing out in stark relief below pallid flesh. Their hair was long and wild and their eyes… their eyes were more the eyes of dolls than of men. Haunted eyes… eyes that had seen things they could never unsee.

Further shocking still was Kawaguchi and Oka. They, at least, were able to put together something of a respectable uniform. Yet their sallow complexions and thinness told all the tale the general needed to know. When even the highest-ranking officers appeared more undead than alive… the true nature of the situation was made unsettlingly clear.

That and Hyakutake had already had a full report of what had happened at the Matanikau River over the past few days. How the Americans had swarmed across and obliterated an entire battalion. Indeed, it had been Hyakutake's order that had withdrawn Maruyama and Nasu's men to more than three kilometers from the river itself.

"General," Kawaguchi bowed. "Welcome to Guadalcanal, sir."

"I see I've come just in time, General," Hyakutake said without rancor. "Things here are far worse than we've been led to believe."

"Yes, sir," Oka bowed.

Kawaguchi managed a thin chuckle, "Far worse, sir. And because of poor support, insufficient equipment, and supplies… it is our men that have had to suffer the most."

Hyakutake nodded. It was clear that it hadn't just been the common soldier. Yet Kawaguchi was careful not to include his own woes in his statement.

"That will change," said Hyakutake. "I will not move against Vandegrift until we have at least 27,000 men here. We will overwhelm them with numbers, as it should have been done already. I don't hold either of you gentlemen responsible."

"Most kind," said Oka, bowing deeply.

"Yes," said Kawaguchi, only nodding. "And might I recommend something, sir?"

"Of course."

"Do not try to cross the Matanikau… the best way to attack the airbase is from the south. A more difficult march… but perhaps the only way."

"I quite agree, General," said Hyakutake. "I've already ordered a battalion of engineers to be brought. We will carve a trail deep in the interior and surprise the Americans from their weakest point. And soon, thanks to Admiral Yamamoto, the Yankees will receive a full demonstration of Japanese naval strength. A full battleship squadron will bombard the field before we take the final steps."

"We wish you luck, sir," Oka said.

"Indeed," said Kawaguchi, not trusting himself to say more.

"I must now rely on Maruyama and Nasu. I regret not having the two of you to guide me," Hyakutake said, and both officers thought he actually meant it. "But you and your men have earned a rest. Recover and get better. Japan has more work to do. For now, I shall take up your burden… and by the end of the month, the Japanese people and the emperor will have a great victory to celebrate!"

Oka smiled and Kawaguchi bowed. Kawaguchi appreciated the new commander's enthusiasm… yet he found it difficult to muster up that level of optimism. He knew better. Guadalcanal was a harsh teacher.

And Hyakutake, too, would learn.

BEFORE YOU GO...

The deeper we go, the bigger things become, eh? Danger, excitement, and tension lay just over the horizons for our brave heroes...

For now, though, thank you for joining me and the Marines once again. I hope that you enjoyed this tale, both its fiction and fact. I look forward to visiting with you again, soon.

Before you go and give this book a 5-star rating and glowing review, please visit my website and join my free email list if you have not done so. Aside from a free ebook, you're also part of an exclusive group that gets early heads-up on books and deals.

www.scottwcook.com

Regards,
Scott W. Cook

OTHER BOOKS BY THIS AUTHOR...

Scott Jarvis, Private Investigator Series
Choices - Book 1
The Ledger - Book 2
Play The Hand You're Dealt - Book 3
Isle of Bones - Book 4
Shadows of Limelight - Book 5
Sins of the Fatherland - Book 6
A Fortune in Blood - Book 7
That Way Lies Madness - Book 8
To Honor We Call You - Book 9
What Lies Beneath - Book 10
Suffer Not Evil - Book 11
He That Covets - Book 12
Whom Predators Fear - Book 13
The Wicked Flee Where None Pursueth - Book 14

A Florida Action Adventure Bundle - Books 1-3

USS *Bull Shark* – WWII Submarine Thriller Series

Operation Snare Drum - Book 1

Leviathan Rising - Book 2

The Cactus Navy - Book 3

Tokyo Express - Book 4

Behavior Reports - Book 5

Seas of Flame - Book 6

Outta the Frying Pan - Book 7

Blood Warm Waters - Book 8

Dig Two Graves - Book 9

Tropical Storm - Book 10

USS *Enterprise* - Naval Adventure Series

Wings of Destiny - Book 1

Wings of Vengeance - Book 2

Wings of Glory - Book 3

Wings of Valor - Book 4

Decker's Marine Raiders Series

Pacific Blood - Book 1

Pacific Guts - Book 2

Pacific Grit - Book 3

Pacific Mettle - Book 4

Pacific Thunder - Book 5

Catherine Cook, an Age of Sail Adventure Series

A Heart of Oak

A Treacherous Wind Blows Foul

The Immortal Dracula Series

The Dead Travel Fast - Book 1

The Blood is the Life - Book 2

The Sword and the Spirit - Book 3

What a Hell We Would Make - Book 4

A Collection of Horror Stories

Whispers From the Dark

Through the Veil of Night

Terrors of the Deep

The Crushing Darkness - Book 1

Made in United States
Troutdale, OR
03/22/2025